Mademoiselle FRANKENSTEIN

BY

ROBIN SOLIT

First edition: May 2025

Cover design by Alejandro Colucci
Interior design by Arjan Van Woensel

HARDCOVER ISBN: 979-8-9916358-5-1
PAPERBACK ISBN: 979-8-9916358-0-6
EBOOK ISBN: 979-8-9916358-2-0
AUDIOBOOK ISBN 979-8-9916358-3-7

www.robinsolit.com

Library of Congress Control Number: 2024927651

Published by Midnight River Press
www. midnightriverpress.com

MIDNIGHT RIVER
PRESS

To Alexi, my beloved son

LAST WILL AND TESTAMENT

On the first day of May in the year One Thousand Seven Hundred and Eighty-One.

In the name of God, Amen. I, Gabriel Galán of the open seas, being weak of body but of perfect memory, calling to mind the mortality of my body and knowing that it is appointed for all men once to die, Do make and ordain this my Last Will and Testament and as touching as such worldly goods as providence has helped me with in this life, I give, devise, and dispose of same in the manner and form following.

First, I recommend my soul to God, who gave it in my body to the earth from whence it came. Should my body plunge into the sea, this, I swear, will be my happiest recompense. Yet, should my body outlast my voyages to the four corners of the world, and should it survive the fury of my crew, who even now are madmen banging on my cabin door, I recommend burial in a decent manner at the discretion of my friends and family.

Second, the ship *Valor*, should it endure its current plight at the outermost end of this earth and be deemed seaworthy, must needs be returned to King Charles of the country of Spain, who bequeathed it to me for the duration of this fearful expedition.

Third, as a man with no earthly house nor plantation nor land nor animal nor funds, I leave my spyglass, compass, sextant, and ship's whistle to my nephews, the sons of my sister, Isabel Arias of Madrid, Spain, to be shared among them as their mother and father resolve.

Fourth, I bestow these desperate writings, my testament, to Master Frederick F., whose whereabouts can be found herein. I urge him, in his manhood, to publish these revelations in the form of a book, that such tragedies not linger silently in his heart, but be diffused out into this great world, that their wonder and woe be shared.

Fifth, to any man who reads my tale at some far future time, I swear that all I heard and recorded is true. I swear it this day and all the days hereafter wherever my soul shall roam.

In witness thereof I hereunto set my hand and seal this day and year.

Captain Gabriel Galán
May 1st, 1781
On the brigantine *Valor*

LETTER I

To Madame ARIAS *– Madrid, Spain*

Boston, Massachusetts
August 11th, 1780

So my treacherous adventure begins. My heart beats with the conviction that my discoveries across the St. Lawrence Gulf and up into the uncharted Northern Pole will astound all who hear of them, for no man has stepped afoot that perilous and mysterious land of ice nor seen the strange peoples and creatures who may call it home.

How I miss you, dear Sister, and the verdant hills of our homeland. Some divine force has imbued me with the strength and spirit for this precarious quest. But for that, I would still now warm myself by your fire and embrace you and all my dear family. But 'tis likewise splendid here in the New World. If only I could show you the clang and clamor of Boston. Soldiers of every ilk fill the streets and the newspapers are full of reports about George Washington and his army. The air smells of blood and war, and I shall be glad to depart.

While waiting for my ship, I have taken to strolling a neighborhood called "The Island of North Boston," an atmospheric place with warrens of narrow streets, crowded boarding houses and taverns, and fine, set-back mansions. I cannot help but think of my dear Cécile, who would now be my wife had illness and cruel fate not intervened. Though years have passed since her death, I have never loved another. When I see a splendid manor here, I fancy Cécile as mistress of such a home and our never-born children frolicking in the street. You have told me many a time to let her rest in God's embrace, but some deaths leave the world a place where the restless souls left behind wander in desolate places. Her death drove me to the sea and I have vowed that, should I discover a lovely island in my travels, I will name it after her. Ambition has taken the place of love, so I now sail to a region where serpents and sirens call, where monstrous sharks and gigantic squid strike terror in the hearts of men, and where I shall be the first man to face creatures of myths and ancient tales and live to tell of it.

Your loving brother,
CAPTAIN GABRIEL GALÁN

LETTER II

To Madame ARIAS – *Madrid, Spain*

Halifax, Nova Scotia
November 28th, 1780

Would that our blessed and enlightened King Charles could see me, his loyal subject, launched into the great unknown. My ship is a sturdy brigantine, sleek enough to follow a coastline, yet rugged enough to brave the Atlantic seas. My sailors are a rough bunch, of various languages, complexions, and ingenious seafaring ways learned from their ancestors. Many were criminals or slaves, but I pay them well by the largesse of the king and they are under the tight control of my sailing master, Mr. Dawson, a hoary fellow who does not spare the whip. Roughness is a necessary quality for he who sails to deep and lonely places. I have also conscripted a cabin boy named Master Percy Lyne, whose father handed him into my care. In addition to his other tasks, he sketches neatly and, with his paper and charcoal, will make our travels, travails, and wonders immortal.

Our first stop was Halifax, for provisions. I have now in my possession a dry box containing a chip log, logline reel, sandglass, whistle, charts, sextant, and of course my spyglass and compass always at my side. These old friends of the sea will be my seafaring lodestars. Oh, Isabel, how heady 'tis to live now a dream that has propelled me these past ten years. I will admit envy of Captain James Cook, who just these few years past navigated toward Antarctica, that other icy clime. He did not reach the Southern Pole, but surely I will surpass him in the north. His two mighty ships, the *Resolution* and the *Adventure*, were admirable but, if I may boast, mine is more splendid yet, so I dubbed it the *Valor*.

What drives explorers, dear Sister? Today the wind is steady and our sails are snapping well, thus I have time to contemplate this question. A man must do what he is called for and drawn to by nature. We desire to test our personal endurance and fortitude. The world is full of wonders, such as mountains that cough fire, rivers that rush up instead of down, and forests of colossal trees beset by ghosts who moan and whisper in incessant tempests. My aspiration is to happen upon something beyond all fantastic knowns, beyond the Egyptian pyramids, beyond the bones of gigantic lizards, beyond the genial people who boil and eat each other and use their mothers' skulls as drinking vessels.

Many a learned man has sought to convince me that this northern place to which I sail is a land of eternal ice and that a ship can only go so far before getting ice-locked, never to return. That scientific proposition presupposes a vast territory of towering mountains higher than the Alps, made of lifeless ice that rises to the sky and stretches underneath to the center of the earth, such that a passage will never be found. Many a pleasant whiskey have I shared with men certain that, even when shining, the sun is so cold that the ice mountains never melt and neither navigable sea nor living landscape run beneath them. The only creatures to ever cross that continent, they say, will be birds.

My stated mission, bestowed by our beloved King Charles,

is to discover a Northwest Passage that will open the northern world to commerce and adventuring. But I hoard a private quest as well, which I feel safe in revealing to you alone. One sun warms our earth, possessing the power to bake the hot African desert, cause trees and flowers to bud in barren territories, cook an egg in an earthen pot, transform even the palest people to a toasted brown, and cause frozen rivers to flow and leap with life. Why should that same sun grow suddenly feeble at any spot on our earth? Why do mapmakers conclude that ice mountains descend to a frigid center of the earth? Perhaps 'tis the opposite and unfathomable fires burn there, thus warming from below as the sun warms from above.

I oftentimes dream of a paradise at the Northern Pole, where winter fades to spring and a living sea beneath laps at beaches and ice floes melt into mighty rivers. A lush landscape arises, populated with trees, flowers, and animal species we knew not before. This ice melt is the purest water on earth, kissed from above and below, and possesses miraculous magnetic qualities. 'Tis not so mad to think so! We already know that northern magnetism causes compasses to snap to life and point up toward heaven, so is it not logical to believe that the waters of the Northern Pole will likewise be touched with magnetic magic and therefore will be fountains of youth? Decrepitude and death will exist no more for those who bathe there. The foundations of science will shake and I shall be the man who harnessed the elemental forces of nature and found the secret to eternal life. Call me not ludicrous; only wait patiently, for my cabin boy and I may yet bring back secrets from the deep.

Your loving brother,
Captain Gabriel Galán

LETTER III

To Madame ARIAS *– Madrid, Spain*

Baffin Island, Northwest Territories
Canada, March 7th, 1781

We have measured our progress along the upper coast
of North America by the presence of great auks sporting
their amusing tuxedo overcoats, so like the coloration of
their penguin cousins in Antarctica. Their funny honking
cries were plentiful enough during the weeks we hugged
the rocky coast around Newfoundland, but we left them
behind as we pressed up into the land of long-ago Vikings.
Would that I could adequately describe the spectacular
nature of this territory. The coastline is indented by plentiful fiords, glaciers, and far-distant jagged mountain peaks
made of ice; 'tis more beautiful than any natural wonder I
have thus far beheld. 'Tis now evident to me why so many
legends originate in these lands, for beauty, mystery, and
terror are bound together in all we see.

Here on ship, however, the ferocity of the waves and gales
have made it necessary to use speaking trumpets in order
to carry on conversations, else our words are torn from our
mouths and flung to the unhappy sky. Dead lights burn on

deck at all times, as do oil lamps below night and day. What chairs we have are lashed to tables, and at times of particularly turbulent seas, we must likewise lash ourselves to our bunks to avoid being tossed out onto the deck. When on duty, I sometimes tie myself high on the mast to search the horizon for I know not what, for there is often no horizon when the sea and ice roil gray-blue and the endless sky is thick with lowering clouds of the same color.

Rats plague us at every turn. They eat the horn buttons off our jackets if we do not take care. Once we set a trap with a scrap of rotten, frozen lettuce procured in Halifax. Pitiful though 'twas, it proved savory enough, for we caught eleven vermin at once and used them to fish these frigid waters for char and pike. 'Tis the fear of all my sailors that soon enough we must choke down the rats themselves for dinner.

So, my ship is now a little matchbox flung about wild seas and towering ice floes that threaten to swamp or crush us at every moment. All day and night we are plagued by the groans of the ship's timbers and the cracks of shifting ice. In our state of extremity, these sounds echo like the agonized cries of men long lost, ghosts of the cold ocean that besieges us.

Still, Sister, I am your fearless,
Captain Gabriel Galán

LETTER IV

To Madame ARIAS *– Madrid, Spain*

At sea in the Northern Pole
April 15th, 1781

'Tis ill-advised, perhaps, to write these letters, as there is no chance to send them from the land of eternal winter, not for many more months or even, it often feels, for years. Still, I feel compelled to write of my experiences, as the lack of a friend to talk to is a torment that has plagued me throughout this journey. I should have brought a brave and learned companion, but knew not the breadth of isolation and loneliness this voyage would entail. These ruffian sailors of many tongues are not fit for confidences and, in any case, are weak from scurvy and other ailments, and are brooding and desirous of abandoning our adventure. I do not feel likewise.

However, at times I fear that those European thinkers I wrote of were correct in their dour prognostications, as we have been ice-locked for a month or more. One cannot count days easily, for when the sun flees this glacial land 'tis eternal night, with only the stars and moon as rough indications as to the passage of time. Sometimes, though, the sky blazes with the sweeping, sailing sheets of green, yellow, and rose-colored lights of the *aurora borealis*. But trapped as we are in the deadly embrace of icebergs, fearful as we are of new, undiscovered dangers, these bands of light seem like the mad scribbling of drunken gods.

After many weeks of dark imprisonment, slivers of sunlight have at last begun to make an appearance. During these brief respites, we crawl on deck and lift our pallid faces to the sky. The ice floes have begun to shift, and narrow fissures of black water circle them like spiderwebs. Hope has sprung up that we have endured and will once again go forth in open seas, where we can harpoon whales and fill our bellies.

I struggle for words, Sister, for I must now relate to you the appearance of a phantom that has pitched us into a furor. We know not if we are beset by fever dreams, for what we saw has confounded even me. It occurred one day as I stood on deck peering through my spyglass at the horizon, though I expected to see naught, for all was everlasting sea and ice and sky. Then there passed before my eye a black blur of something moving. I watched it a moment, then cried "Whale!" with all my might, for I thought the ice had broken sufficiently for a wandering beluga to breach. The harpooners rushed to my side, propelled by dreams of fresh meat.

As this dark shape came closer, we could, to our astonishment, make out its true form, which was that of a sledge pulled by dogs, driven by a man or creature of bewildering proportions, with a long black cape streaming out behind. Then the sledge swerved and vanished behind an iceberg. We fell into a momentary silence, for we knew not what to think. Thus ensued a spirited discussion about the nature of this apparition. Eventually, we deemed it a chimera or ghoul, conjured by our impoverished imaginations, and retired to our bunks, satisfied with this conclusion.

On the second morning following this, however, I came up from below for my morning rounds and saw a throng of sailors, even the weakest of them, leaning over the side of the ship, struggling with something in the sea. My heart leapt for the good of my crew, for I assumed they were man-handling some great, nutritious beast aboard ship. Joining them, however, I saw a broken-down sledge—very like the one we saw before—bumping against the hull. But for one, its dogs were frozen dead and the whole contraption threat-ened to disappear into the churning sea. The sledge was occupied, not by the outsized creature of our fancies, but by a slight human form, perhaps dead, swathed in layers of ice-crusted coats and cloaks.

At last, the crew pulled a poor fellow aboard, exposing for a moment two terrified blue eyes, barely visible in a face sheathed in scarves. The living dog too came aboard but the rest succumbed to a watery grave and went down, sledge and all. At this, the wild-eyed fellow started and, clawing at the side of the ship, threatened to hurl himself into the sea after it. The men restrained him and henceforth he fainted dead away and we feared he had perished.

We carried him to my quarters, where I bid the men lay him on my bunk. He seemed nothing more than a heap of stiff, tattered rags. We tried to rub his arms and legs to rouse his blood, but at our touch his eyes snapped open. He looked at us with pure fury and writhed to dislodge us, burrowing into the furthest corner of the bed.

"Perhaps he is a nameless creature of the north, not a man," I said, and bid my men out of the room, even Mr. Dawson. They went unwillingly, such was their perplexity and curiosity. I poured a cup of brandy and approached the fellow gingerly, fearful he might bite me or fall into a crazed fit. "I am your friend, stranger," I said, "if you will allow it."

He shook so; I believe I heard his bones rattle. Never have I seen such an emaciated, pitiful creature. I held the cup to him and a frozen hand, white as marble, crept out from under his garments. He loosened a length of scarf covering his mouth, then the hand vanished again. The other hand clutched a satchel slung across his chest and he could not be persuaded to part with it. His face emerged a bit more as he leaned forward and I realized he was just a lad, for his cheeks were narrow, with nary a beard to indicate a long time at sea. He let me lift the cup to his lips and drank so greedily that I could see that he'd had no drop for days. The brandy brought him around a little, yet still he shook and threatened to faint again.

I asked if he would come sit by the kitchen stove. He pulled his scarf around his face and succumbed to a state of sobbing despair. I had my men carry him to the stove and once again bid them leave, for curious faces seemed to additionally distress my visitor. The stranger sat long enough to revive in the warmth and even let me feed him a little soup. This effort proved exhausting, however, so we returned him to my cabin, where he fell unconscious and could not be roused.

I took this opportunity to remove his many layers of wet clothing, which I knew would kill him otherwise. I wondered what father would send a boy so young to sea alone. Isabel, I can scarcely disclose to you the shock of what I observed. For under those many layers of dripping garments there lay a young woman, barely past girlhood. Cold and bloodless was she.

I could barely think, but I hastened to clothe her in my warmest attire, causing her to vanish inside their size and bulk. I pulled a heavy woolen watch cap firmly over her head and ears right down to her brows, for her hair was shorn like a convict's, sticking out in all directions. This, of all else, brought tears to my eyes. I could right then have wept over her in sympathy and taken this girl into my arms to warm her with my blood and breath, for such was the way that woeful soul affected my sensibilities.

For some days I ministered to her, not allowing any of my men into the cabin. What with all they had been through, and sick themselves, they would have mutinied at the knowledge of a woman aboard. I tended to my duties when she slept and brought her soup and brandy several times a day. Even asleep, she clung to her satchel, a sorry thing much used. A tinge of color appeared on her cheeks, or perhaps that was my imagining, for she was still alarmingly weak, dispirited, and distraught. She was given to storms of weeping interspersed with long periods of staring out the porthole window with a grievous, suffering countenance.

Her dog responded well to the attentions of the crew, most especially those of Master Percy, the cabin boy. Yet thus far my visitor had spoken not a word, except for feverish, indecipherable utterances as she uneasily slept. In hopes of calming her, I talked to her as I fed her, for though she accepted food, she nevertheless stared at me with great mistrust.

Sometimes, after waking from a frightful dream, she looked at me with mad terror and her eyes flitted to that porthole as if she wished to plunge through it. I spoke to her of Spain, of the beauty of Madrid, its splendid city houses, its artistically laid out gardens, and the vitality and beauty of our people. At times I spoke in Spanish, at times in English. I knew not if she understood my words, but my chatter did calm her, as 'twould a child.

Three days after her arrival, as I leaned toward her with a spoonful of soup, she whispered, "Thank you, Captain," in slightly accented English. The sound and gentle lilt so disarmed me that 'twas then I who could not speak.

April 16th, 1781

Sister, I will continue my story in these journal pages, as my tale has much to unfold, more than any letter could contain. Perhaps one day you will read these pages and know your brother all the better for the manner in which I tell it. I pray that you then understand the inevitability of my growing to love my poor guest. No, there was no growing; from the first moment my gaze fell upon those unnerving, half-mad eyes with their eyelashes white and heavy with frozen snow, from that moment, my blood ran hot. Could I have ripped out my pounding heart and given it to her, I would have. My world now dwelt in her slight frame. My men, ill and restless in our ice-locked state, became inconvenient shadows to me.

As my quest has been propelled by a desire to discover unknown things, I have now reached my first epiphany: man can, with the deepest adoration, love a woman with no name, no history, and scarce a word exchanged. I love my visitor, not chastely, as one loves a child, nor fondly, as one loves a sister or mother or cousin. No, the ferocity of this love causes me physical pain and has so crazed me that I could howl at the cold moon. I cannot confide in my men, nor even my visitor herself, for I do not believe she could bear another's fevered state. At rare moments I silently beseech Cécile's heavenly spirit to forgive me, as I have near forgotten her. Our love now seems, I am ashamed to say, a childish dalliance.

My visitor was preoccupied as to the whereabouts of that other sledge and its monstrous occupant, and begged me to allow her on deck, though she barely had the strength for it. I had not questioned her overmuch about what event had propelled those two sledges to this barren, lonely continent. At times, I thought she desired to unburden herself of this curse that caused her so much torment, yet she restrained herself. And so I waited, though I knew not how many days of life she had left, so afflicted was she in body and soul.

I relented and created a false identity so she might pass on deck as a young lad, as we had mistaken her at first. I gave her the name of John Willoughby, a common enough name in the colonies, son of a bookkeeper in Connecticut. I swelled with pride at having thought of this ruse, for it elicited a smile from her, which I had scarce ever seen. I told the men that Young John suffered from a severe contagion of lice and the itch, so they stayed well enough away and squelched their inquisitiveness.

Swathed in heavy clothing and scarves, she cut a dire, tragic figure, scanning the frozen landscape for that mysterious being. While we gazed out toward the horizon, she let me babble on about gradations of ice: that fast ice is attached to land, drift ice moves at will, frazil ice is thin plates suspended in water, slush is water-saturated snow, and shuga is spongy white ice lumps. She listened politely but all the while scanned the terrain with great anxiety.

Though ignorant of the identity of that which terrified her, I comforted her as I was able. "Surely that fearful thing has gone to a watery grave," I said, "for no lone traveler, as you yourself know, can survive here for long."

At moments, she seemed to accept this account; at other times she only fell to weeping and whispered, "You know not of what you speak, Monsieur." My heart broke at her calling me Monsieur, for I feared she saw me merely as an elderly gentleman, so well had I hidden my hot-blooded fervor.

Amongst all the tough and world-weary men aboard my ship, only the cabin boy guessed my visitor's true identity. I discovered this when I saw him sketching her profile as she gazed out to sea. Though little of her face or form were exposed, his sketch nevertheless depicted an unmistakably female figure. I grabbed him roughly and pulled him behind a high coil of rope that we might have a bit of privacy, even as I kept one eye on my visitor, lest she attempt to leap into the sea.

"What possessed you to draw Mr. Willoughby in this way?" I asked.

"Why sir," he replied, "surely our traveler is a girl, for I see it in her face and manner." His expression was quite absent of guile.

"Do the other men see her thus?" I asked.

"No, sir, 'tis only me, sir."

I relaxed my grip and leaned close to him. "Let this be our sworn secret, lad." He nodded and scampered away, fearful of somehow arousing another fit of anger in me.

Henceforth he became my visitor's secret shadow. I often let him into my quarters, where he drew many a sketch of this wretched, shorn stranger—her affecting face, her wringing hands, and her delicate body tangled in a hurricane of restless blankets.

I must admit that Master Percy had a markedly salubrious effect on my guest. She gazed at him often with tender affection, and once I saw her reach to straighten a lock of hair that fell across his forehead. He instinctively leaned toward her at the touch, as a child leans to his mother. At this, my visitor hid her face in her hands, burst into sobs, and could not be comforted for many an hour. Shame fills me, for I must confess to an appalling jealousy at the tender rapport between woman and boy. I knew it to be nothing akin to the fire burning within me. Yet so impassioned was that fire that I would, I believe, have cast a hateful eye at any creature on earth who deigned to glance at her.

April 19th, 1781

Yesterday, my visitor awoke greatly weakened, more even than on the first day she appeared—that phantasm from the sea. Alas, I sensed the angel of death hovering outside the porthole window. I sat near her, took her hands, and willed my warmth to give her strength. She did not flinch from my closeness and indeed a little color rose in her cheeks.

I gave her a sip of brandy, for that is all she would take now. "Captain Galán," she said, "I have seen these days that you are eager to hear my miserable tale. I have kept my counsel, sire, because I knew not if I had the fortitude to tell it, nor if any man or woman had the strength to hear it. For 'tis terrible indeed, beyond any nightmare ever dreamed of in fitful human sleep, yet it rises within me with desperate urgency to be told."

I had never heard her speak so many sentences, and so surprised was I by the urgent, whispering musicality of her speech that I scarcely heeded the warning in her words. Just then, Mr. Dawson pounded on my cabin door and summoned me above, for a terrific storm had blown in from the north, which I had not noticed due to the enchantment in my little cabin. I threw on my outer clothes and bounded up the ladder to the deck, only to encounter a storm wilder than any so far on our long journey, as spring storms can sometimes be.

The melting fissures between the ice floes had not expanded enough for the ship to sail but had loosened sufficiently to cause shifting and careening into each other with tremendous force in the fierce wind. In the dark, they clashed like behemoths from ancient worlds. Flayed by cutting ice rain, my men and I struggled hour after hour to keep the *Valor* upright.

Having witnessed two apparitions driving sledges across

the frozen sea, we now saw or thought we saw all manner of beings. When nearby ice floes crashed together, huge waves of icy saltwater exploded up into the night sky like dragons and sea serpents flinging us about with flicks of their watery tails. At some points of exhaustion, I'm sure I saw red burning eyes and heard the cries of primordial languages.

At last, the wind died down, the sea creatures drew back under the sea, and a tentative sun came out. Men had collapsed and, I feared, died on deck. My hands were bleeding from the ropes and my face was peeled raw from the stinging ice. I tore off my outer clothes and stumbled to my bunk, improper though 'twas to occupy it with a lady abed. I had slept in my captain's chair since she arrived, but there was no stopping my poor body from nearly falling atop her now. She was awake and pulled herself into the corner so as to allow me space. She scarcely occupied a sliver anyway. She pulled blankets over me as I had done for her so often, and I could not help but smile a little at this.

"Tell me your story," I said, barely able to muster the words.

"Tomorrow," she said. "I will tell it tomorrow."

I gazed at her, and even in the extremity of her pallor and thinness and unkempt hair and expression of loss and despair—even with all that—she was the most beautiful, ephemeral girl I had ever beheld. I wished to gaze upon her for a hundred years, but sleep pulled me toward unconsciousness.

"I do not even know your name," I said.

"Océane," she whispered. "My name is Mademoiselle Océane Frankenstein."

CHAPTER I

I woke before dawn and checked upon my men, who stumbled about the deck putting things right after the storm. I could scarcely wait for my visitor to speak. Returning to my cabin, I saw her upending the contents of her leather bag. From it fluttered numerous letters wrapped in ribbons and other bits of paper and ephemera. She held them close and began her story, reading selected letters when her story impelled it. Sister, I strive to record all faithfully herein, though 'twas a flood of words:

Captain Galán, the story of life is the story of exile. My people come from faraway nations and have been blown about by the winds of fate. For many generations, the ancestors on my mother's side lived and died in their beloved homeland of Portugal. Their farmland ran red with the blood of countless wars until at last they fled in terror during an Ottoman military campaign more gruesome than any before. They sought peace in the La Chaussée area of Poitou, France and joined the passionate Huguenot nobility and bourgeoisie settled there.

And in that place began the family tradition of *materia medica*. No one in any town is more beloved than an apothecary who can ease a fever, tame the pains of childbirth, and dispense a secret potion for a lazy lover. Thus began generations of practice in the use of ergot, mushrooms, *psychotria viridis*, laudanum, and all the other herbs, minerals, animal parts, blossoms, and roots which, by exacting methods, became the elixirs seen in the shop of every apothecary.

In time, war again interrupted this pacific existence, forcing my ancestors to sail the terrible journey to a wild and wooded colony they heard tell of in New France, North America, a region called Acadia. Perhaps you have been there? 'Twas a utopia where French people lived peaceably with the Mi'kmaq, who dwelt there from before time, working the abundant fields and expansive forests, and fishing the sea overflowing with the crustaceans that kings dine upon. There the newcomers lived in airy houses built in the French style and continued their trade as apothecaries.

My mother was born there and named Beatrix Belfleur, and never did a kindlier woman live. All I know of her life in that innocence of Acadia has been told to me, for I never knew her. I shall tell you of this in time, for the distressing tale requires courage, which just now I lack. I shall tell you an easier tale awhile.

My father's people too abandoned their homeland. In their case 'twas Germany, land of castles and mysteries. They sailed across the great sea to the New World, toiled in work camps to pay off their passage, then settled with the Palatines in the Hudson River Valley of the colony of New

York. A restive people, they did not hold onto the visions and ways of their homeland. Some moved to Pennsylvania, where, eager to be Americans, they joined militias and broke horses for the carts and carriages making way into the wilds of this new land. Those who stayed in New York became newspapermen and solicitors.

Edgar Frankenstein, my father, was sent back to Germany for a medical education at the age of fourteen. After three years he returned, the pride of the New World Frankensteins, well trained in the surgical arts. He resided in the house of his cousin in Boston, Massachusetts, and began his profession in that city of knowledge.

Now strengthened, I shall continue to speak of my mother. She had the happiest of childhoods. Acadian children grew up strong then, for in their isolation they did not perish from the illnesses and plagues that inflicted others. 'Twas a paradise, with an endless bounty of cattle, sheep, and pigs; numerous grains, vegetables, and fruits; hemp and flax for cloth and ropes; gaspereau, cod, and shad from the sea; and the mysterious forests of pine, fir, cedar, beech, birch, spruce, and larch. Never did an Acadian back then go hungry nor want for any of the simple comforts of life. From the youngest age, my mother learned the ways of gathering herbs and flowers and drying them in the sun.

How my parents met, I know not. In my imaginings, they were drawn together by the mysteries of destiny, which can never be altered. My mother suffered the death of several newborn babes before me. In later years, I saw their simple headstones, wept over them, and put flowers at their feet: Malo, Seraphim, and Marie-Thérèse.

My parents gave me the spark of life during *Le Grand Dérangement*. Hell came to Acadia in the form of men in red coats who pillaged and burned every house and field until all was ash, then drove my people with whip and musket onto ships reserved for prisoners and slaves. Amongst those were my parents and there I was banished, too, flowering in my mother's womb.

Those ships were meant to exile us to rural areas in other colonies or Britain or France, but stagnated out at sea for four long winter months. Unable to disembark, my people suffered every pestilence known to mankind, spread by the ships' sailors, dying by the countless hundreds of disease, cold, and starvation. In agony, they perished in that cursed place and were flung overboard to die again in a different way, for in the manner of my people, if we are not properly buried in God's great earth, our souls will never rest.

Endless slashing wind and cyclones of snow blew across the Atlantic that winter, sent by furious gods. Those months aboard the death ship never left my father. For the rest of his life, the remembrance drowned him in harrowing dreams. His surgical expertise on board was restricted mainly to the officers, as helpless he watched his own people deteriorate and expire from numerous unyielding diseases and deprivations—among them stench, fumes, vomiting, mouth rot, seasickness, fever, dysentery, boils, foul water, and scrofula.

Then came the day of my birth. Women big with child on those ships hid their bellies, for if the shipmasters caught sight of a newborn, 'twas ripped from its mother's arms and never seen again.

Because my father ministered to officers, he frequented their comfortable quarters and spent more time on deck than other exiles, thus he witnessed both the ease of officer life and the fate of those dragged up from below, which left a great bitterness in his soul. Many a time in later years, the spirits of sleep cursed him with visions of infants thrown naked and wailing into the thunderous winter sea, where they took their first and last breath, slipping down to cold, troubled graves, bereft of name, alone. How greatly he suffered from the remembrance of his own beloved Beatrix Belfleur, also big with child, and how, at her most perilous time, he was forbidden to attend to her, as the first mate required bleeding for some minor malady. These tales were told to me many a time and this is how evils become history, so as I grew I too suffered dreams of these little ones who choked and died and could not rest.

'Tis wrong to say that I never knew my mother. I saw her once and she saw me. Eye to eye and breath to breath we rested and she gave me my name, Océane, girl of the sea, for she dreamed of another sea, lapping at the shores of home, lazy in summer, sharing its bounty of strange and beautiful creatures who swam and crept and leapt into the hands of all who lived in the paradise called Acadia. She whispered to me all that day, half-delirious, so my father tells, naming flowers and roots and berries and secret recipes for healing elixirs. She coughed and bled, endured many maladies, and burned with fever, but still she whispered to and stroked me, and called me beautiful and held me next to her skin. Those hours guided my life in ways that you shall see.

I never cried. To this day, my father says that saved my life. That day, the sun slipped down behind the horizon and my mother weakened. A shipmaster came below for his nightly inspections, seeking the dead and dying and newly born. Anticipating this examination, my father hid me in the folds of a blanket, while up on deck he tended to a shipman's rum-sickness. I slept, sustained by the remembrance of my mother's skin and kisses.

The shipmaster kicked a crumpled form here and there, and at the sound of an ill and crying child, he gestured with his musket for his guard to snatch that child by a foot, strip off its clothes, take it upstairs, and fling it overboard. That night, the shipmaster kicked my mother, where-upon her coat slipped open and he saw a pool of blood surrounding her. He did not realize this was childbirth blood, so extensive was it. My mother barely cringed at his kick, and in an instant a sailor yanked at her helpless body and pulled her upstairs.

On deck, my father saw her emerge from below, now dragged by her hair, her mouth open in a silent scream. Before he could react, two shipmen heaved her up and over, cursing her for being French. Into the deep she went. My father hung over the side, half-blind with tears and rage, but he saw her reach for him, saw the shock and anguish in her eyes, saw his love, his bride, vanish into the bitter, unforgiving sea.

In a corner below deck, a huddled, hooded figure sat silent. Two days before, she had given birth to a stillborn boy so small and translucent that his blue heart showed through his skin. He was seized out of her arms with such violence that all nearby heard his bones snap. Unwilling to go on deck in an icy storm, the sailor opened a nearby porthole and stuffed the infant out into the hungry sea with no more thought than if 'twere a rat. Lost and lost that little boy was, for he never saw his mother's eyes nor heard her sweet voice, and his soul was now doomed to amaranthine wandering, for my people believe that babies who go down in the sea are eaten by monsters.

His mother, mute in her grief, witnessed my birth. How it must have torn at her to see a living babe feel a mother's breath and embrace. She watched my father hide me and saw my mother dragged upstairs. In my father's absence, she crawled to where I lay, now stirring and hungry, sheltered me in her garments, and put me to her breast. Surely I knew that this was not my true mother, whose scent and dark eyes I will remember evermore, but life will have its way, so I nursed and felt that woman's tears upon my head.

My father returned, shaking with the agony of his loss,

and felt around for me, crying aloud when I was not there. The silent woman tugged his sleeve, opened her coat, and pulled his hand toward me. Hesitantly, he put his hand on my head and knew 'twas me. "Océane," he whispered, and crumpled sobbing at the woman's side.

That was my first day of life.

You may say that I cannot possibly know such things, but I do. I know because that woman, Mimikej Poulette, married my father and became my beloved second mother. A Mi'kmaq native woman, she knew the ways of both Acadians and her ancient people. In my baby way, I called her Mimi, and so was she known to me ever after.

As the years passed, a hundred, nay, a thousand times she told me of that ship, of her helpless boy who never drew breath, and how she came to be my second mother. And a hundred, nay, a thousand times my father spoke of his Beatrix Belfleur, such that I know every sigh and tear, every smile and song she sang with the other women of Acadia as they carded wool, bloodied their fingers sewing thick leather shoes, and cooked great pots of corn and crackling for winter nights.

She had a temper, too, I heard, and had been known to blaspheme the sheep when, by nature of their dumbness, they wandered in circles on the dirt roads, forgetting to move aside for passing horses and carts. 'Twas this quality I loved the most, for humans are more themselves in their imperfections, and so I loved her more for hers.

When, many years later, I had a formal birth certificate, my father wrote my name as "Océane Frankenstein dit Belfleur," in the Acadian style of honoring both father and mother.

Forevermore, Acadians, scattered far and wide, told tales of *Le Grand Dérangement*—that merciless expulsion from their Garden of Eden, of the ships of death, of starvation, of babies shoved out porthole windows, of their troubled little souls crying out from the dark of the Atlantic Ocean, exiled from God and man.

CHAPTER II

At last, those gruesome ships docked at Newport, Rhode Island, far from their intended destination of the Cajun settlements in New Orleans, Louisiana. Even so, passengers were forced to remain on those stinking ships while authorities argued about what to do. The only respite was release from the fetid decks below to breathe fresh air.

Though the air was sweet, the Acadians trembled for fear of future imprisonment, indentured servitude, or–because of official indecision–sailing to sea again to be dumped overboard en masse. Many crumpled to their knees, so long had it been since they used their legs. In years to come, my father spoke of what he saw during those waiting days–sailors spitting and cursing and whipping recalcitrant people, traders bargaining for ships, barrels, chocolate, textiles, clothes, bottles, sugar, and molasses.

Newport teemed with *nouveau riche* from an influx of Portuguese, homeland of my mother's people. New factories belched black smoke from the making of sperm oil and sper-maceti candles. Silent gray-clad ladies in modest bonnets seemed by some heavenly intervention to float unscathed and untouched as they picked their way amongst merchants and pirates who shouted the livelong day, for in that place the Society of Friends found shelter from persecution.

In the days of waiting, my father and Mimi watched the activities of the triangle trade—sugar and molasses brought by captives from the Caribbean to be distilled into rum, which was then shipped to West Africa in exchange for captives for the New World slave trade—black men shackled, scarred, bought and sold, sold and bought again.

I consider those days on deck my introduction to new, heady elements of life: a spring breeze, children playing on the pier, the scent of roasted chestnuts and peppermints and beer purveyed in carts alongside the ships, and pale yellow spring sunlight that startled my newborn eyes. Then horses and empty hay wagons lined up on the dock and my people walked, limped, or were unceremoniously dragged off the death ships and loaded into buckboards, some dying on the spot from rough handling.

As people from different ships merged, they cried out names in a search for missing family members. A few fell into each other's arms, but most stood disconsolate, their thin voices vanishing in the general din. Soldiers emptied the ships by flinging the dead in heaps on the plainstones. My father told me that the last Newport voice he heard was a bilious roar from the dock: "Smells like money, boys!"

The wagons headed southwest. When the caravan stopped for water, people and horses stuck their heads into troughs or hastened to nearby creeks to drink. My father felt a strange, wild rush of energy. At a water stop some distance into the countryside, he took Mimi's hand and, with me in her arms, they fled into a dense growth of trees. They had scarcely exchanged five words, yet she did not give me back to him and go her way.

Breathless, they sank down at the foot of a tree. The wagons moved on; the sound of horses' hooves and wagon wheels grew dim, then silent. As they huddled there, dizzy with hunger, weak with ship ailments, plagued by ghosts, a mild breeze passed over them. They leaned their heads back against the smooth gray-white tree trunk and looked up. The leaves were newborn, not the flagrant sturdy green leaves of summer, but a light and delicate green, quivering, trembling, and dancing in the pale sun. True too for the next tree and the next and the next, as far as they could see, for they had landed in a grove of quaking aspen, whose slender trunks and whispering leaves seemed to bestow grace upon them. They rested and felt the good of the earth that had kept its innocence during their months at sea.

For a long time, they had a marriage largely conducted in pantomime. He spoke English and German; she, French and her native Mi'kmaq language. Over time, they patched together an amalgam of tongues, but in the aspen grove that day, they were strangers, bound together only by the thread of my life.

During their long journey back to Acadia, my father's medical services were their calling card. Though he had no equipment with him, he had his knowledge, which together with Mimi's ways with unguents and soporifics made them highly prized dinner guests. Townspeople and rural folk gave us clothes when ours were rags, food when we were hungry, and passed on news of the day.

As Mimi filled out, so did I, drinking the warm, blue milk meant for her lost boy until I became quite a roly-poly little creature who everyone was eager to jiggle or sing to as my father and Mimi ate. We dozed on clean hay, listening to the night noises of cows and horses shuffling in their pens.

One farmer gave us a goat named Tutta, and in midsummer a textile merchant gave us a horse, so great was his gratitude after my father removed his daughter's appendix using a hunting knife, a needle, catgut thread, whiskey to stupefy the child, and fire to burnish the knife and needle, after which Mimi dressed the wound with honey and willow bark. The child came out of her whiskey stupor, smiled at her parents, and all was well.

Gently did my father try to disabuse villagers of old-time home remedies, such as using grated chocolate to stop bleeding wounds; moss to treat gunpowder wounds; saffron, goat's milk, and salt for jaundice; and the burning and eating of toads to prevent smallpox.

As we passed further north through lush, unsettled territories, my father and Mimi traveled in a state of blessed amnesia. For a time, they let memories of the death ships wash away in gentle summer rains and waterfalls. Neither bears nor wild hogs nor mosquitoes nor wasps nor snakes bothered us, nor did we meet anyone who wished us harm.

My father's beard grew like a lumberjack's and Mimi let her hair flow free, black and silky from rainwater. She now rode horseback like a forest queen in a storybook, for a grateful family who had nothing else to give pressed upon her an elaborate wedding dress. My father bid her keep it in its brown paper wrapping, but she wanted to wear it and so she did. I remember the intricate white lace of that dress, for I spent my days in a little basket Mimi strapped to her back. I clung to her shoulders as we rode and thus became familiar with every tiny flower and ribbon and fine stitching of that dress.

The natural world became my universe: gentle oak, elm, walnut, maple, and fir trees; wildflowers, vines, and berry bushes; and the creatures living in those woods—squirrels, deer, raccoons, rabbits, and foxes. Every bird on God's green earth surrounded us with the riot of whistles, tweets, caws, shrieks, chirps, and cries.

In those dense backwoods, we spent the nights on the mossy ground alongside creeks, lakes, and rivers, and heard the raucous ricochet of frogs passing worried messages back and forth across the water in a great din. There too I saw my first fireflies, which in my young eyes were stars. Thus those lazy months of forgetfulness passed, a pacific interlude of which my father spoke with tears of happy remembrance in later years.

We arrived on the home soil of Acadia along with a modest number of countrymen, stragglers all, returning to their beloved environments on Prince Edward Island, Cape Breton Island, Nova Scotia, and onward up to the Gaspé Peninsula and along the lush banks of the St. John River, even as far as the mysterious and lonely Magdalen Islands. This was the time of starting over.

Returning Acadians oftentimes fell upon their knees to kiss the rich soil of their homeland, laughing, crying, even stuffing their pockets with handfuls of dirt, pine needles, and little stones—whatever earthly good they first came upon. Even I, set down on the ground beside my rejoicing people, scooped up a handful in my fat baby fist and ate a bit of leaf and 'twas interesting and good.

Thus I joined the river of time, back to the time before time when dirt itself became the aspect that binds people to place, the power of dominion of homeland. Have not all men knelt, full of gratitude for the sweet earth of home—be it desert, forest, farmland, or ice—do not all kneel and thank their ancestors' bones beneath their feet, thank the mysterious force that keeps us from falling up into the terrifying black abyss beyond the stars, thank the bounty of food and water, thank the clay, the dust, the earth, our beloved earth?

There I passed the innocent years of childhood. Adults

labored from dawn to dark to rebuild burned-out houses and boats, corral farm animals that had exiled themselves into the wilds of the forestland, and replant farmlands, so the children of my time were free. Gone was the carefully plaited hair of my mother and her mother; gone the confining layers of frocks meant to establish and maintain the sanctity of girlhood; gone the boys' stiff Sunday suits, unwilling shoes, and slicked-back hair.

While doing our chores of collecting water and firewood, we dallied in rich forests and stripped naked to frolic in streams and lakes. Likely we were the only Acadians before or ever after who experienced the yellow delight of a full-body sunbath or a naked leap into a waterfall pool. So too were we likely the only ones to see the nakedness of our friends—girls and boys—as free as the goodly sprites, fairies, elves, and moss folk we were sure accompanied us on our explorations. 'Twas there I got my first inkling of the wonders and mysteries of the human body. Skin, sinews, heartbeat, breath.

Mimi and I traversed those forests and meadows, for they were her true homeland. In town, she was industrious and reserved, not given to expansive conversation. Out in the wild, though, she looked tall and willowy, and told me stories of her people, of their expertise with fish and game, of their role as guides for European sportsmen and naturalists, of their part in the fur trade. Along the way, we stopped at Mi'kmaq camps and ate in the cozy confines of their wigwams. Mimi and the other women spoke rapidly, their language unknown to me. They dazzled my child's eye, for they spoke more expressively than French Acadians and decorated themselves with shells, feathers, and beads.

During those rambles, we filled our baskets with many of the innocent, deadly, life-giving, sleep-inducing, dream-disturbing, stinging, soothing, fragrant, and stinking curiosities of apothecary. Mimi knew much of herbs and potions, and my father wished to honor the inheritance of my first mother, his beloved Beatrix Belfleur. 'Twas my task from my earliest years to sort flowers; I learned the names and scents of all. And so the knowledge of those two mothers was passed on to me and thus was born my interest in the alchemy of wild things, the conjuring ways of natural elements and animal parts, what each does to the human body, and how they can become something altogether different when combined.

For my father, the placid days of his journey to repatriation soon ended. My mother's spirit haunted and tormented him. He begged Mimi for potions to give him peace and she tried many a concoction, but he could not shake his tormenting guilt over the sight of his beloved staring into his eyes as she was flung to her watery grave.

Seeking to exorcise his demons, he worked harder than any man, helping with the tasks of building and harvesting even as he doctored the many people who traveled by boat, cart, horse, and foot to seek his treatments. Beloved by all, he carried his sorrow secretly, visible only in his body—gaunt, with great shadows under his eyes from sleeplessness— which others mistook for a kind of religious devotion to his healing arts.

In my child's eyes, I only saw an imposing figure, a man who knew all I yearned to know and was kind to me in an absent-minded manner. He knew not how his shadow cast itself upon my actions evermore and I scarce knew myself until 'twas too late.

CHAPTER III

When I was five years old, my father and I moved to Boston so he could perfect the many new surgical arts developed since his schooling in Germany. Mimi remained in Acadia, for reasons I did not understand until much later. Our journey took place during a desolate and icy November. We traveled overland as my father would not step upon a ship with me ever again. 'Twas a sturdy closed coach, a rare comfort provided by the medical institute that hired my father; thus we had it to ourselves.

My father slept steadily, as if a sleeping sickness came over him or 'twas all his sleepless nights saved up. He was not plagued by nightmares, for nary a furrowed brow did I see, nor hear any groans or anguished cries. This long slumber did not distress me; it provided me with something I had never known—uninterrupted, leisurely contact with some-one of my own blood. My good father—devotedly working, pursued by demons—'twas all I knew of him until then. Now

I had the luxury of observing him without his knowing, my first minute examination of any grown person.

How I marveled at his shaggy eyebrows pointing this way and that, and the tiny stubbles of beard on his cheeks that darkened every day. His hands were a wonderment of complexity—knobby bones, rolling blue veins, and skin rough enough to hack down a tree, yet tender enough to sew a perfect catgut seam. I turned his hands and studied the lines running crossway on his palms, how they formed a little cup if you scrunched them all up together. Comparing them with mine, I wondered why his had so many lines and mine so few.

As always, he smelled of tobacco and medicinal soap. I breathed this in and leaned against him hour by hour, nestling under his coat, dreaming, gazing out at the slushy landscape. People vanish; this I knew in an embryonic way. Hence, I clung the more to that beloved, exhausted man. I grew up during those days, years older I think, rousing my father for hot stew and beer at nighttime tavern stops, helping him remove his coat and boots as he tumbled onto rude, bug-ridden cots to sleep yet more. Everything was backward; I was his keeper and his mother, and briefly he let it be so.

A few days shy of Boston, a carriage wheel broke. My father emerged from his slumber that we might travel on foot to the nearest village and arrange for repairs. Shortly before they were complete, we grew restless and, although the weather was a misery of sleet and slush, we climbed a high hill in hopes of viewing the larger landscape. Stopping to rest at the leeward side of a sheltering pine, we saw to our surprise a wet, shivering boy perhaps a few years older than me, likewise seeking refuge from the sleet that now blew sideways in a heightening wind.

"Ho there," my father said, "who do you belong to, young

fellow?" The lad seemed about to loudly claim that tree as his, but the question disarmed him, so he closed his mouth and said nothing. And nothing is what he said for many a week, though he did shake his head no or nod yes when addressed. My father wrapped his coat around the boy and we took him back to the tavern.

Word spread across the village and people came to look him over, but no one laid claim to him or expressed any knowledge of him. He shook his head when asked if his parents were living, thus it became clear he was an orphan, a wanderer living on wits and luck. My father bid him climb into our carriage and on we went. Man and boy both lapsed into sleep, leaving me alone with my thoughts about boys and men. Men are sweeter when they sleep.

So we three began a new life in a house on Commonwealth Avenue in Boston. In time, the boy spoke and in a highborn manner, too, though many a year passed before we heard the story of his origin. His name was Cristophé Savoie—he of the black, black hair and blue, blue eyes—and he became my cousin, my friend and companion, my fellow explorer.

My father enrolled us in school. I learned to braid my own hair, dress myself smartly in a smock and heavy wool stockings, and off I went with my books, a proper Boston girl, holding Cristophé's hand. We spoke English and picked up reading and sums quickly. After school, I reverted to my free Acadian ways, roaming the city, blending in easily in a crowded, young city awash with urchins. Some were lost or abandoned, some had fathers, some even mothers—those rare and mythical creatures in a city full of restless soldiers on wild-eyed horses thundering down streets and byways.

Like all city urchins, Cristophé and I became expert at snatching chestnuts, fruit, and other savories from food carts. Curiosity led us to the harbor and its environs, the most interesting part of the city. 'Twas too risky to wander amongst the crush of humanity around the docks, so we sat upon a stone wall across the street or climbed into the branches of a nearby tree. There we watched the great heaving sailing ships from far-off lands and people in unusual garb conducting business in numerous languages.

Cristophé evidenced a great interest in adult concerns, often sat in on the spirited conversations my father had with prominent men and, for a child, took matters of state with unusual seriousness. One day, we observed the unloading of a slave ship—a noisy, shocking undertaking—and he described at some length the buying and selling of human beings. Though common thereabouts and in the colonies, this was unfamiliar, as Acadia had no slaves, nor any people in chains, nor even dogs or horses in chains. Childhood innocence serves its sweet, insulating purpose but 'tis fragile, for the world of men is barbarous and loud about it.

Boston Harbor was my real schoolhouse, for 'twas there I first understood that I was not immortal. Now is the same as forever for small children; it takes time to grasp the truth. This realization occurred when a tremendous thunderstorm swept across the harbor. Great crashes of thunder rolled over the sea, rain came down in torrents, and winds blew such that the rigging on the great ships set up an awful clatter and empty barrels tipped over, rumbled down the streets, and fell into the harbor. The sky was inky blue and jagged sheets of lightning blinded us, then vanished, leaving stars of light upon our eyeballs.

We sought protection from the rain and found a spot under the canopy of an overturned sweet bun cart. I held Cristophé's hand, reveling in the chaos, the flooding, the crashing of ship hulls against the docks, and each frightening thunderbolt. "God is angry!" shouted Cristophé in my ear. I nodded, believing this to be true, and to this day I believe that nature's manifestations reflect the mood of the gods, not the God of Christian faith, but the ancient gods of storybooks. Even now, Captain, does it not seem that the old gods disapprove of your voyage and have locked you in ice that you might proceed no further?

During that long-ago storm, a streak of lightning hit a man fishing off the pier. His clothes caught fire, then exploded off his body. The crown of his hat blasted off and spiraled out to sea. I scrambled from under the awning and ran to him, as did numerous others. There I saw a wondrous sight. He was naked. Red spidery flowers slowly bloomed across his head, neck, and torso, first as tiny roses, then broadening into feathery, fernlike designs, gracefully trailing off at his waist.

Men tried to rouse him, slapping and shaking him smartly. They put their ears to his chest for long minutes then gave up, declaring him dead. I could not hear their words, only watch as one does a theatrical. For a long time after that day, I thought that bloomed on everyone's skin when they died, and how perfect and magical that was.

As I gazed at his lifeless body, I was struck by a different kind of thunderbolt, the knowledge that death is the fate of all who live, including me. I sat in a puddle and wailed. No one paid me the slightest attention because of the roar of the storm and the enthralling spectacle of the poor young naked dead man before us.

Another man pushed through the crowd carrying a medical bag like my father's. He knelt down and covered the dead man's mouth in a huge kiss. Shocked men in the crowd hustled their women away lest they witness this barbarity. The doctor, if that is what he was, pressed upon the young man's chest then kissed him again, these two motions over and over as the storm howled unabated. That chest rose and fell, rose and fell until at last the dead man coughed, pushed the kissing man away, vomited blood, and sat up, bewildered, still covered with ferns and roses. My memory fades then, except that while I witnessed this event, a fantastic world revealed itself to me, one that forged my life, as you shall see.

Thus ended our free and easy city afternoons, for the kissing man was indeed a surgeon who happened to know my father and had seen us at various picnics and church events. Cristophé was dispatched to study at the Academy Charity School in Pennsylvania, boarding with Frankenstein relatives in that city. Now seven years old, I was sent to the Ursuline Academy in New Orleans, a boarding school-hospital-orphanage whose nuns welcomed displaced Acadians, freed slaves, girls from Central and South America, native peoples, and daughters of enlightened wealthy colonists who believed in a civilized, spiritual, and just society.

In that building on Chartres Street in the Vieux Carré, I turned into a different girl, dressed in ribboned dresses, adopting perfect manners, graceful movements, and a cultured speaking and singing voice in French and English. My mind abandoned its childish dimensions and grew huge and hungry for knowledge of many disciplines beyond what the religious, historical, and literary schoolbooks offered me.

I longed for Cristophé and my father, and wrote many anguished letters expressing my tearful state. My father replied with exhortations to calm myself and take to nature whenever possible. Cristophé scrawled brief excited utterances about the glories of soldiering, for the atmosphere was changing, 'twas thick with anger and turmoil between the New World–impatient to shed its old master–and the Old World–loath to relinquish any power or territory, so eager schoolboys now studied the history of war, military tactics, and weapons.

My loneliness was assuaged in my third year at the Ursuline Academy, for I found the greatest friend of my life–Lara Eaux, a Cajun girl born under my same moon, daughter of a textile merchant in the north Louisiana Territory. We looked like sisters so we pretended thus, dressing and braiding our hair identically. We walked holding hands, whispered our secrets and dreams, and were rarely without each other. A truer, kinder friend has never lived.

Thus I became civilized. No more did I run about nor find myself in deliriums of joy over the physical and sensory world. I learned to move with a kind of chaste and elevated beauty that comes from a life of the mind, a life with nuns. But whatever my delicate manner, my inner whirlwind of curiosity about the why of everything in life and death perished not, not even to this cursed day.

Mimi did not relocate to Boston with us, for she was happy in her homeland. While I was in New Orleans, my brother Freddy was born, to our great excitement and joy. Perhaps a year after his birth, my father sent me a letter containing a pastel portrait of Mimi and Freddy—she in a stiff brocade dress, many necklaces, and her hair flowing long and free, and baby Freddy seated on her lap, a captivating, heavenly baby.

Lara and I traveled to Acadia several summers in a row that we might delight in the company of Mimi, my father, Cristophé, and darling Freddy who, as he learned to crawl and walk, developed a fascination with animals and at the slightest opportunity visited the barnyard beasts. We were permitted these voyages because my father relented sufficiently to allow me on non-ocean-going boats and Lara's aunt, Madam Boloq, traveled as our chaperone. How beautiful was the Mississippi River! We puzzled out our girlish theories of life as Madam Boloq played cards with other chaperones and kept a diligent eye on us. We were not free to run about the ship, as young ladies from Catholic school must walk decorously.

Several Christmas holidays we visited Cristophé at the

Frankenstein home in the territory of Pennsylvania. That brooding youth had become a model New American: bold, tall, smart, amusing, immensely handsome, fearless, confident, and courtly in a style well approved by Lara. He recited epic battle verses in a most affecting manner, which the boisterous Philadelphia clan found worthy of many rounds of spirits.

Listening to him, I feared him blind to the dangers of bayonet and rifle, but still I loved him and he was the boy I knew best in all the world. When we were children, Mimi and my father wished for us to marry and as the years passed, he became less my beloved friend, more my beloved, and so 'twas agreed with a kiss on the back of my hand and the promise of a dreamed-of future of peace and happiness.

Despite these diversions, I became miserable in my perfectly clean and orderly life, and grew restive with desires that had no name but which I felt as unruly, dangerous, and vital undercurrents in my nature. I installed myself in the good graces of the school hospital, offering myself as an assistant of the lowest sort—washing foul bandages in tubs of boiling water, discarding purulent refuse, serving water to the parched, blankets to the shivering, and feeding goat's milk in little rubber teats to orphan babies sometimes left on the grounds. Birth, death, torturous pain, fever dreams, black canker, pleurisy—these became a field of study far more absorbing than the literature, languages, and histories of the classroom.

A portrait near the entryway of the hospital particularly caught my interest, a small gold plaque bearing the name *Sister Francis Xavier* and this inscription: *Blessed Is She Who Has Dominion Over The Elixirs That Ease The Maladies Of Body And Soul That Are Visited Upon God's Poor Multitudes.* Next to it hung a drawing of a nun in a white habit with a cotton mask over her mouth, such that only her eyes and cheeks were visible. Numerous tiny bottles stood in rows in a cabinet behind her and she was busy grinding something in a little stone bowl like the one Mimi used.

After a year or more of making myself silently useful there, the school arranged a formal course of study in Apothecary Arts and, in memory of beloved Sister Xavier, treated me most indulgently in pursuing these interests.

My dearest Lara was more inclined toward ancient Greek and Roman myths. She knew every tale of gods and goddesses of the sky, sea, earth, and beneath in the fires of the underworld. Muses, furies, winds, gorgons, fates, nymphs, monsters—these were her bedfellows. Oftentimes at night, I climbed into her bed and she whispered tales in such a dramatic fashion that sleep eluded me the whole night through. As we grew, she added the study of ethics, ontology, rhetoric, and aesthetics, and urged me to elevate my studies to these higher arts rather than the lower order of flesh and blood.

My father, however, encouraged my inquiries, so much so that he sent me a trunk full of items devoted to the topic of medicine. The trunk itself caused great curiosity, for 'twas from a London bookshop and elaborately painted with the names of children's copybooks from some former use: *Strokes, Easy Letters, Long Letters, Short Words, Figures, Sentences, Maxims, Morals and Precepts*, and so on.

Inside were these four items: *Pharmacopoeia Extemporanae or A Body of Medicines: Containing a Thousand Select Prescripts, Answering Most Intentions of Cure, To Which Are Added Useful Scholia, a Catalogue of Remedies, and Copious Index*; *The Anatomy of Melancholy, What It Is: With All the Kinds, Causes, Symptomes, Prognostickes, and Several Cures of It*; a set of anatomical fugitive sheets with beautifully printed naked figures that revealed layer by layer by lifting thin tabs like an advent calendar, each layer showing more intricate, delicate depictions of the flesh beneath; and finally a small carved ivory anatomical figure of a woman with a removable torso, thus revealing the lungs and intestines.

My classmates lost interest quickly and you may say that these were scarcely gifts suitable for a girl of eleven years, but they marked the end of my childhood and I was not sorry for it. They opened a door to a world of mysteries and curiosities that I eagerly embraced, though I knew not many of the tiny, copious words in these books, half in Latin. Unknowingly then, my father set me more firmly upon a road I gladly followed from that day forward.

The words I could read enchanted me in their evocative sound, such as "ague," "dropsy," "the purples," "mortification," "apoplexy," "scales," "strangury." These words seemed religious to me, words that might be used to describe the suffering of saints in ancient paintings. The frontispiece of one of those books contained the motto *Primum non nocere*, an oath I later violated beyond imagining.

CHAPTER IV

When we were thirteen years of age, Lara's father took her out of school, news she received in an unwelcome letter. "Daughter," he wrote, "Now you must take your knowledge of sums and bookkeeping and work in our shop, as your mother is poorly and can no longer lift bolts of fabric or kneel at the dressmaker's form. Say farewell to the kindly nuns who could not love you more. I shall send a cart for you two days hence."

We read this letter numerous times, trying to recast the words, but at last fell upon each other and wept until we near fainted, and so my dearest bosom friend returned to a life without philosophies and old gods, without sophists and theories of justice.

A state of constant weeping descended upon me. None of my usual preoccupations interested me, not books nor medicine nor apothecary. Many a day I left Ursuline unbidden and wandered the city alone. My old ways of childhood freedom on this earth returned to me and I felt great constriction at a school that had cared for and taught me much this long while. I felt no fear of man nor place nor soldiers nor cannons gathering in nearby farmers' fields, for I cared for nothing and no one. My family ceased to receive letters from me but they worried not, concluding only that I was intent in my studies.

I often visited Saint Peter's Cemetery outside the French Quarter, where I read headstones and contemplated the lives of those slumbering below, based on their names, age, and the achingly sincere words upon the stone. From there I wandered to the river, observed the elemental forces of the Mississippi, and pondered other great rivers of the world—the Amazon, Nile, Congo, Lena, Obi—those mothers of the sea.

At times, I watched men dig holes in odd places along the riverbank, at the edges of cemeteries, and where the city faded into woods, searching, as rumor had it, for treasure buried in those locations by long-ago pirates. At gloomy moments, meditating on my discontents, I wished to surrender to the river, to let it take me to the unknowable ocean full of salty tears from all the poor wretches on God's earth.

Without Lara—my daily touchstone, my steadying, gentle friend—my darker self was left unchecked. I desired not to go to Acadia, nor even Boston, for my family knew not the depth of my brooding contemplations and I hesitated to speak of it for 'twas all whirling and complex, mystical and thrilling, dangerous and morbid and captivating.

While boys are lost to thoughts of war, girls too live secret lives. Who had I to confide in? Who could calm the disorder of my confusion about life and death and the imagined place in between that so occupied my thoughts? I read of conditions named "apparent death," "suspended animation," and "coma." In the hospital, I saw people faint and appear lifeless, yet they proved not so, and often I heard doctors describe "restoring" patients to life. Why then, I wondered, can we not bring back beloveds from the other side? My father could have likely answered me in full, but his extreme sensibilities made me cautious to stir up thoughts that might cause him pain.

A year passed. The more time I spent in the hospital, the more I learned of medicine and apothecary, the more my dreams grew like my father's, plagued by the ghost of Beatrix Belfleur. Many a dark and lonely night in my solitary cot I suffered from the memory of her fevered skin against mine, of those desperate hours in the death ship, all I knew of her, nothing evermore. Whereas in younger years I did not consider the actual moment of her death, I now knew enough to imagine her lungs filling with saltwater and the gasping, hopeless agony of God's sweet breath departing with shocking, choking suffocation.

I grew pale and thin and now bled excessively every month in a woman's way such that several times I fainted dead away in the hospital ward at sights that never caused me to swoon before. Please forgive these blunt expressions, Captain, but 'tis all true. My newfound breasts ached with a tender sensitivity that made me beg the nuns to loosen my stays and stop the womanly bleeding, too, only to have them avoid my questions with a shame I did not understand. Why must girls be punished thus when boys rise up strong as wolves to become presidents and kings?

All was amiss with my body and soul and I could not be comforted. This became evident to the nuns at Ursuline, so they wrote to my father regarding my daily absences and sorrowful response to the loss of Lara, and he wrote back thusly.

To Mademoiselle OCÉANE
FRANKENSTEIN DIT BELFLEUR

Boston, Massachusetts
January 12th, 1774

I have exchanged letters with your Ursuline Academy teachers about your school sorrows, which you did not confide to me, and they give me great concern. From my vantage point of age, I can assure you that friends such as Lara are often friends for life, and I believe she shall be, too. In my fatherly ignorance, I have not understood the depth and sensitivity of your nature. If you are still fascinated by the books I sent you and your work in the Ursuline hospital, I encourage you to follow that interest in healing, which you have rightly inherited from your natural mother and me and our many forefathers.

The war needs good nurses. I bid you return to Acadia and study those books well for one year, adding to your own education, then I shall happily welcome you back to Boston to help me in my practice. You will be of special advantage because of your knowledge of apothecary, for 'tis a rare nurse who knows those secret formulas. One year, dear Océane, my girl of the sea, and we shall join together for the benefit of the sick and lame. While I think this plan most sound, I have not discussed it with Cristophé, who as your betrothed may frown upon such a future for a young lady, so I leave it to you to enlighten him as you wish.

Your loving father,
DOCTOR EDGAR FRANKENSTEIN

I took the contents of this letter to heart and thus I bid
goodbye to that cloister of my girlhood and returned to the
loving arms of Mimi and Freddy, now a charming boy with
curly hair who looked much like my father. I went reluctantly,
for I yearned to go in a direction other than into the bosom
of my childhood, yet I knew not where. Cristophé had finished school and joined a militia; I scarce felt I knew him,
for he had moved into a man's world, of which I knew little.
My father sent a Philadelphia Frankenstein cousin named
Nicolas to accompany me north, for nary an aunt nor female
cousin desired to sail up the Mississippi River in winter.
Perhaps five and twenty, Nicolas was an enormous fellow—
bigger than any man I had ever cast eyes upon. At first, he
did not think much of me, for weepy, morbid schoolgirls
are a bother to men.

He grabbed my trunk, waved me on, and charged off
toward the dock, whereupon I was forced to run after him in
an indelicate fashion, for his legs were long and he covered
ground at an astonishing speed. I beseeched him several
times to wait but he ignored me and I thought him most
ill-tempered. I soon discovered, however, that he was deaf, to
his everlasting sorrow, for this forbade him from soldiering,
his heart's desire, for which otherwise his imposing figure
was admirably suited. This malady made him an unusual
sailing companion. Though largely silent, he understood
me well and read my expressions with great sympathy.

Not long after we set sail, I observed a putrid burn on his
wrist from a fire. He let me drain its foul contents as I had
learned in the hospital, clean it, and bind it with a strip of
my petticoat. This relieved him greatly and soon he became
my affectionate companion and ever after swooped me
into his arms and called me Dr. Missy Océane in a strange
booming off-key voice that quickly became dear to me. By
family agreement, he became my faithful shadow, protector,

helper, and witness to the misadventures to come.

The Mississippi River in winter well matched my dreary state of mind. Cold gray days stretched out and I was wracked with dreams of drowning mothers wrapped in bolts of cotton and linen, so conflated were my longings for my first mother and my most beloved friend. Mimi met us at the dock and I saw that she was great with child, which forthwith cast Nicolas into a state of crippling embarrassment. He refused to look directly at her.

However, her condition excited me, for I felt a child would be an excellent companion and friend to Freddy—an eager, intelligent boy—for though he played with other children, Mimi was his only kin in that part of the vast New World and this, I know, can write a story upon the soul of a child to last a whole life long.

Mimi was quiet on the subject of the impending child, her countenance rather forbidding, such that I dared not broach the topic. Neither did Mimi's friends nor Mi'kmaq relatives mention it, nor even the women who were also round-bellied and therefore by nature had much to discuss out of the earshot of men. I could not understand this and was driven to question Freddy, but he was puzzled at my query and so I did not press it.

Many a year had passed since I spent a winter in Acadia, but I had not forgotten the icy sea and winds. Even in the severest snowstorms, I walked my familiar childhood forests with my faithful Nicolas trailing behind. To my child's eye, those deep woods had been intimate, friendly groves, cir-cumscribed by the paths, brooks, and clearings familiar to all children there. Now, though, I traversed deeply into their mysterious, wintery environs, enclosed in muffled silence.

Each room at the Ursuline Academy contained a plaque inscribed with the words *Know Thyself* and by this, the nuns intended us to explore the benevolent nature of our hearts and souls that we might grow into good, just, thoughtful people. But I knew myself not. As I roamed the stark Acadian landscape mulling over the philosophies I had learned, the answers seemed then like a book hiding behind another book hiding behind another book.

The snow began to melt into mud when Mimi bid me come walking with her one day as we had many a year ago, to her secluded places of roots and bark. She would not allow Nicolas along, for she thought escorts unnecessary in that pacific land. I begged her not to go that day for the forest was mucky, dripping, dark, and altogether unpleasant. Her back ached and her ankles had swollen painfully, and she seemed but days away from giving birth. Acadian women, though, often walk long distances into the forest as their time grows near in the belief that this shortens nature's process of bringing new life into the world.

Mimi knew that I myself was bleeding in a woman's way just then and wished to counsel me. "This will be you one day soon," she said, placing her hand on her belly.

"Oh, not for many a year," I said, "for Cristophé is fighting and I..." I trailed off, unsure as to the end of that thought. Surely I wished it for myself some distant day, yet right then I felt a sudden horror at the physicality of it. Mimi, who usually smelled of lavender or jasmine or the deep and pungent scents of moss or unguents, smelled of sweat and blood and incipient milk and something sour and terrible. I had smelled that in the Ursuline hospital and felt a sick, cold dread encountering it again.

Mimi began to shake, so I bid her sit upon the ground, which she did with great difficulty. "Océane," she said, "there are joys and mysteries and terrors in this world that you know nothing of. You must be careful! Some day, you will love a man and 'twill tear you to pieces and threaten to destroy you. Love has an awful, dark power just behind the light." She was breathless and holding her belly.

"But I love Cristophé," I said, "and that love is simple and pleasant and knows no darkness."

"Not that kind of love," she replied, then took to rocking back and forth with her arm circling her belly. Whimpering, she began to speak to the child within. "You will be the one beloved child of all my life," she said, "you and none other." She murmured this over and over, oblivious of me.

Tears stung my eyes, for though I was not of her blood, I had suckled at her breast and thought I knew well her love for me. And what of Freddy, who had come from her body no less than this one would? I felt a misery that I cannot describe. Mimi was in her own world now, moaning and whispering to the child within in the language of her ancestors. Her voice had a resonance and aching love I had never heard.

I left her there, so hurt was I. "She is delirious and knows not what she says," I told myself, but my pain turned into ire and I strode a long distance along the sloppy trail until I heard a creek running softly. I flung myself upon its bank though 'twas muddy and cold. My anger turned back to heartache and I sobbed a long while, for was I not truly motherless and had been all my years, mistaking Mimi's good affection and responsible care for something other than 'twas? At last, exhausted, I fell asleep.

I awoke to find the sun in a different place and guilt overtook me for having left Mimi alone. Hurriedly, I retraced my steps or thought I did, but I went in misdirections several times. My remorse grew into panic until at last I came upon her. All seemed calm. I heard her breathing and was flooded with relief, so I fell upon her, kissed her, and wrapped her in my arms.

Eventually, I dried my tears and pulled back enough to see a babe in her lap, not one hour old. I saw he was a boy and stared with wonderment at his appearance, for he did not resemble a Frankenstein in any manner. A beautiful child, his hair was straight and black, his eyes black like Mimi's, and his skin a deep chestnut, darker than hers, very much like the Mi'kmaq warriors who shared their blessed Acadia with us. He was of good size but unnaturally quiescent and languid. He watched Mimi as she lovingly tended to him and once again I was hit with a wave of melancholy, for this was the look my father described to me many a time—the look of motherlove on the face of the beautiful Beatrix Belfleur.

A week passed and the boy would not suckle. Mimi and her friends tried every midwifery trick they knew, but that little one would not take goat's milk nor cow's milk, nor the milk of other nursing mothers. Mimi devised many herbal potions and dribbled them into his mouth, but he only coughed and the liquid came back out. And so that boy, named Henri, died in a manner ghastly to observe. He perished, not in agony, but dried up like an autumn leaf losing its beauty and life bit by bit, day by day, until it crumbles, drifts to the ground, and turns to dust.

Mimi wrapped him in a shroud of flowered fabric and asked me to accompany her to the burial ground, only me, though private burial was not the custom of Acadia. Near day's end, we set out in a cart and horse and rode past the city's usual cemetery where my mother's people doze for all eternity. A winding path through the woods ended at the top of a hill. Mimi said I should turn in a circle and view the hill from every angle.

At first, it appeared a nondescript slope recovering from winter's sleep—stones and dirt, grass and weeds not yet a hand's height. I looked at Mimi quizzically but she was stern as stone and bid me look again. The pink and orange streaks of sunset shifted a bit and in that momentarily renewed sunlight I saw that the hill was covered with little wooden crosses in straight rows, crosses such as Acadian mothers make for children's graves, their small branches intertwined and tied with bits of leather or strips of long-faded muslin from the garment they wore the day the child died, each cross marking the resting place of one Acadian babe.

Mimi walked halfway down the hill, stepping between the rows, and I followed. A wind had come up and blew the bits of faded fabric like little flags—tiny, sad flags snapping in lonely harmony. Mimi stopped at one particular row and I near bumped into her, so closely was I following. "Mine," she said. She walked along the row, counting each one. "Six," she said. "These six are my babies, yet none as precious as this one who slumbers in my arms."

Why was this one so special to her? Why was that hillside covered with the graves of little babies? I felt about to faint as she buried her most beloved boy and put his cross in place. At last, she rose and spoke in a bitter, flat voice, gesturing over the breadth of the hill. "Look unto your life, Océane," she said. The sunset colors were gone and now the world seemed made of secrets and lies. I lost consciousness and fell to the earth.

CHAPTER V

Thus my year of personal study commenced. Mimi was kind and generous to me. We spoke not of her row of dead babies nor were there visible shadows of anything she said in the woods the day of Henri's birth. Did she forget? To this day I harbor a silent, simmering ache over it. I believe that words spoken at such a time in such a manner carry a raw truth, which discussion could twist into something less potent, a mere misunderstanding. In an odd way, I did not want to water it down, for some things in life ought to be remembered in their stark clarity, which in normal social intercourse is rarely heard.

The patina of the Ursuline Academy had followed me to the simple land of Acadia. People knew I read, and when they saw my trunk of learned books they left me to myself rather than expecting me to share the usual domestic chores. Though I had acquiesced to my father's wishes, I was nevertheless tormented by a desire to be elsewhere, for the world was large and full of astonishments I wished to explore.

My hours spent with Freddy and my books then became my solace. Freddy's interest in animals had grown and we often sat side by side learning about our favorite subjects; likewise, we amused ourselves with jackstraws and marbles. When my mind grew weary of book learning, I took to other occupations. I had witnessed in the school hospital that sewing is a vital component of medical intervention, so I asked Mimi to expand my knowledge of this most humble handicraft that I might employ it in my future endeavors. She taught me embroidery stitches for joining, seaming, and patching, as well as decorative, intricate stitches for I knew not what particular use.

At last, the seasons went around and I kissed Freddy and Mimi goodbye and sailed from Halifax to Boston with Nicolas and Cristophé, who got leave from General Washington's Continental Army to travel by my side. With both men accompanying me, my father surrendered his fear of oceangoing ships and permitted a sea voyage at the tail end of winter. In any case, going overland would have been impossible, for Acadia was still buried in snow. Winter followed that ship, which took quite severe punishment from the cold and icy waves.

Cristophé—he of the black, black hair and blue, blue eyes—was tall now, a full man, calm and self-assured with the posture of a soldier. I had to adjust and get to know him a different way. During the day we huddled on deckchairs, bundled up in heavy blankets. The sun was bright and cold, and we talked for hours, nursing cups of hot chocolate, with Nicolas always keeping watch.

I told Cristophé of my father's wishes that I follow in his footsteps, as much as a girl is able, and how agreeable this was to me.

"'Tis not a safe world for girls to go into such professions," he said. "You have seen little of the horrors of the world. Your school clinic with its protective walls and teachers on every side is hardly comparable to nursing in a rough city, for patients will be far more ill with serious maladies that you are sure to encounter in Boston, especially during wartime. Let us marry sooner than planned. Let me care for you with the proper love and devotion."

"Oh," I said, "I greatly doubt I shall be in danger. Father will likely use me as an apothecary apprentice and I shall be safely ensconced in a back room full of flowers and other wonderments of nature. You will be in the Army for many a month, perhaps even many a year. If we were to marry now, I would pine away terribly and, as a wife, have the protection of no man while you are soldiering. If we wait, you can take up your musket and three-corner hat and freely become the brave and noble man you desire—an honor that will follow you all your life—and I will be safe under my father's tutelage."

My reply lacked complete candor for, though my love was true, I was urged on by a compulsion to freely find my way in this world a little longer. He took me in his arms and we resolved to go our separate ways for now and promised to write to each other, as we were able. By that conversation, I discovered that a decision could leave one sorrowful and elated in equal measure. Experience henceforth, however, taught me that 'tis not exactly true; time throws emotions off-kilter and there is no such thing as equal measure.

I lay alone in my cabin at night, lonely and tossed about by my fears and preoccupations. Neither of my companions could stay in my cabin with me, though I would have let them if convention had permitted it. Cristophé told me that Nicolas attempted to spend the nights crouched outside my door in the narrow hallway but was forbidden from this endeavor, for so bulky was he that others could not pass by. Thus he was relegated to Cristophé's cabin in wakeful misery for want of being able to protect me.

'Tis a shadowy world in a half-empty little cabin in a very large ship when one, in the normal course of her life, has rarely spent a night alone. I clutched my blanket close, to no avail, for I felt my mother alive in me every night on that voyage, trapped in a ship like that very one in which I reclined, trapped in the underbelly of man's cruelty, a swatch of fabric stuffed in her mouth to absorb the screams of childbirth.

Still, by day, with my two men beside me, I was reassured and felt my heart quicken as we approached Boston Harbor. 'Twas full of British, French, and American warships milling around every which way, spread far out toward the horizon. Some had cannons with little curls of smoke coiling upward. We were able to disembark only after the greatest difficulty.

The streets were choked with a terrifying crush of armed soldiers; we were hard-pressed to wind our way to my father's house. Nothing therein was as expected. The air was abuzz with excitement. My father's medical kit and numerous other cases were stacked by the front door. He greeted us warmly and bid me immediately don my plainest dress, most shielding bonnet, warmest cloak, and sturdiest shoes. He and Cristophé disappeared into the library and emerged in fine waistcoats, breeches, and long blue coats with white facings, linings, and buttons, and three-corner hats. Leather straps crossed over their chests while satchels, canteens, and muskets hung from their shoulders.

Tears sprang into my eyes when I saw them and I could scarcely breathe, for they looked so strong and dashing, and already half gone to the hell-bent fields of war. I saw a longing expression steal over Nicolas's face, so greatly did he wish to be a soldier. Cristophé took my hands, kissed them repeatedly, and explained that he must report to his regiment with all haste, for due to high seas our ship returned behind schedule and he was expected forthwith. He stroked my face, held me tenderly, whispered I hardly knew what, then departed.

I fell to my knees and wept, despairing that I would ever see him again. Lofty theories of courage are fine, but the realities of a loaded musket and goodbye kiss are something quite another. Nicolas led me to a chair and my father came to comfort me.

"You are going, too, Father?" I asked. "Must I see you for only this moment, then lose you, too?"

"The fighting is such that I cannot heal the wounded here; I must join General Washington's Continental Army as a surgeon. Do not let your heart drop, for if you wish it, you and Nicolas may accompany me. I have registered you, for women oftentimes follow troops as water carriers, laundresses, seamstresses, and nurses. You will be at my side to nurse men as they fall on the field or from illness, and never will you find a greater university than a battlefield.

"If you desire it, you will see and experience things that will sear themselves on your sensibilities and cause you great despair and difficulty. You, protected schoolgirl that you have been, is this what you choose? Say no and I shall kiss you most heartily and leave you here with Nicolas to mix and dispense apothecary elixirs, a most worthy employment of its own. Say yes and you will see the world anew which, I do believe, dear girl, is something you long for."

I put my hand in his and my heart filled with love for this man opening life to me.

CHAPTER VI

Thus three winters passed. Miles beyond counting, days beyond counting, I walked behind soldiers alongside other camp followers—women and children keeping after their men, beasts of burden carrying sacks of laundry or large straw baskets of pots and kettles and other camp supplies strapped to their backs. Sometimes young children peeked out from the baskets, war babies.

On we walked, clad in rags, skin browned by the sun, every vestige of feminine fancy gone. Behind us clattered wagons containing the larger weapons of war and heavy supplies, and behind them, livestock seized now and then from nearby farms, though in that last, fiercest winter even those creatures grew scarce, for farmers ate all their sheep and cows and even their dogs.

Nicolas walked at my side, seemingly impervious to the vicissitudes of war and weather, well-loved by all, for he often took on the burden of a woman who seemed especially spent and about to faint.

Doctoring in wartime is an intimate occupation. The usual womanly reserve is of no use, nor are the pretensions of privacy that exist in hospitals, such as shielding bedclothes, screens, and separate cots, which do not exist on battlefields. Every man who fell in battle or from illness or starvation or sheer despair was stripped naked before my eyes. Every shape and color and station of man passed through my hands and I lost all the shyness and ignorance that goes with virginal maidenhood.

Men often clung to me, wept in wretched agony, cursed God and man, and begged for clothes, blankets, shoes, and food. Many a soldier called out for his mother with his last breath, and for this I felt the greatest sympathy for reasons you well know by now.

Some good days our marches took us through lush forests. As we passed through these dense, unsettled woods, the war receded. The drummer boy ceased playing; we proceeded quietly and did not talk, and even the wagon wheels tread lighter on the forest floor. We felt sensitive, like children, to the forest creatures, the rustle of leaves, the small talk of running brooks, and the dappled sunshine, and would have gladly set down our arms and woes and curled up on the warm ground to sleep for a century that we might awaken to a peaceful world of plenty, if such would ever again absolve this earth of blood and horror.

My father spoke truly, for it took me some time to cease fainting or vomiting at the wounds I witnessed, mortal wounds that men visited upon each other in God's beautiful meadows where butterflies, field mice, and bees went about their blessedly simple business. During those early weeks, he kindly had me tend to apothecary supplies and so I prepared stimulants, rubefacients, caustics, salts, emetics, purgatives, blistering compounds, maggots, and bloodletting equipment.

I wrote to Lara and Cristophé, when I had a location for
him. My letters were not entirely forthcoming, for I believe
all war letters are highly selective in their content so as to
shield the recipients from truths too appalling to bear. Nay,
I did not write about being eternally bathed in the splash
of blood and every other body fluid; nor of handing instruments still bloody from the last man to my father that he
might separate men from their limbs; nor of my growing
skill in stitching up wrists, shoulders, ankles, and thighs after
amputations; nor of summers plagued by rattlesnakes and
mosquitoes; nor of heavy thunderstorms with winds strong
enough to uproot trees and turn battlefields and camps
into swamps; nor of barefoot men, women, and children
who, though not wounded, suffered from ringworm and
the seeping stings of hornets that seemed to organize into
their own infernal armies; nor of winters marked by blue
feet and misery; nor of soldiers dying slow, tortuous deaths
from the effects of cannonballs, grapeshot, musket balls,
bayonets, sabers, and knives; nor of soldiers drowned in
river rapids, trampled by horses, or accidentally struck by
axes in camp; nor of women running out onto battlefields
to strip clothes and weapons from the barely dead to give
to their soldier husbands; nor of the particular afflictions
of the itch, smallpox, lice, dysentery, bilious fever, malaria,
apoplexy, chilblains, pleurisy, boils, abscesses, and gangrene;
nor of how some days so many died of smallpox that not
enough living survived to bury the dead, so we lay them
side by side under God's open sky and left the worms to
do the rest. Patriotism is brother to barbarity; let no man
tell you otherwise.

Instead, I wrote letters about the tents called Flying Hospitals that men set up in every camp, complete with a surgeon's table and fresh straw over the floor for men to lie
upon and be tended to. I wrote too of the generosity of the

French, who provided mercury compounds, laudanum, lavender spirits, opium, arsenic, cream of tartar, tincture of myrrh, quinine bark, vinegar, camphor, turpentine, lint compresses, ligatures, tourniquets, scalpels, and jalap, and how country people gave over their last rum and whiskey for use as a surgery narcotic. I wrote to Mimi of the official daily rations for each man: one pound of beef or fish or pork, one pound of bread or flour, one pint of milk, one quart of spruce beer or cider, as well as three pints of beans or peas and one pint of Indian meal per week, so she might be comforted that Father was adequately fed—though, in fact, this was rarely true.

I did confess that, at night, my father and I sometimes drank a cup of spirits to numb our realization that medical interventions themselves often seemed to kill patients in alarming numbers, with shocking rapidity. My father often despaired of this and fell into black states of mind that lasted for months, which I tried to relieve by working close by his side. Sometimes—as in that gilded carriage so long ago—I was his mother, urging him to rest and clean himself, and for one moment to look up from his work to heaven's blue sky and find the beauty there.

I wrote of the wheelbarrows, springless wagons, carts, and stretchers made of blankets or coats used to carry the wounded off the battlefield; and of my habit of tending to wounded men at dawn, before marches or battles commenced, by shaving them, bathing their hands and feet, and combing their hair, and how in that quiet time of day soldiers confided their secrets and sorrows. I wrote of the brave women who often stepped across fields of blood to collect the empty canteens of their husbands and returned with them filled with fresh water.

'Twas during those years that I came to attain an extensive knowledge of the body's every organ, tissue, sinew, and vessel. If not too exhausted, I kept a candle burning at night and studied the anatomical fugitive sheets my father sent me until they became frayed and marked by dirty or bloody fingerprints. Even with the candle snuffed, I could draw maps of the flow and pathways of things—how vessels were an elaborate tree, with the heart as the center, and how lightly that fragile heart was protected from blows and weapons, how a touch on a nerve in one part of the body caused a strong response in another distant part, how every person had the same construction inside, regardless of the differences in their exteriors.

Always I came around to questions of whether death was final or if an undiscovered land existed between life and death. At last, I spoke to my father of this. He answered in historical terms, telling me that even ancient peoples feared vivisepulture and that corpses have been revived because of accidentally dropped coffins, rough handling by grave robbers, initiation of embalming, and attempted dissection.

People, he told me, have drowned and come back to life after being rolled about on top of barrels. Even we, he reminded me, had given up on soldiers whose lives had surely ceased, only to have them groan and move about when prepared for burial. Round and round this discussion went and still we ended up in the same place we began: life and death contain mysteries man can never know. For months, I dreamed that a living boy in a shallow grave sat up, breathed, and shrieked with confusion and horror.

During my third year in the war, I became ill with a spiritual fever, a fever of my psyche. I drew back from everyone, even my father, caring for nothing and no one, nor even if I lived or died. My world was composed of every stinking body fluid and effluvia. The earth's surface was covered end to end with seeping, weeping, suffering corpses. God yawned in a corner somewhere. Man was violent and cruel;

women birthed dead and dying babies. Children everywhere looked like haunted skeletons. Water tasted like poison. Poison tasted like water.

In this soul-sickness, I took a pony and cart and turned my back on the battlefield, carrying only my small apothecary cabinet, books, and letters. I spoke to no one. The pony poked along a narrow woodland path. Many an hour passed and the breath of night came close before I heard my faithful Nicolas rushing behind me. I near collapsed upon seeing his dear face. He led me to a soft bed of pine needles in the darkening forest, patted me on the back with his big, awkward hand, and said, "Doctor Missy Océane."

I fell to weeping and felt poisonous and evil, as if I myself were contaminated by every horror in this world, for neither man nor woman nor any living creature can retain purity of heart and soul in war. I slept a day and night around. Nicolas did not awaken me, but huddled with me, protecting me from cold rain, cannonades, and nightmares of hell and damnation.

On we went, staying off well-trodden roads when possible. Weeks passed thus and I gave no mind to my father or Cristophé or anyone dear to me. Let them think me dead, for so I felt. November drew near and we were faint from hunger as we passed through wide countryside with spread-out farms, mostly deserted, for game had gone to ground for the winter.

One day as a cold storm gathered, we climbed a high hill, where Nicolas saw a farmhouse at some distance. At the sight of this, he hastened toward the house with his empty rucksack in the hope of begging a potato or rutabaga or finding half-rotten apples at the base of a tree in the yard.

After he left, I was overswept with vast loneliness. The sky turned gray and a sleet storm blew fast and angry across the landscape. My mind was confused; time stretched and constricted. Perhaps I was really on that other hill, in that other storm when my father slept and slept, and in my childish innocence I cared for him and we found beloved Cristophé. Or that other hill covered with the graves of babies, where little bits of fabric waved at the sunset.

I got down from the cart and rushed out into the open field, into the fullness of the storm, and screamed curses—for I had learned many rich turns of phrase in the Army—screaming until my voice cracked and departed, then I stripped off my clothes and stood naked in the raging wind and needles of ice. Wordless, I begged God to take my life, for death in life is no life at all, but nothing happened. Soon enough, the indifferent thunder rolled on and I fainted dead away.

When I awoke, I was wrapped in a blanket, lying on a straw mat before a fire. I saw Nicolas and another man seated at a kitchen table. A kettle bubbled over the fire and something smelled good. One may wish to die, but the stomach has its own ideas. I rose and Nicolas turned toward me. He smiled with a joy that I had never seen in him and excitedly waved about a card covered with little pictures. The other man went to stir the kettle before I got a good look at him. Nicolas bid me sit near him, took one of my hands in his, and began to make shapes with his fingers against my palm. He was snorting and laughing such that I laughed, too, to my surprise—though I had no understanding of the meaning of this.

"'Tis the American Manual Alphabet, if I may show thee," said the other man. He put a bowl of soup in front of me and I saw him fully. He was beautiful. I cannot equivocate nor temper that. A lock of hair fell over his forehead and his eyes were big with golden lights and long eyelashes. His clothes were simple, clean, and well fitting, an astonishing sight during wartime. His shirt had all its buttons and he appeared in robust health.

He sat beside me and pulled a book close, a children's alphabet book. "Eat, friend," he said. Flushed with shame about my filthy, unkempt appearance, I ate my soup with impolite alacrity nevertheless, for 'twas rich with onions, potatoes, parsnips, and meat, perhaps rabbit. "My name is Moses Dalton," he said. "Thy friend came to my door carrying thee—cold, wet, and insensible." As I ate, Nicolas pointed at the card and book, and continued to wave his fingers in the air. This, the stranger explained, was a method of opening the world of speech to those who could not hear by spelling words with finger speech.

"Thou and thy devoted friend are welcome here, Océane," he said, and smiled at my surprise. "Thy friend told me thy name is Doctor Missy Océane. In the manner of my people, we use proper names, not titles; so pray do not take offense. Likewise, I beg thee call me Moses and tell me the name of thy intrepid friend."

Thus began an interlude in my life that I will never forget, for I understood at that moment that whether I knew Moses Dalton for a day or a year or a life entire, our time together would be as a golden dream, a fairy tale, a wonderment, alive inside me for all eternity and even evermore after that until the time after time when all is gone but for the swirling breath of ancient gods.

CHAPTER VII

'Tis hard to keep joy unspoken, so during that time I wrote the following letter, that my family might know I still walked this earth:

To MIMIKEJ POULETTE

Near Saratoga, New York
December 20th, 1778

As you may know, Nicolas and I left camp last fall. Perhaps Father, Cristophé, or Lara have inquired as to whether I am with you in Acadia, for I am ashamed to admit that I have not written to them. Could I explain this self-excommunication, I would. Perchance 'twas melancholia creeping upon me, stealing my affections and affiliations.

I believe that the time will come when I am able to explain this impulse; I will then beg forgiveness from all I love for troubling them with worry, as I do beg you today if you have experienced even one disquieting moment on my behalf. My health is blooming and my spirit recovering from nostalgia, that spiritual plague of many a soldier, in a manner I shall now describe.

With winter setting in, plagued by hunger, Nicolas and I were kindly taken in by a Quaker, a man named Moses Dalton. While the war left me believing in neither miracles nor thaumaturgy, I am hard-pressed not to ascribe this to some kind of divine intervention.

Do you know of Quakers, also hereabouts called the Society of Friends? They are distinctive in their manner of dress, bearing, and speech, which reflect their belief in simplicity and equality. They have no hierarchy, nor titles, nor leaders, nor followers. I have never addressed him as "Mr. Dalton" for this reason and he too only calls me "Océane" in their familiar manner, even from the moment we first met.

Quakers are opposed to slavery and in this, they are kin to Acadians. Their spirits are tempered by tranquility, love of land, and silence. Moses has described to me religious services marked by neither minister nor priest, but long periods of community silence broken only when and if any member wishes to speak. Imagine any group of people we know who would be comfortable sitting for an hour or two in holy silence, without the lubricating effects of audible prayer, scripture readings, sermons, songs, or the other comforting traditions of Christian service! In their speech, they use "thee" and "thou" and "thy" and "thine" in the ancient manner. I think you would find them and their ways most agreeable, for by their beliefs they strip away the false praise, status, and rivalry evident in most human societies.

They are not without laws or rules. They disowned Moses for the crime of joining General Washington's Continental Army to take up arms in the war. 'Tis why he dwells no longer in the salutary company of his Quaker family and companions, instead living this past year in an abandoned farm in a territory little occupied except by regiments marching through. We are in the northern New York colony, some miles away from a town decimated by war such that many shops along the main street are burned-out shells.

Farms far and wide were seized, sacked, and burned by Redcoats, their occupants having fled or been killed defending themselves. Then the soldiers moved on as battlefields shifted. The village is beginning to rise again, such that 'tis possible to buy necessaries. Moses brought with him his people's knowledge of botany and zoology, set up a laboratory in the tower of a likewise abandoned and partially burned chantry called the First Parish Church, filled it with many curiosities of nature collected hereabouts, and has absorbed himself in writing a book of catalogs, sketches, and precise and poetic descriptions of each entity, along with explorations of its cycle of life and death.

Do you see then how destiny has stepped into my life? For not only have I grown to love Moses, but our minds are singularly aligned in our interests and passions. Perhaps you remember when, on the birth day of your poor dear Henri, you warned me that a certain kind of love can be so deep that it cannot be contained and will, in the end, tear you up and destroy you? I understand this now, for I believe that describes the profound, captivating love I have for Moses, except that he is so kind and good, steady and laudable in every way, that surely 'twill not end in devastation.

A blacksmith married us in the simple manner of his people. Nicolas has caused no impediment to our union, though in the past he has sent many a man cowering in fear for even glancing at me a certain way. Nay, he loves Moses, who forthwith from our first day taught Nicolas a magic method of conversing by using finger positions for each letter of the alphabet. Now that dear fellow chatters all day, though he scarce utters a word!

Moses—I could speak his name a thousand times a day and never tire of it. Likewise, I could tenderly kiss and touch and lie with him in the good glory of nakedness and never feel shame nor hesitance. Again, I beg your forgiveness, Mimi, for I was shocked and even silently thought ill of you upon seeing Henri, who did not resemble Father in any way.

Now I understand that a woman is helpless in the face of love and that you uttered that warning because you loved another man, Henri's father. How you must have suffered, loving someone other than your wedded husband. I understand now why, when your belly was heavy with Henri, you and your friends were oddly silent, for 'twas far more complicated than I could fathom. And too I understand your fevered attachment to that quiet babe, for "that" kind of love made him all the more precious to you. I curse the naiveté that kept me from being able to truly know and comfort you. How can love that deep ever be wrong, given as a gift from God, if there is a God, which I have come to severely doubt, for war is surely a godless state of man?

You will caution me that I am betrothed to Cristophé and I swear that I do love him pure and true, but not in the manner I am describing here. I will free him from our engagement at some future time, but for now, I want to bask in the perfection of this farmhouse, which Moses and Nicolas are bringing back to life with every manner of fruit, vegetable, and flower. This springtime past, the land around us was a riot of cherry and apple blossoms and sweet green grass springing from winter's desolate earth.

My belly is swelling with a baby, Mimi! How overjoyed I am, yet too I suffer from nightmares filled with sneaking fears and forebodings that this harmony and abundance cannot endure. Moses knows everything I studied, all I did and saw during the war, and he intuitively understands even my most private preoccupations, for we speak as one natural philosopher to another. My father would cry out in wonderment at the fullness of his laboratory, for before we arrived he transported much equipment from Charleston in the South Carolina Territory, including a microscope, a marvel I had never before seen.

Quakers have a view of life and death in which life and love are mysteries that man is unable to penetrate; they possess a timeless quality that cannot be destroyed by death nor constrained by time and space. Heaven is the here and now. In our secluded sanctuary of farm and church, surely my heaven is now. Moses and I see ourselves as adventurers in the riddles of the earth and this is a delirious, reckless, divine state. Is this the sublime state about which you warned me? Such exaltations cannot be for ill, for even our unborn child seems to us made of clay and seas and trees and rain and mountains and every glory of this earth.

Mimi, I beg you keep these revelations to yourself for the present. Please be so kind, though, as to let Father know that I am recovering from war shock and will write to and see him in due time. He will no doubt pass these glad tidings on to Cristophé and Lara.

I sign off as your dear,
OCÉANE FRANKENSTEIN DIT BELFLEUR

My heart eased upon writing this letter, but never did I send it, for reasons you shall soon see. But please allow me a sip of spirits, Captain Galán, for my story now becomes more confounding. 'Tis to my benefit that you have allowed Master Percy to stay here throughout, but I beg you now reconsider, for 'tis a grisly tale I tell. I see he is a most perceptive child and, if you deem him sturdy enough to bear my words, 'twill be a solace to me that he remain. Do remember, though, that I have warned you thus.

In the fall, near a year after my arrival at the farm, a bewildered calf stood outside our kitchen window and, mooing pitifully, stared at us big-eyed as we ate. Moses and Nicolas cajoled her into the barn and spent the night washing her and tending to deep bramble scratches and a chewed-off ear. They named her Penny, talked downright lovey-dovey to her, and fed her potato mash from their fingers with such devotion I could not help but be convinced what a fine father and uncle they would be. Sometimes when war and death are all around, one is eager to pour affection on any innocent living thing that fate brings to your side.

I checked on them at dawn and there they all slept, sprawled on the barn floor. The calf lay curled up with her face close to theirs. I sat awhile nearby; how peaceful was the sound of Nicolas's snores mingled with the first conversations of early birds. Morning gave a hint of a cold, sunny day. They woke, shook off bits of straw, and seemed altogether sheepish about their bovine love the night before.

One day we went on a fishing expedition, with Penny ambling after us as if she were a dog. She drank deeply from the creek and frolicked about, tripping over roots and rocks in her lightness of spirit. I sat at the creek's edge and took charge of our supply of worms. The men baited their hooks and settled down to wait. Nicolas balanced his fishing pole between his knees while he and Moses practiced the finger alphabet in lively, silent conversation. They laughed and jostled like boys, and the morning passed in this delightful manner. The last of the autumn leaves had fallen and now lay as a carpet of red and yellow dust. The baby, whom we decided we would name Eugénie or Solomon, kicked gently inside me.

Sire, yet again I hesitate to continue, yet again my story falters here, for I fear that no one can bear the weight of my vile and tragic tale, even secondhand. I beg you lower me overboard when I have finished, for 'twould be a fitting end to my wretched life. Promise me this even if your promise be a lie, for 'twill comfort me well enough that I may continue.

Nicolas had gone off to gather rabbits and squirrels from our traps when a small contingent of British cavalry then came upon us. The soldiers were thin and none too healthy, for smallpox scars marred some of their faces, yet their coats were smartly buttoned and their hats had red feathers on the crown. Nicolas had taken with him the hunting musket in case a deer crossed his path, thus we had no gun. Moses had a gutted trout in one hand and his knife in the other, and appeared outwardly unperturbed. But he moved to shield me with his body and even though I could not see his face, I felt the pounding of his heart.

"Greetings, friends," he said, "will thee sit awhile and share our catch, for we plan to cook and dine right here by God's abundant stream?"

The soldiers' horses were restless, anxious to drink from the creek, but the men held them back until their eyes bulged and their muzzles dripped with foam. My baby flipped about in a frantic, unnatural manner and I was struck with a terror so great that spots appeared before my eyes and I heard a great roaring in my ears.

The foremost soldier dismounted, handed his reins to the fellow beside him, charged forward, and bayonetted Moses through and through. I can scarce speak these words I am about to say aloud, for I saw the blade come out of his back, saw it, and thought perhaps 'twould plunge into me—and I wished it so, if wish can be the word. But 'twas not cruel enough, nay, for the soldier grabbed Moses's hunting knife, slit my beloved's throat, and even as he lay bleeding–dying–on the forest floor, the soldier slashed his beautiful face with deep cuts to the bone.

Because Moses no longer shielded me, the men saw my pregnant state, muttered, grew nervous, and urged the killer–splashed with blood–to mount his horse and hasten away. The horses reared up as the soldiers jerked their reins hard, and in the confusion a horse kicked me, hitting my body entire, knocking me down. As they turned to leave, I heard one clear sentence: "Quakers... dirty thee and thou cowards."

My fall knocked the wind out of me until at last I gasped and crawled over to Moses, who lay with his eyes open. I shook him, crying out his name repeatedly. Penny wandered over and nuzzled my hand, the little bell around her neck tinkling. The curse upon that harrowing day was not yet complete, for a river of blood and water then flowed from inside me, down my leg; sharp pains flattened me. I screamed and wept, and my tears were made of rage and hate and nothing other.

Nicolas returned with an armful of rabbits, wild carrots, cattails, and chicory. Upon taking in the scene, he fell upon Moses, felt his cooling flesh, and let out a bellow that sent Penny crashing into the woods. He tried to come near me as I squatted on the ground with my skirt lifted, but I snarled at him in a feral manner and, comprehending what was happening, he turned away in mortification. Scarlet from shame, choking on rage for not being there in our time of trouble, he held Moses in his arms, his fingers desperate to speak to those blessed hands I so loved.

I gave birth by the darkening riverside and, like the babies on that Acadian hillside and so many babies on God's bedeviled earth, she died before she lived. The moon rose, shimmered on the creek, and I saw her face, little Eugénie, and there within her my mother's face as I remember in my bones. She was peaceful, my girl, and the whole forest grew soft and reverent in her presence. How pretty was she! A pretty, beautiful, innocent, perfect, plump girl.

Eventually, Nicolas and I gathered our dead. He followed me gingerly, afraid of my blank expression. Across the sleeping fields we went, now white with frost. Penny stuck close by, letting out anxious moos now and then, wondering why she was out at this cold, unfamiliar hour. We did not stop at the farmhouse, but carried them to our church and lay them on a pew. I placed the baby in the crook of her father's arm in a careful tableau, feeling strangely placid. What good was wailing and fussing? Surely, if my beloveds merely slept, as it seemed they must, I too should sleep, for dreamland called me then with its dear oblivion. I arranged Moses's cloak over them but not over their faces. Nicolas and I lay upon adjoining pews. "May beautiful dreams come," I said to Nicolas, but of course he did not reply.

In the morning I awoke hungry and clear-eyed. You may well say that the night robbed me of my senses, but by the twisted logic of grief, I felt I had just found them. What other reason could there be for my years of study in apothecary and medicine? What of those war years practicing surgery and nursing under my father's tutelage? That day, all the stars seemed aligned, for I concluded that whereas my beloveds might be deemed dead, they were not sincerely dead. Truly, they did not look sincerely dead. If you ask me what medical book discerns these terms, I cannot point to one. 'Tis something I concocted within myself, based on all I knew and felt. Yea, I felt a thrilling confidence that I could bring my beloveds back from a twilight land between life and death.

Snow had fallen while we slept in the nave. We proceeded to the farmhouse for food and supplies in the pure beauty of a first snowfall of gentle, lazy flakes, and collected items

I thought useful into a wheelbarrow. Nicolas made many trips back and forth, transporting wood and barn boards to fix holes in the roof and board up broken windows. All the equipment went up into the bell tower laboratory, even a large metal pig trough we used as a makeshift fire pit.

While we arranged things into a functioning operating theater, Moses and Eugénie remained below in the nave, for the cold there was most beneficial as a hedge against putrefaction. You may wonder how in God's good name a girl such as myself, in those circumstances, could think in this coldly reasoned manner. 'Twas not in God's good name, that is why, nor was anything I ever did from that day to this.

My initial efforts proved futile. I lacked the courage to disarrange their cherished, beautiful bodies and thus performed only known procedures, such as rubbing them vigorously with ammonia and spirit of rosemary, then with salt, then with a cloth steeped in brandy, then inserting a feather into their mouths, way down into their throats, then placing a bottle of boiling water against the heels of their feet. There is a reason known procedures are everlastingly antiquated, for the more we attempt, the more means must evolve.

I gave up on these simple endeavors but did not give up hope. I bound them in shrouds made of bedsheets and allowed Nicolas to take them to a burial spot I knew to be covered with wildflowers in summer. Poor man, the ground was close to frozen and it took a full day and night with an axe to dig deep enough. When 'twas done and their bodies were given to the earth, he collapsed like a giant bear and would not rise until I lay down in the snow next to him, nose to nose. I whispered, "Please," that he might read my lips, after which he held my hand for a long time.

What he did not yet know was that I had placed my beloveds' hearts in a glass jar and secreted it in a corner of the church nave with snow packed all around, for 'twas necessary for my next plan, which came upon me like an incubus in the night. If hearts be the seat of the soul and core of life, I would use them to try again, a different way. So prodigious was this plan—you may call it maniacal, satanic, impious, wicked, though I did not—that for some time I sought to erase it from my mind. I did, in fact, attempt to run from it.

Winter began in earnest. I left home and traversed the surrounding territory bundled in my cloak, a deerskin hat Moses made, and tall moccasins I had taken some time since from a dead soldier. Likewise clad, Nicolas followed me, though I bid him go back. Penny too trailed behind, a blanket strapped around her scrawny belly, content to have us within sight. For several weeks, we lived like trappers, subsisting on roots and game, walking dawn to dusk through mysterious, unsettled forests, up many a hill, beside many an icy river, across endless frozen farmlands and meadows.

When the white winter moon beckoned, we kept on through the night. In the stark beauty of the landscape, my disposition altered. The poisonous whirlwind of rage and hate and bitterness cooled a bit. Instead, I suffered from the sorrow and anguish that fills all hearts when beloveds die. Then that ebbed somewhat, too, and was replaced by a kind of strange, clean serenity. For some days, I did not question this feeling, nor try to explain it to myself. I let it occupy my sensibilities and rest my spirit. Soon, though, I faced myself and understood that this weird, austere peacefulness is something that washes over a person when they have made up their mind about something so fateful that nothing can dissuade, divert, or destroy it.

By then, the snow was too deep, the nights too bitter, so we circled back to the farmhouse, now containing a soft dusting of snow inside from fissures in the roof. We lit a fire, swept the floor, and set a huge pot of squirrel stew bubbling on the fire, ample for many a day. We tried to settle Penny in the barn, but so accustomed had she grown to walking by our side that alone, she bellowed for hours, so we took pity on her and ensconced her in the shed off the kitchen.

My program could not proceed without Nicolas, yet I feared for him should he unknowingly embark upon it without discerning his part. I had not let him observe my efforts to bring Moses and Eugénie back to life, but he likely had some sense of it. My finger alphabet spelling was simple, but I painstakingly worked out the following: "I will make the hearts of Moses and baby live again. Will you help? We must work with dead. Very bad. Yes or no?"

He gazed at me for quite a while after I posed the question, the first time he had fully engaged thus since his woe of observing me giving birth, and his face alit with hope. "Doctor Missy Océane," he said in his odd, endearing voice, and nodded his assent.

The church belfry had three large bells that hung high above in the dome, leaving ample room on the floor below to create an aciurgy. Nicolas remade two pews into a long, sturdy table. Moses's botany and zoology equipment stood clean and gleaming. I ventured by necessity into surrounding towns that only Moses had previously visited, for during my period of retreat, I had no desire to mix with others. We had a bit of money and traded farm equipment and jarred goods for kettles, glassware, copper wire, miles of catgut, herbs and apothecary elixirs, sewing needles, lamp oil, and knives, transporting them on a sledge pulled by Penny, who was pleased now to be of use.

As the preparations neared completion, I grew impatient, for I had determined to create a human being animated by my beloveds' hearts. Given Moses's qualities—his noble heart, his intelligence, his splendid, upright goodness—and my baby's perfect purity and dear nature of childhood, I imagined a being more godly than man, indeed as tender and kind as Aphrodite, as brave as Apollo, as wise as Athena, formed by fire, water, earth, and air. Only a Christian God can create life, you say? 'Tis not so, and henceforth I became God's uninvited, unlikely apprentice—a nobody, no mother's child, no child's mother.

I decided upon my fresh course having concluded that my failed initial experiments to restore life to my darlings stemmed from the hot grief and reverence with which I conducted my efforts. I had failed to use the rigorous, painstaking methods I knew so well. Tears and hope are insufficient remedies. I avowed to courageously work with blood, bone, and sinew as I had on the battlefield. Reason and methodology are in themselves not cold-blooded, for the study of anatomy bestowed upon me a joyous belief that the grand and glorious complexity of the human body could be mastered and tamed.

CHAPTER VIII

Captain, war litters the land with corpses. I beg you to bear this in mind as I continue. Nicolas and I set out one moonless night on a macabre mission, having borrowed two full-grown oxen from a neighbor's field, returning them the next day and none the wiser, for Penny was too young and small to bear a load such as we had in mind. We yoked them to an empty hay wagon and proceeded to a distant encampment. Nausea swept over me, so sick and anxious was I about our impending task. Nicolas, evermore quiet, was a special kind of quiet I found most unsettling.

After many an hour, we heard the nighttime snores of soldiers in their thin tents in the snow, and groans and cries of the injured and lonely. These sounds gave me the greatest sorrow, for they brought back a life that, because of Moses, had come to seem a long-gone nightmare.

We tied the oxen to a tree on one side of an open field on the Patriots' side. From the manner in which cannons and other accouterments of war were set up, 'twas clear 'twould soon be aflame with cannonballs and musket smoke and hundreds of men racing toward their fate. I did not fear encountering Father or Cristophé, so fixed was I upon our lugubrious errand. Nothing was the slightest bit odd about people lingering by a wagon on the outskirts of a battlefield, for 'tis how camp followers transport the dead and injured to the Flying Hospital or the grave.

A cruelly bright winter sun rose that morning and with it, a mad crush of men rushed forth with hearts and weapons blazing. Redcoats are terrifying in their discipline. They march in perfect straight lines that stretch across the field, and even when a man marching mere inches from them is hit, they step over him and surge on at a controlled speed, unwavering in their confidence. Half the men in General Washington's Continental Army, Cristophé once told me, are under the age of sixteen, and I knew this to be true, for so many who passed through my hands were tender boys. From whence does the courage of boys come when the enemy is thus smartly comported?

Nicolas and I waited an hour as men and weapons clashed in full frenzy, and then likewise stepped onto the field, splashing through bloody snow and mud, collecting the dead. Dressed as the other women camp followers in a worn dress and rag wrapped around my head, I blended in with them, for they too came to help or rob fallen soldiers. We did not steal any man's belongings; only perhaps you may say we stole the men themselves, men of every color and size. I gestured to this man and that, using I know not what criteria in the maelstrom—we even collected two women who had taken musket balls and, horribly, a naked child who alas had wandered onto the field in confusion.

After loading ten or so bodies into the wagon, we threw empty grain sacks over them for concealment should passers-by come upon us. Nicolas then slapped the oxen smartly and we proceeded away. By the time we traversed far enough from camp that 'twas no longer audible, the feverish exertion of our quest drained out and we grew lethargic. Even the oxen pulled their load in a slow, dejected manner. The day and distance passed in this way.

Placing the corpses in the church nave proved an awful endeavor, for it required us to strip and wash them, thus encountering their personal possessions—letters creased from frequent readings, small sketches of a woman and child, a watch fob, a home-sewn waistcoat with a name embroidered inside. Thus we learned something of their identities, which I had not anticipated. I put these items in a basket by the door.

At last, those warriors rested, each on a separate pew, arms crossed if there were arms, eyes closed, naked in the cold, with a little snow drifting over them from above. I spread cloves, camphor, and ginger all about to neutralize the effluvium inevitable in such a dark undertaking. 'Twas only when, exhausted, I went up onto the balcony to sit awhile and gazed down that I appreciated the majesty of man's variety. All perished on a single day on a single patch of land, yet they ranged in color from pinkest pink to brownest brown, all locked in man's mad, eternal fixation on bloodshed—Dutch, English, Swedish, French, German, Spanish, Swiss, Scots-Irish, native peoples, and African slaves fighting for their freedom of a different kind.

Let me not describe the full particulars of how my creature came to be. Numerous blizzards passed over the landscape that winter, well suited to my mood and undertaking, for the residents of surrounding towns and farms were kept away by towering snowdrifts and the unforgiving winter wasteland. At times, I felt like a Daughter of Night or a Fury, come forth to shriek in anguish for all that I lost. By lamp oil and candlelight, I toiled in the high tower until Nicolas forcibly dragged me away and fed me with a spoon as if I were an invalid. At other, quieter times, that belfry was my secret kingdom, where bells once rang in innocent days and now hung silent.

I summoned all I had learned—from curative materials hiding in mysterious forests; to schoolgirl observations of blood and pain and fevers; to the anatomical categories of name, description, place, temperature, virtues, and time, which now in my notebook I applied most assiduously to each element big and small that went into my creation, so that these meticulous notations might sidestep the passion and disarray that contributed to my grievous first failure; to the study of each Latin name on my father's charts; to the surgical and medical interventions of the battlefield—these were the compendium of knowledge that now guided my hand.

I felt that this creature in the making would hereafter be my voice, expressing my pain and promise and loneliness, my hope and desire for my beloveds' hearts to beat eternally and show all men that God, who disappoints a thousandfold, does not have the last word in the creation of life.

When I was exhausted beyond all ability to stand another moment at my operating table, too weary to return to the farmhouse for sleep, Nicolas led me to a stack of blankets in the belfry where Moses used to rest and read during his labors. I knew not if my creature, fashioned from the flesh and bone of corpses, would even be human, and of this I worried much. When I was able to sleep, I dreamed of winged, many-limbed freaks that flew across the sky like Icarus, or giants who disappeared like smoke into the pits of hell, or monstrous babies shrieking and shedding tears that drowned the earth.

I made my creature some eight-and-a-half to nine feet tall—a colossus—for two credible reasons. Having lived these years with Nicolas, having observed how others responded to his immense size with wonder and awe, I wished to also create someone whose proportion would best reflect the fullness of his glory, in the manner of a Greek or Egyptian statue. Too, though my hands were small and agile, the microscopic nature of human vessels prohibits their feasible recreation without instruments that do not yet exist. Thus this being—if indeed he ever sprang to life—would be bigger than Nicolas, bigger than any living man.

After several weeks in the quietude of my belfry laboratory, I realized that never before had I worked on my own. 'Twas the first time without Father or a cherished friend or teacher to guide my actions, restrain my worser impulses, or rescue me when my knowledge or courage failed. These bubbling flasks, beakers, fire pots, hacksaws, knives, and other implements were more extensive than any I had handled before. 'Twas no tepid experiment, I knew. 'Twould be a towering success or catastrophic failure. Little did I know there is such a thing as catastrophic success.

People need something to believe in. So habituated had I been to the ever-presence of God that the lack of belief in his existence added to the loneliness I already felt for all my beloveds, dead and alive. He to whom I once said my childhood prayers, my battlefield prayers, my unborn baby prayers, had forsaken me and all who sought his goodly protection.

Sometimes, when my eyes blurred from the exquisitely close work of sewing vessels, organs, and muscles, I put down my instruments and sat at a little window seat Nicolas built for me that I might gaze at Penny wandering in the field below and the open landscape that disappeared into far-off woods. I lived like a nun on tea and simple winter soups.

Week after week, snowstorms raged, shaking the remaining window glass and setting the bells into an ominous slow motion, too slight to sound. When the weather was too algid for man and beast, Nicolas brought Penny into the vestibule, where I could hear her knocking around and calling out affable little yoo-hoos. I visited her when I wished to let her breathe on me with damp, sticky breath that smelled of oats, my friend who filled my mind with peace and comforted me with her funny ways.

In my mind's eye, my creature was a quilt, pieced and stitched from the soldiers lying in the cold nave. I extracted the healthiest parts of each, determining this by examining their tissue through Moses's microscope. I had a vision of the whole emblazoned in my mind and sketches all over the walls and floor. I dare not and will not describe the slaughterhouse conditions in the nave as time passed. I did my best to negate the fetid quality of the air in the belfry—worse even than the nave below—by burning flower-tinctured oils in the lamps. Still, there were layers of odors: from snow and cold to rosewood and lavender to the unmistakable smell of decay and earth and blood.

Nicolas did all I requested; never did he recoil, though after we buried Moses and the baby, his plump face never regained its round and gentle expression. He carried his sorrow in his cast-down eyes and the drawn lines around his mouth. Perhaps I looked like that, too. I had not seen myself in a looking glass in many a month, not since I saw my face reflected in the creek on the day of our fateful fishing expedition. I will say that I had every lush signifier of womanly beauty that day. Still a girl, I wore my hair in a long, loose braid, as I had before the war. 'Twas my vanity, my hair, my feminine grace. I washed it in rainwater and tied it with ribbons, and 'twas that brief loveliness that looked back at me the day my world collapsed.

When grief overcame me as I toiled on my ill-fated project, when my thoughts were tormented by visions of hillsides of babies planted in the earth–unbloomed buds–or of my lost beloveds or of soldiers crying out for their mothers, when these thoughts overcame me much, I brewed potions of ergot, mushrooms, psychotria viridis, or laudanum.

I took only small amounts to induce light waking fancies. Remembrances of Acadian tales and bits of songs drifted through my mind, along with visions of childhood spirits such as cloud people, dryads, and firebirds. Ergot in particular produced a recurrent vision of a seahorse floating among gentle seagrass–have you heard of seahorses?–tiny, delicate creatures living in the warm waters of faraway placid seas. Why this vision came to me I know not, so contrary was its angelic physiognomy to the bloody, godless task at hand.

Can you bear to hear yet more? Mimi and my father would sicken if they ever knew how their lessons benefited my undertaking. I used plain catgut to sew my creature's interior stitching with the neat, surgical stitches my father taught me. For the exterior, as in a quilt, many visible seams were necessary to connect piece to piece. For these I employed Mimi's embroidery stitches in a decorative fashion, using catgut soaked in yellow quercitron powder from black oak trees and indigo blue from a fabric shop in town, both procured when I sent Nicolas for supplies. For double strength, I used these bright strands for the lace running stitch, raised lattice bands, double-darning stitches at the elbows and knees for flexibility, and doubled-over looped edges throughout the torso and legs.

The face was difficult, for I strove to make it pleasing, even beautiful, with prominent cheekbones, symmetrical brows, and a stately nose. The eyes were different colors, one hazel, one blue. The scalp was crowned with waves of lush, dark hair. Once I was satisfied with the harmony and stability of his physiognomy, I embroidered a lacy pattern of ferns and roses such as the one I beheld long since when that

Boston man was struck by lightning, for I never forgot its beauty and magical qualities. For this, I used double knot, single feather, seeding, tulip, and twisting chain stitches. This resulted in a startling design such as I had seen in books on the tattooed faces of men in faraway lands.

I had no fear of my creation, for creating life, was not this already the province of my body? Women, from the mystery and awe of our bodies, we create life. As my task neared an end, however, the methodical reasoning I hoped would prevail throughout began to erode. Fatigue, doubt, and afterthoughts crept over and agitated me. I dropped things, burned things, miscalculated, did over, grew furious, threw things, wept. The belfry laboratory that had been so neat became strewn with innards, discarded instruments, tipped-over jars and tubes, over-boiling pots, and abandoned letters that I had begun many a night to Father, Cristophé, and Lara, only to give up for want of being able to tell the truth.

These chaotic surroundings matched my inner turmoil, and near the very end I lost my nerve. I fled to the nave and fell upon my belly on the altar stairs. 'Twas the dark night of my soul, Captain. Bits of that poem came to me and I murmured what I could: *On a dark night... I went forth without being observed... In darkness and concealment... In secret when none saw me... Oh, night more lovely than dawn... Oh, night that joined beloved with lover... There he stayed sleeping, and I caressed him.* I lay there in a valley of blood and unused eyes, arms and legs and severed heads, stench and decay and endless slop of entrails—all I had rejected in the making of my creature. 'Twas a foul graveyard and none but I was the profane gatekeeper of that stinking necropolis.

Still, even this stopped me not. I collected the final vessel from its hiding place and implanted those two hearts into my creature's chest, connecting the smaller one to the big that it too might also carry life's blood and share its soul and spirit. This marked the moment to animate my being. Mother Nature extended no friendly hand that night, for 'twas the darkest dark of the new year and a dreadful blizzard blew down from the north, from the land of eternal ice in which I now find myself. Every object in my laboratory rattled from that bitter, shrieking wind; even the church struggled to keep from flying off into black, starless nothingness. I heard Penny's plaintive moos and the sound of her restless path around and around the vestibule, and 'twas the only touchstone that kept me steadily bound to my task.

I shall not describe my exact method of giving him *vis vitae*, lest you or others seek to emulate my dire transgression. Suffice it to say that it involved a complex elixir of herbs and medicines infused into the creature's bloodstream, an enormous collection of linked glass Leyden jars, and, at the last, the kiss of life. The infusion progressed well, but the Leyden jars, once provoked by copper wires, imparted a tremendous jolt and spray of sparks. The stench of burning flesh and hair filled the room, and my creature's skin burst apart in places, not fatally—if such is the word for one who does not live—but leaving black, necrotic fissures in many spots, including two on his face.

I nevertheless put my mouth on his, opened his lips, and blew full breaths of life into him. My body trembled such that I could barely stand. He tasted like cloves, which I had rubbed all over him in an effort to... well, surely you can fathom why. I breathed and breathed until I grew faint. Still I breathed and breathed. Night began to think about giving way to day but the storm roared anew, the church shook, the bells swayed. At long last, I felt flutters in the creature's chest, weak, then stronger, then a breath, then nothing, then three breaths, then nothing, then breath after breath after breath, raw and ragged. His eyelashes quivered, his chest convulsed, one eye opened and gazed upon me, ice blue.

CHAPTER IX

The other eye opened. No longer was it hazel. Instead, 'twas a most unnatural lavender, for the shock of the Leyden jars must have altered its hue. An odd silence fell, as if the earth itself was stunned by this new creation. 'Twas not really silence, for the storm had not ceased, but by some mechanism of shock, my ears heard it not. Time became a peculiar thing—stretched, almost lazy. Those eyes blinked, adjusting to the flickers of candles and lamplight.

Nicolas and I stood still as garden sculptures. Tears glistened, then slowly rolled down the sides of the creature's face, disappearing into his ears. Of all the moments I foresaw when my creation first came to life, this was unimaginable. So astonished and touched was I that tears gathered in my own eyes and spilled down my cheeks in a flood of sorrow such as I had not truly felt since this long nightmare began— the direct nightmare of my beloveds' deaths, back to the nightmare of the war, back to the nightmare of the death

ships, back to my forebearers in Acadia and Portugal and
Germany, back to the ancient ancestors of us all, all who
have wept from time immemorial for the joy and grief of
being alive. My tears were quiet, though, as I held my skirt
crumpled against my mouth to muffle the sound.

As I stared, thunderstruck, the creature sat up, his
knees drawn in, a hand extended. Once I saw a sketch of
an immense marble statue and 'twas exactly like my creature in that moment—a naked man, huge of haunches, with
long, muscular arms and legs, knees up—one more than
the other—with enormous feet, one hand outstretched, a
large head crowned with waves of hair, gazing into a far
distance. That book of statues was in my father's study in
Boston and I studied it many a time for its magnificence,
its transcendence of mere mortal form, though I knew not
why it so enchanted me at the time.

This living form before me, however much it resembled
that perfect being in aspect and unknowable expression,
was marred by the very process of creation. Those spark
fissures, though not many, were suppurating and leaking
trails of purulence, including the two on his face. His hair
had half burned away, his scalp singed in those patches.
For all my meticulous work, several stitches on one ear had
loosened, causing it to hang lower than the other.

Most notably, his skin, which without life's blood had
evidenced only pale differences in color relative to each
donor—those ten donors all represented somewhere in the
landscape of his body—had taken on bold, rich hues, result-
ing in a creature of every human color, stitched together
with blue and gold thread. Several stitches too had come
undone on his torso, not enough to cause deep gaps, just
sagging here and there, as when a fabric hem likewise
unravels. Nicolas, I saw, was alarmed at the overall effect
and sidled toward me a bit from the shadows in which he

stood, as if ready to protect me from this startling creature.

My gaze was fixed upon our new companion—if that he be—for upright he was far fiercer than I thought. In time, he haltingly turned sideways in a clumsy manner and sat upon the edge of the table looking at his surroundings, trying to get his eyes to work, one arm still outstretched. At last, his gaze settled upon me and I was shot through with awe, terror, and wonder. I knew not if he possessed consciousness or the spirits and souls of my beloveds.

Though I know not why—perhaps 'twas the gesture of a mother—I picked up a piece of bread and jam from my nearby dinner plate and inched forward to lay it on his open palm, then stepped back. He contemplated it for some time. I could not tell if his eyes were focused upon its particularities. Perhaps not, for he let it slip to the floor, raised his arms toward the sky, and let out a scream such as humans have likely neither uttered nor heard.

Captain, now in this quiet, nighttime moment in your quarters, I shall endeavor to describe it, though at the time 'twas like a bull had knocked me down. Was it even a scream? 'Twas neither a cry nor shriek, nor bellow, nor roar, nor wail. 'Twas a howl, as if every wolf, fox, hound, and coyote cried out at once, not in rage or hunger, but in eternal loneliness. So deafening was this that all the laboratory glassware shook and broke, as did the few remaining windowpanes, causing the outside to rush inside. The icy tempest blew through the belfry, extinguished all the candles, and set the lamps swaying wildly on their hooks. The bells above swung in larger and larger circles, then began to clang in thundering succession. Penny took up mooing.

The creature stumbled to his feet, clutching his head as if the sound of the bells tore at his senses. He vomited some kind of dense, black, putrid stuff. A lamp fell with a clatter and ignited a straw mat on the floor. The incoming wind avulsed the flame in jagged spikes. Nicolas, who clearly felt the vibration of the bells in his feet, charged forward to grab a bucket of water to douse the fire. This sudden motion gave the creature, who had seemingly not noticed him before, a terrible fright. He knew not how to coordinate his limbs and thus swung his arms in every direction, one blow striking Nicolas across the chest, throwing him off balance such that my dear friend fell backward down the long staircase, landing in the nave with a hideous clamor.

The whole world was a frozen, fiery hell of bells and whirling snow and screams, yet even in all this I could scarce take my eyes off the phantasmagoria of the huge, naked, dazed figure of my creature, fixed in a crouch, my living being there in a whirl of wobbling lamplight and licking fire and incoming snow and a column of moonlight that lit up all his colors and wounds, and in that moment I saw, with the devil's own eyes, that he was beautiful.

What manner of person am I that such a thought should pass through me when my faithful companion lay at the foot of the stairs? I shook myself from whatever spell I was under and clattered downstairs, the creature not far behind, unsteady, hesitant. I bumped right into the bulk of Nicolas and knelt beside him feeling for a beating heart, but 'twas no life there. His neck was broken, his body already cooling.

A long time passed—or it seemed a long time—and still I huddled at his side, sobbing, cursing my newborn creature, who in his first moments had ended a life, intentionally or not. When I looked up, my creature was in the balcony with a lantern in his hand, staring down at the rubble from my grand experiment, trying to understand. I saw he could not fathom it.

He descended there and lingered at a stack of soldiers' garments, blankets, and belongings. I could only see him then as a dark apparition, such was the light there, but I saw him wrap himself in a sweep of black cloaks and pull a hood over his head like a monk, and by this I knew he had consciousness in the form of shame over his nakedness. His body threw an immense black shape upon the wall and I could not even see his figure anymore, just the shadow.

Things grew quiet, as everything that could fall or be broken had already broken, and the storm had abated somewhat, causing the bells to slow down and eventually emit just an occasional clang. Penny mooed from the vestibule and knocked her head against the door repeatedly, so I went to her like a phantasm and buried my face in the warmth of her neck.

Glancing back into the nave, I saw the giant shadow slump slowly to the floor. My creature was giving in to sleep or death. My sensibilities had reached their limits. I too wrapped myself in a cloak and trudged back to the farmhouse, Penny at my side. She was happy to be out, even though dawn had not yet arrived and the storm blew with moderate force. The snow was knee-high and soft enough to sink into, thus each step was an achingly slow endeavor. I looked back at the church once. All was in darkness except for a flickering light in the belfry, the fire burning itself out. I cared not.

That night, I had the following dream: I sat at a large dinner table, such as at the Ursuline Academy. My dinner companions were clean, neatly dressed girls with excellent posture and identical hair ribbons, red for Christmastime. Each girl had a large bowl of gumbo, and in my dream I could clearly taste and smell its roux base, okra, onions, filé powder, catfish, crabs, shrimp, and rice. Several pretty plates of sweet calas waited on a side table for dessert. We sipped coffee, though in reality we were not permitted this at school. We ate with perfect manners.

Whereupon the girls turned into everyone I knew—Father,

Mimi, Moses, Cristophé, Lara, Nicolas, Freddy, Beatrix Belfleur, and babies, too—Mimi's unliving baby from the death ship, her Mi'kmaq baby Henri, her row of babies on the hillside, and my beautiful baby Eugénie. Yet another change, for everyone turned into the dead soldiers Nicolas and I had taken from the battlefield, but they were alive and screaming, naked and stitched all over with blue and yellow thread. Their bodies broke into hideous, bloody pieces as I had dissected them and, before I woke, I was alone in a desolate forest with no life but my own—even then, I was a ghost.

CHAPTER X

Captain, my tale about that little burned-out church is not quite done and I shall confess it soon. 'Tis enough to chill your soul. What a devoted listener you are! You owe me nothing, nor are bound in any way to hear me to the end. Should you wish me to cease at any time, I beg you say so, for only my words are keeping me alive and, once silent, I shall surely take my final breath and find my waiting place in hell.

Shortly after my creature came to life—if life it be called—I left that territory and proceeded to my father's house in Boston. Never before had I walked this earth alone. In his absence, Nicolas followed me as a ghost; many a time I turned reflexively to wave to him behind me, for naught. A kind post-rider stopped for me on a rainy day and let me sit behind him as his horse galloped across the landscape. Though I knew him not, nor he knew me, I put my arms around him as one must under such circumstances and found comfort in his simple warm humanity.

My father had completed his war service and thus was present when I knocked upon the red door I had not seen since before the war. So astonished was he at my wan, bedraggled appearance that, before I scarce said a word, he embraced the breath out of me, put me to bed, and wrote to Cristophé and Lara, pleading with them to come give me solace and comfort, as I was weak and ill and greatly disturbed in my spirits.

I lay abed while awaiting the arrival of my friends, a bed that inhabited a world so different from mine those years past, for 'twas an island of its own, a high, four-poster with fine sheets, a down coverlet, and numerous pillows in silk cases decorated with embroidered violets. While comfortable, dwelling there for weeks was not truly beneficial, for though it provided much-needed physical rest, my mind was a constant ferment of calamitous thoughts, of life lost, love lost, and death defied. I even suffered for days over Penny with the little bell around her neck, whom I had abandoned in a neighbor's field that they might adopt her, and happily so, for cows were scarce and greatly valued. Still, I wept upon realizing that they would likely eat her eventually; such was the dire lack of meat in those parts.

I told my father nothing of my deepest sorrows and misadventures, nor even of my ecstatic times with Moses. Let him think me still a maiden, let all but Mimi—sworn to secrecy—who knew me from my former world think me a maiden. He too had nostalgia from the war and perhaps harbored secrets of his own. He had not recovered much since I stood by his side in the battlefields—still thin with great dark circles under his eyes, haunted, skittish, sleeping poorly. I bid him play checkers with me, as we used to, and in this kind of companionable way we spent many hours together, though not sincerely together as we once were.

Cristophé–he of the blue, blue eyes–was no longer he of the black, black hair. Though young, a good deal of silver now mixed amongst his curls. Instead of making him look older–for his face looked much the same–he now had a somewhat magical appearance, as if accidentally brushed by Father Time as he passed by. Otherwise, his years as a soldier had changed him remarkably little, in the sense that he had no nervous conditions such as Father and myself–no nightmares, nor fits of gloom, nor distrust in the goodness of people. His faith was not childish, nor religious, but that of a true soldier, born to fight with bravery that was not blind and with a love of freedom that was not selfish.

I learned this as we sat by the fire in the evenings, warming ourselves from the gentle chill of spring, for firelight is always a truth serum. I learned this on the battlefield when men lay down their weapons and huddled around fires, poking at the flames, speaking of secrets to their fellow soldiers. There in the bosom of we who loved him, Cristophé softened his stoic soldier's reticence and told us of private things long a mystery.

"I am a descendant of Christopher Columbus," he said. "From my earliest years, I heard tales of the Atlantic Ocean, its profound darkness, frequent storms, violent winds, and the innumerable monsters that inhabit it. I have studied ancient maps and there 'tis called the 'Sea of Darkness.' Those maps invariably contain colorful drawings of fearsome mythological figures with upraised arms, warning against voyages from the old land to the new.

"Every child knows the stories of the great explorations of Christopher Columbus. 'Tis a history in which an ordinary man can have difficulty finding room of his own, for the shadow of a great ancestor both shelters and obscures those who follow. And so down the generations until my father, Bartolomeo Columbus, came to the New World as a young man, married, and sought his fortune. He, however, had a fatal flaw. This has caused me some consternation in my life, for do we all not wonder if the flaws and fates of our parents reflect themselves in us?"

We rushed to assure him that he had no fatal flaw; we who knew him best knew that no finer man could be found. At this, he was overcome with emotion. We comforted him with gentle words and touches until he was able to continue.

"My father carried his family history with excessive pride. He could not reconcile himself to the more modest circumstances of most who dwell in the colonies. He undertook many endeavors—merchant, farmer, and trapper—but soon abandoned them as beneath him. So bitter had he become that he gave me my mother's surname when I was born, that I might escape that curse.

"His wife, my mother, also came from highborn people and had a delicate nature. She too failed to adapt, but in a different way. He took to drink, gambling, and thievery; she became morose and quit the tasks of mothering and domestic activities. My early years, then, were greatly confused. I heard many stories of my great ancestor—for whom, as you see, I am named these many generations later—and my mother taught me proper speech, reading, and writing, yet too life was full of fits of drunken rage from my father and storms of tears or despair from my mother. When I was eight years of age, my poor mother waded into a river and drowned. No sibling lived past infancy, so I had neither brother nor sister to turn to.

"I accompanied my father on one of his nefarious errands, though I knew not and know not the details of it, for he had demonstrated for some time that he wished to make me his accomplice. We stopped overnight at the tavern in that little town where you also stopped. My father drank and roared for several days. Unable to pay for room and board, he fled before dawn one day with two horses and a fine carriage, leaving me behind. I had neither money nor any knowledge of where I was, so I climbed that hill and sat there for two days and nights, ashamed and hungry. Then God smiled upon me, for you two came along and I began the magnificent life the Frankensteins so generously offered me. I have sought to forget what came before, except for my given name and the fantastic stories of Christopher Columbus, for I often dream of him on the battlefield and consider my courage his."

He lifted his gaze from the fire and looked at us with a face so full of love and strength and calmness that I went to him, sat on the arm of his chair, pressed my cheek against him, and whispered, "You are my beloved," which threw me into a state of mortification, for when I said it, my life with Moses and my creature vanished for a moment, then I felt a horrible, cheating despair, for I was not pure enough for Cristophé.

My secrets weighed me down such that I retired to my bed and stayed there some days, trying to drown myself in sleep. Again and again, I dreamed of that seahorse floating like a lovely little ocean angel amongst gently waving seagrass. At last, I understood the meaning of that dream: 'twas Eugénie, my precious baby, living far from me, drifting evermore in a warm, blue-green sea, innocent of all the ills on earth.

Before I plunged back into complete despondency, however, Lara arrived. Just as the years had changed me greatly, so too had she become a woman, though we were barely eighteen years of age. My soft, ethereal schoolgirl friend had become lovely and graceful, though touched by sorrows, as was evident from time to time in almost imperceptible sighs and unfocused gazes out the window. We all have our sorrows, for none go to their grave without suffering the pains and lamentations that are the essence of the human condition.

In the intervening years, Lara's mother had died of consumption and her two militiamen brothers died at the Battle of Baton Rouge. Her father's shop caught fire and, without funds to rebuild, he now contented himself by carving and selling bird decoys out of cypress roots in the far reaches of bayou country. She herself worked as a textile weaver on a massive loom, creating cotton cloth.

"'Tis hard on the hands," she said, "but the soft clacking of the looms allows me to dream." She smiled, brightened, leaned close, and spoke *sotto voce*. "Remember how I loved the gods and goddesses?" she asked. "Neptune, Venus, Apollo, Demeter, Luna... and nymphs, monsters, muses, fairies... all of them. Well, I write stories at night, as if these beings live now in the shape of humans."

"Oh, dear friend," I cried, "that is the happiest endeavor I could have dreamed of for you and your literate soul!" I hugged her and held her hand, and once again we were twelve, whispering secrets. She reached into her apron pocket and drew out a small parchment book bound with purple ribbons, entitled *Le Cabinet Des Fées* by Mademoiselle Lara Eaux.

"For you," she said, and urged it upon me. The book had been printed on a press and was a beautiful thing to behold. Tears welled up in my eyes—happy tears for my friend who, confined to a textile mill, nevertheless kept the joy of youth whereas I, by my desperate actions, had lost my childhood forever. As in our schoolgirl days, she was an excellent antidote to my morbid sensibility. Though I trusted her, I did not confide in her for some time, for I feared losing her love if she knew the magnitude of my aberrations. She too, I think, wished to fill this time at my father's house with ordinary pleasures with which we were all at ease.

As such, my dear friend and I took it upon ourselves to

cook for my father, though he had a cook who had done her best to coax him to eat like a proper Bostonian, serving him porridge, lobster pie, ham, clam chowder, cheeses, baked beans, and beer. We found diverting pleasure in preparing Acadian food to tempt his palate—buckwheat griddlecakes, clam *fricot*, salt cod *beignets*, corn soup, and sugar pie. Lara and Cristophé did the shopping, for I was too anemic and disheartened for this task, but the preparation was a joint undertaking and this we enjoyed for many a week. The men ate with gusto, as warms every woman's heart. Even so, I felt an oppressive presentiment that my creature was near.

As May came to a close, my father and Cristophé sent us by horse and cart to the seaside village of Newburyport for sea air away from the constant war turmoil in Boston. On the way there, we passed a splendid European stagecoach drawn by six white horses decorated with white feathers. The carriage top was thrown back, revealing a man and woman dressed in wedding finery, attended to by four outriders, a footman, and a coachman, all attired in new liveries. Neither of us had ever seen such a display of wealth and it gave us much to contemplate and wonder over.

We resided in a boarding house near the Merrimack River and spent many a congenial day along its banks, watching lazy ferries carry people, goods, and horses from one side to the other. The air was sweet and we took great delight in strolling past fields of wildflowers—their colors pastel, like watercolor paintings—and gazing into the pretty windows of bakeries, bookshops, and dress shops.

"I want to tell you of my beau," Lara said during one of these excursions. "His name is Lanoix Juchereau de St. Denis. His father is a Creole solicitor, a very prosperous, educated gentleman living in the Saint John River Parish of Louisiana. His family is known for their exquisite manner of dress and sophisticated soirees, such as musical, literary, and artistic lectures and presentations, much like Europeans in their ancestral times."

She proceeded to tell me how every Saturday she went to the marketplace and wandered among the fishmongers and flower girls and men hawking great slabs of meat. She carried with her a basket containing copies of her fanciful stories, selling them to those with a little extra money for such an extravagance. To each customer, she gave a sweet-meat, for she had learned in her parents' shop that people would travel far and wide for something free. There came Lanoix one day to buy a book, then many a Saturday and many a book, whatever the weather, until he waited around the marketplace until her basket was empty, then walked her to her rooming house, talking of his family and his genteel way of life.

Many months passed this way. She walked upon a cloud of love as, it appeared, did he. One day, in a burst of passion, he promised to marry her and thus sealed, though they did not speak much of it again, there commenced stolen rhapsodies of amorous congress in private places that he knew, and only when she bled. When I heard this last my heart sank, for only a man with much experience with women and less than noble intentions would conduct himself thus. I do not know if Lara understood its import, for most maidens are kept naïve about these matters until their wedding day. I took her hand but did not interrupt and she continued.

"One day we had a picnic on a large promontory over-looking the landscape. Lanoix was unnaturally quiet. He showed me an architectural drawing of an expansive French colonial-style mansion surrounded by draping oak trees and vast fields disappearing into the distance. 'Twas soon to be built, he told me, on River Road near Destrehan, so that his father might broaden his sugar and indigo crops and amplify his business in the slave trade.

"'To be honest,' he said—and dear Océane, you know 'tis always heart-sinking when someone says those words—'To be honest, I am eager for this, for I share my father's view about dark men who come from far away, for did God not create them to serve those who truly advance culture?' I stared at him then, for having spoken those few words, he no longer even looked the same to me—that is, he did, but my eyes saw a different man. Love mixed with revulsion in the very same instant. I felt sick unto vomiting and only barely kept my composure. This man who had been in the most secret valleys of my God-given body and soul!

"He continued: 'I know that Cajuns abhor slavery, back from the old times in Acadia. Maybe you are even secretly mixed-blood; 'tis what my father would say. My family has great contempt for anti-slavers. For this reason, I can neither present you to my people nor marry you.'"

He turned toward her and in his face she saw his father's living enmity and beneath it his anguish that, a prisoner to its principles, he would not, could not but embrace it, and even beneath that she saw his love for her and his shame that love prevailed over nothing in his life. She left him on that rock, stopped going to that marketplace, and never saw him again. My dear Lara wept as she related this and I tried to comfort her by telling her that surely she would soon meet a far better man to respect her sensibilities and share her beliefs.

Her confidences encouraged me to tell her of Moses and Eugénie, of our bucolic life on the farm, of his death, her birth, their burial in the frozen ground, and the death of Nicolas, too. Though I longed to, I could not bring myself to tell her of my creature. I lied as to the manner of Nicolas's death, the same story about an accidental fall I told Father and Cristophé—perhaps 'twas even the truth. I covered my omissions with tales of Penny and the great and good things

I had learned about Quakers until I found myself prattling and ceased talking altogether and fell into a melancholy state that lasted for some time.

But I confess all to you, sire, for before I leave this wretched earth, I desire for one soul to know my story before it disperses into dust, as all things must, thus I shall continue by returning to complete the story of my creature's creation, though you may spurn me once the words are spoke.

I returned to the church a day after my creature's birth, if such it be called. Wisps of smoke still rose from the belfry fire. Penny had wandered there before me, her dinging bell the only sound. The church had a hollow feeling, its nave deserted except for the carnage my experiment left behind. Nicolas still lay at the foot of the belfry stairs and I was overcome with a riot of thoughts. Shivering on a stair near his body, I still could not fathom whether my creature had killed my poor dear friend in a mindless rage or whether 'twas caused by reflexive fear, such as when an animal rears up at an unexpected fright.

I could neither carry nor drag Nicolas outside for burial. Must he then lie there for all eternity, his spirit and soul adrift? Where was my creature? Dead? Gone? I climbed up to the belfry. The roof had burned away, leaving the rest exposed to the sky. The bells hung in their proper places, though the ropes were charred, as were the beams that held them. I contemplated the quiet, snow-covered landscape; 'twas impossible to consider a future.

Forthwith, the church shook, someone thundered up the staircase, and there my creature stood, the first I had seen him by daylight. What a fearsome being! His wounds and burns were yet more evident and the lacy pattern on his face was unexpectedly bright and shocking, the more so for the two places split open from the Leyden jar sparks, from which drizzled trails of reddish liquid.

A look came over him that, even contorted by stitches, I can describe as anguished. He pulled a shiny plate from under his cloak, which I recognized as the collection platter upon which the chalice stood on the altar below. He held it up and observed his face in its reflection, then threw off his cloak and changed the position of the glass until his body, piece by piece, was mirrored on the shiny surface and there I too saw its unnatural construction, its bits of unraveled thread, its oozing wounds, its patchwork of colors.

Horror and shame grew in his expression as he conducted this inspection, which I saw was for my benefit—a wordless bewilderment about what or who he was, a loathing for his own being, for which I had labored so hard. His perusal complete, he wrapped himself in the cloak again and rocked back and forth, his face distorted.

I went to him and put my hand in his—his first human touch—and led him to a scattering of straw and blankets, bidding him rest upon it. I put my cloak under his head as a pillow, though his patchy, half-burnt scalp and hair were abhorrent. I lay down next to him. You may call me mad for that and 'tis true. So utterly did I believe that he was the reincarnation of my beloveds that I placed my hand over his heart—his hearts—which beat with a thundering regularity that astonished me. His body was warm, hot even, and he smelled of blood and ash, of rain and smoke and earth and sickness and death and bursting, bursting life.

So much did I ache and long for my beloved husband that I lay atop my creature, bare skin to skin, and murmured I know not what, for I believed that Moses would show himself to me. My creature reacted as a man does, as ten men, for he possessed the power of all of whom he was composed; I feared I would die from his bruising kisses and embraces and—I can only confess this as I near my last day—I feared I would die from pleasure.

After some time, I awoke as from a stupor, a spell, trembling with cold and nausea and mortification, for my body bore contusions, scratches, a black eye, a swollen lip, red fingermarks on my hips, a bite on one shoulder, and one arm hung askew, painfully sprained. Oh, I wished to disappear from this earth right then, for 'twas clear to me that this creature was not my Moses, nor did he contain the gentle spirit of an innocent babe. Nay, he was a misbegotten monster and I his obscene maker.

CHAPTER XI

Lara and I remained in Newburyport through the summer and took to watercolor painting at the river's edge and in the meadows. My arm and other wounds had healed and I was much strengthened. Lara was an exquisite painter, attested to by the enchanting paintings in her fairy books. My skills were poor though my enthusiasm great, but dear Lara noted that practice would improve my work over the course of the summer.

We thought about the goddess Persephone, how despite her dire woes in the underworld, she faithfully painted all the entrancing flowers on earth, and so we used her as our inspiration. This occupation lightened my heart, for how can life be dark when one spends their days on a picnic blanket in a meadow or riverside redolent with bachelor's buttons, buttercups, Jack-in-the-Pulpits, goldenseal, and the many other flowers with which Mother Nature adorns herself? Butterflies and bees kept us company by day, fireflies and peepers at river's edge by night.

We talked of happy times and laughed much while recalling amusing or naughty moments of our lives. This lighter
conversational path proved a natural remedy for the tragedies we both endured. Still, my creature dwelled in an
atramentous moiety of my mind. I started at every sudden
noise and half the shadows cast by summer trees looked to
me like apparitions.

One evening, then the next, the sun took on an unnatural
crimson hue at dawn and dusk, and the moon glowed pink at
night. 'Twas surrounded by heavy purple clouds intermixed
with jagged fuchsia streaks of light. A sense of foreboding
spread amongst the townspeople and fishermen noted that
codfish were behaving strangely–wriggling about on deck
less than usual and covered with a thin, ashy scum.

Lara and I lay in our beds those two nights and, inspired
by this spooky natural occurrence, she whispered stories
of ghosts and demons, of footfalls on the stairs, of hags and
harpies and ogres until I burst into tears. Shocked and
remorseful, she climbed into my bed, stroked my hand,
and wiped my nose, begging forgiveness a hundred times
as I begged her forgiveness likewise a hundred times for
being a big baby, when all along I knew she had only lightly
prodded the looming, tangible terrors of my life.

At dawn the next day, we settled ourselves at a particularly
lovely spot on the riverbank, ate a bit of bread and cheese
wrapped in our handkerchiefs, and watched dawn arrive
while people stretched and went about their morning tasks.
Within an hour, the sun came up a deep, brassy red. The
sky turned yellow and a mass of rust-tinted clouds blew in
from the west and began to blot out the still-rising sun. The
sky then dimmed and turned hazy and copper-colored. This
muddy mass of shadow and fog increased as the morning
passed, and by noon the entire firmament was obscured by

midnight darkness. We could not even see the white paper of our painting books when we held them just a few inches from our eyes.

People ran into churches and taverns. Men got drunk and went hallooing through the streets, encouraging women to throw off their clothes and dance, for this was surely the end of days. Some lit candles and prayed for hours, weeping about sin, guilt, and redemption. Cows bellowed and fled to their barnyard stalls, chickens went to roost, frogs began to croak, and all went berserk during the blackest day and night ever witnessed by man or beast. It began to rain then, a flood full of mud and flakes that stank like a malt-house or coal-kin.

Lara and I fled in terror and got separated while pushing through the panicked townsfolk. People could not help but run into each other and lose all sense of street names, where their houses were, or who might be standing nose to nose with them at any given moment. Desperately, I called Lara's name, but all around me people likewise screamed for their children and mates. The entire sky, land, river, and sea were black and choking.

I tried to get away from that terrifying oppression by pushing through town, down a long street, touching the clapboards of one house or shop to the next to guide my way along. The houses then grew scarce and I continued on a path that led me forward by the sound of little pebbles crunching under my feet, then I scrambled uphill, blind, arms outstretched, then through a grove of fruit trees, feeling for their trunks, then out the other side up, up another hill.

What propelled me thus? Guilt, sin, and no redemption, for surely this foul eternal darkness was God's punishment; surely He, whom I had cursed, had awakened and seen my unholy creation. Up and up I climbed until the ground became slabs of bare, jagged rocks. I found a promontory and crawled under a rock ledge to escape the rain, which dropped objects from the sky like a biblical plague, perhaps even frogs and locusts.

Utter darkness tells no time. A minute is an hour is all eternity. After some time crouching under that rocky ledge, I felt the presence of another, maybe a stray dog or fellow citizen likewise wandering as I was. I stepped again into that tempest and saw a small light. For a moment, I thought the moon had returned, but 'twas a lantern giving off warped, distorted light as the dirty rain dripped down its glass sides. It took quite a while for my eyes to adjust, but I soon detected a looming shape in the flickering illumination. My heart beat erratically and I knew it to be my creature.

That filthy muck from heaven poured down upon my head and inside my clothes. The furious, upside-down world infected me with a poisonous loathing for this being to whom Nicolas gave his life and, had I a gun, I would have shot him then and there but, nay, 'tis not the whole truth, for I felt an equal desire to speak to him. I greatly wished to know his nature.

"Creature," I said. I had to raise my voice much in the clamor of the storm, and I believe it came out as a scream. "Creature, have you a soul?" He stared and I saw tears join the rain pouring down his face, for never had he heard my voice nor, I believe, had any person spoken to him in his brief life; perhaps the sound hurt his sensibilities, whatever they may be.

"Creature," I called out again. "Are you man or beast? Can you speak? Do you think and reason?" Still the silence grew, black as the midnight day. His cloak was black, too, so the only things visible were his hand holding the lantern, his face with those unsettling, odd-colored eyes, and the dim outline of his body. He seemed to shrink a little and struck me then as a dumb animal, a lost and wretched beast. My anger dissipated; instead, I felt unwilling compassion and continued more quietly. "Do you know who I am? Do you know from whence you came? Are you my beloved? For 'tis only that I care for."

At this, he flung the lantern at me. It caught me on the side of the head and knocked me over. The glass broke, the light extinguished, and a glass shard buried itself in my leg. I cried out and clutched my wound. In the darkness, I felt him gone. I crawled back under the ledge, bound my leg with strips from my dress, fell into a much-disturbed sleep, and hid there until the sun came up, innocent and yellow, as if nothing had happened. The sky was blue, morning birds sang, and butterflies awoke in the meadows as I limped back to town. The only lingering sign that the darkness had been more than a collective nightmare was a blanket of dust or ash over everything; four or five inches of thick ash lined the banks of the Merrimack River, and the trees, plants, and grasses showed no hint of their natural summer green.

Newburyport was peculiarly quiet. People looked at me strangely as I made my way to the boarding house, to Lara. A queasy sensation overtook my stomach as I neared a small group of people looking downward in a sober manner, even more so when a minister broke away and came toward me. He put his arm around my shoulder and led me to the park, murmuring words I could not quite catch. People moved aside and there Lara lay on a bench, dead pale, dead, my dearest friend. Did she drown in that midnight noon? Or trip and fall upon the cobblestone streets? I stared from face to face, kind strangers, rumpled and confounded from the dark day before.

"Her neck is broken," said the minister. I heard that and bent to kiss her cheek—bloodless as a white rose—and saw there a scrap of blue thread. I stood wild-eyed, flooded with the knowledge that my creature had done this, done it with aforethought to hurt me.

"She is bleeding," someone said, and indeed I was, for the bandage around my leg had loosened and blood trickled to the ground, drop by drop, until it seemed that all my life's blood was gone. Black spots flickered before my eyes. I succumbed to that dim nowhere between life and death and blacked out.

How desperate I was then, for what had I? Neither friend, protector, husband, mother, nor child. And so I found a new friend in a laudanum concoction I mixed from opium, saffron, castor, ambergris, musk, and nutmeg. To this, I added psilocybin mushrooms and rum. I kept a brown bottle of this in my apron pocket and for some time my sensibilities floated in a miasma of dreams and visions, remembrances and forgetfulness.

'Twas in my pocket when, after several melancholy months at my father's house, he decided to send me to a nunnery in Montréal. This came about when he wrote to the Quebec City branch of the Ursuline Academy regarding my predicament. They recommended a plan to ensconce me in a cloister where I might rest and gingerly apply myself to apothecary work, as my health permitted. How old must a woman be before her father stops sending her places? All women round the world know the answer to that; he will do so until she has a husband who will then prevent her from going places. So, I made my way north, still under the dreamy influence of laudanum, reflecting on the only time in my life when I determined my own direction. 'Twas the journey that led me to Moses, to my free and happy year with my beloved.

After much contemplation about the nature of freedom, I entered Montréal resolved to go my own way instead, for my fury and shame required open space, solitude, and the expiation of nature to wash away my sorrows. I ceased imbibing the contents of my brown bottle, hired a dappled horse named Jack and a covered cart, purchased supplies, and headed farther north alone. I found these preparations easy, for men shrink and become solicitous in the face of widows' anguish, and often think them witches or of other evil origin. I was soon some distance from the city, with only curls of smoke from chimneys and blacksmith shops visible behind me as I wandered alongside the St. Lawrence River.

Jack proved physically strong with good endurance, but was rather sour-tempered and distrustful in nature. Bereft of Nicolas, I had to learn how to handle a horse and conveyance, and many a time Jack halted because of my confusing tug on the reins and mixed-up verbal exhortations. Still, we came to an understanding and thus proceeded.

After some weeks, a downpour of many days' duration began and I therefore stopped at an abandoned hunters' hut with rusted traps scattered about. I stared out the slatted window to amuse myself, but such a thick fog obscured the landscape day and night that I began to contemplate the nature of fog itself.

I wrestled about turning myself in to a magistrate to confess the existence of a murderous creature I had set upon the world, that he might track and destroy him. Yet I hesitated, for who would believe me? Who would believe the nature of my invention? And had I myself not committed crimes against God and man by grave robbing, mutilation, and unholy experiments? As I stewed in my furies and doubts, Mother Nature echoed my sentiments, for even when a patch of fog cleared for a moment, 'twas evident that the river had overflowed its banks and rushed carelessly across adjacent fields.

I nevertheless came to the end of my patience with that meager hut and began to load my belongings back into the cart. I heard much splashing and commotion in the river, perhaps an animal coming ashore after being swept away in its swollen waters—possibly a donkey, or an ox. Then the fog swallowed all sound again and I went about my business until a sense of dread came over me. I turned and saw a specter emerge from the fog. There in the doorway, dragging behind him a cloak and leather bag, stood my creature like a Prince of Darkness—naked, towering, wet, muscular, scarred, enfolded in silver fog, utterly beautiful.

"Hurt," he said, and collapsed at my feet.

CHAPTER XII

I stared at his senseless body, took up the knife I wore at my waist, and placed the tip directly over a pulsing artery in his neck. How easily I could spill his blood, yet my hand shook. I found myself surveying his body as I would a soldier on the battlefield. His original sores had putrefied and he had suffered many abrasions and insect attacks. His skin now drooped dangerously near the sutures that seared away during his creation, and the adjacent areas were red and swollen. Whatever hatred burned in me for the deaths of my friends, if I plunged my knifepoint thus, 'twould be the end of this creature, yes, but likewise the death—the sincere death—of my beloveds' hearts, which still I half-dreamed might corporealize in the body of he whom I created.

I felt I might go mad from indecision, but in the end, I had not the fortitude to inflict death upon this being who asked not for life and now required aid. In that moment, I was swamped with unbidden sympathy for this illegitimate being. I let out a cry of confusion. Jack started as he grazed and kept a suspicious eye on me.

Though my creature near filled the hut in its entirety, making it difficult to maneuver around him, I covered him and went about the business of cleaning, draining, and sewing his wounds. One wrist appeared to be broken, so I set it with two straight branches and a sturdy wrapping. His eyes fluttered and he became cognizant of my ministrations, but not enough to grow agitated or push me away. I mixed pastes and unguents to seal his wounds, then brought my instruments close to his face, which I approached with trepidation. I had ministered to the facial wounds of many soldiers and knew that such repairs caused even the most restless patients to grow still and compliant. Perhaps they feared mutilation of their features or were lulled by the soft touch.

The intricate embroidery of ferns and roses had held up well, its delicate lines and whorls intact despite whatever life my creature had been living. It took some long time to debride the two wounds that interrupted that peculiar tattoo, if I may call it that. He was well awake during this and watched me with those unsettling blue and violet eyes. At last, I finished my efforts and packed up my medical supplies.

He grew restive and tearful. I mixed him a cup of water with a strong dose of laudanum. His gestures were disordered so I held the cup to his lips and was startled to behold him peering at me trustingly, as a child might. My heart leapt as I wondered if this innocent expression was perchance the spirit of my darling girl, my Eugénie. This confounded me and added to the tumult I already felt from this man or monster, lover or beast, so much so that I too downed a draft of laudanum and so we drifted for some hours in a strange, companionable, dreamy silence.

I felt an ebbing of the loneliness that had haunted me since the death of my beloveds, perhaps even the loneliness that afflicted me since Beatrix Belfleur and those few fleeting hours of tender motherlove, then no more. I knew not the depth and breadth of that desolation until I curled up in the corner of that hut, an arm's length from my accomplice, he who lived only by my hand and my compulsion to chase grief to its hiding places. Tears slid down my cheeks, but gently, like pain melting.

When I came back to myself, I gazed out the doorway of the hut and saw that the fog had cleared and the moon hovered over the river, now churning with uneasy, muddy force. My creature still floated in an in-between state, so I quietly gathered my things, hitched Jack to the cart and proceeded across the wet grass. Night can be forgiving and this night gladly cooperated with my wish to leave my creature behind, for the moon guided me and the stars kept me company. I held the reins loosely and half-dozed as we plodded forward with no particular destination.

Some hours later, Jack reared up, throwing me from my perch. There appeared before me my creature yet again, cloaked, scowling, all traces of languor gone. "Hear me, Océane," he said, "for you made me, scarred me, breathed into me, gave me spirit and soul if those I possess; thus you will hear me and never leave until my last word is spoke."

My mind tripped over the meaning in his words—his words!—for he spoke in a voice deep as doom, ragged with misery, broken, with crackles and little gulps of air, as if his speaking and breathing were not quite in harmony. He bid me sit under a tree and paced before me, gathering his thoughts, then spoke for many an hour.

"When I awoke, scalding fire raced through my body and the sweet scent of flowers and a soft mouth on mine, then breath filling me, boiling, strangling, choking breath. Thunder rumbled and my heart seized, scorching, every part burned, hurt, stretched in all directions, excruciating bursts, burning, hurting, fire, then I saw bells up, up and in me was why? Why? A ghastly shriek, sorrow, error, terror, despair... Why? Why? Mud flowed from my mouth, why? Something came at me, bear or beast, to hurt, to hurt me, my arms and legs all tangled, I hit him, and down to the bottom that bear fell. Then in another place blood everywhere, feet and eyes, hands and heads, confusion all, all went black.

"You were there, I know! Burning, pulling, aching, my body, blue and yellow lines this way and that, confusion. Do I belong to myself? So many parts and colors I had, many parts divided, fighting, pulling, me, not me. And you, you! A girl everywhere near me, next to me, you, your skin, your mouth on me a different way, fire, heat, pain, and flowers, why? Then hurting pleasure, anguish, confusion, snow, yes, cold night snow, burning, tearing flesh and there I slept or died a day or night, then back I went and there the bells again, a man below sprawled all wrong, 'twas that bear now with a man's face all wrong, oh, tearing, fiery flesh and there I slept or died again.

"Later, or on a different day, I saw him still there, a man but first a bear. I hit him, knocked him to go away, never on purpose, your friend, broken on the stairs. Pain, burning, I lifted him up so surprisingly strong was I, lifted him big though he was and saw in his face a kind person and hot grief boiled. I took him then deep into the snow, dug a snow cave there, lay him there, and sorrow, sorrow, death or life, I tried to ask but found no voice then, all was silence but a night bird, an owl, a wolf cry, quiet snow, good night silence, then I lay beside him, bear or man, silence, silence. I smelled of rotten things, foul things, forests, decay. Sorry, sorry I said to your friend, still no voice, sorry, sorry, please rest now. I took his hand and cold we lay until I know not when.

"Once more, I returned to my birthplace, up where the

great bells crashed, embers, smoke, sparks, broken glass, snarls of wire, scattered flesh upon the floor, but you were gone. I tried, I think, to think a thought, but memories fought, jumbles of words, deeds, places, faces, I could not make sense. I tried to see a before, but no before belonged to me, only fractures, sensations, lamentations, burnings, yearnings. I cast my eyes upon a disordered pile of hay and blankets on the floor, half-burned, stinking of wet ashes, there where you lay with me. There I sat, oh cries of pain, for my skin tore in places when I moved, my insides seeped to my outsides.

"The bells swung a little when my body thudded to the floor. I clutched a handful of ashes that I might somehow find you there. I had no words then, but speechless I yearned for you. Did I not know your face and touch? Did we not share primordial sensations, whispers, colors, lights, choking, breathing, life bubbling down hundreds of roadways from head to feet, yet whose, whose life? I cried bitter tears then, for 'twas all ash, all cold ash. I was alone in a world of snow and confusion. Man or beast, you ask? Who knows me when I know not myself?"

I wept listening to him, for I then understood what prompted his tears and screams as he first drew breath— the agony of life abounding. I had not known of nor anticipated his physical pain. What inhumane directive led me to ignore that possibility? I cringed from shame and guilt even as I surveyed the landscape to see how I might escape this terrifying being. He read my thoughts, scowled, and continued speaking.

"I took a few items from the tower, things I could not quite name then, but which became of great use to me in later wanderings—a tinder box with flint and steel, a compass, a knife, candles, a tin cup, papers, and other random things. These I placed in a rawhide bag, which I tied around my body. I then ventured out into the snowy landscape. I covered a long distance and the air did clear my mind some little bit as time passed.

"Never have you been far from my thoughts, my maker—I shall call you that ever after, for is that not what you are? Yours was the face I first gazed upon and your mouth twice I felt breathe into me. Has mother's milk ever touched my lips? Have I a father, sister, brother, cousin, or any human companion? Again, again I ask: Am I man or beast or some unnatural being in between?

"I examined my body for the source of my many burning pains and sensitivities. In that search, I did not find that secret mark all children possess, where once a rope connected them to their mother. What I do possess is a most unusual variety of skin colorations—skin of slave owners, skin of slaves, skin of soldiers, skin of native peoples—which in my travels I have compared to others. In those people, I did see numerous tones and colors, but each person to a single color. I know this single color too from jagged remembrances of people I never knew, yet did know throughout a life I never lived yet did live.

"How sick I feel, for these thoughts and inquiries have no answers, yet forever buzz around my mind like wasps, stinging, poisoning, never quiet. I do not know my name or origin, but I know my skin possesses the colors of men from many lands; this makes me not a man but a monstrosity. Because of my silence until now, you may have thought your creation dumb, but I am no fool, for I see the many blue and yellow lines all over me in no logical pattern and this I know is absent in all other men. My days and nights are plagued by a fury of different colors pulling, burning, ripping, yet other men do not cry out from this. These matters torment me without end, thus I ask as you asked me: Have I a soul? A spirit? Why do you cry at these questions? Answer me not if you care not. I will tell you my story and perhaps one day you will repay me likewise with your secrets.

"My first encounter with other men occurred when hunger drove me to approach a town. Instinctively, I kept my presence to the outskirts as a wild creature might. There was much merriment in the town square, which stirred a tumbling incoherence in my memory—apples, children, rum, loaves of bread split open with cheese inside. These drew me close, yet regardless of my tremendous size, I felt delicate and shy, and feared to reveal myself.

"One noisy group crowded in front of a curtained theatrical booth watching several wooden dolls dancing on strings. I was most captivated by this—how merry, funny, and dramatic they were, with voices from behind the curtain reciting rude poetry, and making the dolls whack each other with sticks, shriek, and sing blue songs. The children laughed and clapped, and so too did the adults enjoy themselves mightily. Though my skin ached and burned and boiled so that I could scarce keep from screaming, I too felt my spirits lift and wished to sit near those happy people.

"Another doll appeared from behind the curtain, a greatly fat fellow with a misshapen body and grotesque visage. Thereupon onlookers hissed, threw pebbles, and taunted him, then threw larger and larger rocks such that the people behind the curtain were impelled to withdraw their wooden players and close the whole thing down. I retreated to the forest, stealing bread and other food from the carts abandoned by their owners. Long I pondered the source of their mocking ways and a great melancholy crept over me, for it occurred to me that if joyous townspeople throw rocks at ugly wooden dolls, what might they do to one such as me?"

CHAPTER XIII

"Fragments stirred within my troubled mind for many days and weeks, my maker. I heard voices around me, causing me to whirl about and cast darting looks in every direction, only to find no one, yet still I heard them talk to me. At length, by taking up residence high in a sturdy tree that I might watch all my surroundings at once in search of those who seemed to creep behind my shoulder, I came to understand that those voices were within me, a multitude of voices, a constant crowd of visions and memories that did not belong together.

"Is not a man one thing? Can men not confidently call themselves farmer, poet, woodworker, teacher, or book-keeper? Inside my mind 'tis as if many men live at once; that is, I know pieces of things, but not one whole of anything. If required, I can build half a chair but no more, teach sums but not long division, blow in a harmonica but know only half a tune, plant tobacco but know not its purpose. My mind is full of shadows of wives, children, cousins, mates, yet they are strangers to each other and live in disparate places.

"My maker, does every man's body feel at odds with itself? Many a time have I seen men stride about this green earth, supple, muscular, every part in harmony with every other part. Often have I secretly followed such men or women as they went about their simple walks, unworried as to the mechanics of their knees, the beating of their heart, and the mysterious workings of every element that makes men sigh and smile and know their name and live at ease inside themselves.

"Once I saw a naked man swimming in a lake. How serene he was! Before long, he shook off the water and lay upon the bank that the sun might dry him. How strong he was and sleek; God made him well, for he was not marred by cuts and lines and gaps and mad, uneven slices of color such as I am. He propped himself against a willow tree, watched a family of ducks paddle by, and began to whistle. This sound awoke in me a great surprise, a pain of aching memory and confusion, for I knew that simple country tune and a few words. So lilting and childlike was the tune, so much did the words touch my tormented soul, that my eyes burned and tears of fire scalded my cheeks. Those snippets came to me thusly:

> *A froggie would a-wooing go,*
> *mm mm mm mm*
> *A froggie would a-wooing go,*
> *with a rolly polly po*
> *Off he set with his opera hat,*
> *hi ho hi ho, mm mm mm mm...*

"In time, I learned to quiet the chaos in my mind by reciting aloud passages from books. I had no books in my possession nor knew how I learned this skill nor any other thing that whirled through my mind. Still, I could proclaim like a schoolboy from books I could not identify, speaking pages and pages to the trees and flowers. Thus I amused many a squirrel and deer I passed in my travels, though I do believe my voice is harsh and halting even when I strive to modulate it.

"One story especially gave cheer, about the misfortunes of a seafaring man on a deserted island. No matter how low his spirit, he prevailed by his wits and ingenuity, and never ceased his conjectures on the nature of life. Many a day I puzzled over how I came to memorize those pages, plentiful enough to keep me company in my lone and dreary travels. I rambled in circles, for neither sun nor moon could then orient me and I had no destination.

"When tired, I passed in and out of a strange state I cannot call awake or asleep, a middle zone, for I never truly sleep in the blessed serenity I know to be plentiful in the lives of ordinary men. By instinct, I knew I ought to sleep by day and wander by night, but the sun was balm to me, and so I learned to move quietly, and taught myself or somehow knew how to light a fire, catch beasts of field and forest, and build an arbor of thick branches to keep out rain and snow.

"One day, I came upon a regiment of soldiers marching through a thickly wooded landscape. Immediately, I felt a kinship and knew the name of every weapon and item each soldier carried—a musket slung on his right side with a leather or tin cartridge box containing twenty to thirty rounds of ammunition and a musket tool. On his left side a bayonet in a leather scabbard attached to a linen or leather shoulder strap. Each soldier also hauled a haversack of linen containing food rations and eating utensils—even these I knew to the last detail!—a wrought iron fork, a pewter or horn spoon, a knife, a plate, and a cup. Then too a canteen of wood or tin. A knapsack held extra clothing and items such as a razor, a tinderbox with flint and steel, candleholders, a comb, a mirror, a fishhook and twine.

"The drummer boy banged out a familiar cadence and so compelling was that sound that at once I crashed through the woods near them in eagerness and joy and marched along in a parallel path. How good my limbs felt at that moment!–arms and legs swinging, head high. However, at the sight of me, all nearby took a terrible fright, drew back in horror, and fell into a disarray of people, carts, and animals. I reached out to those close by in innocent brotherhood and happiness and tried to speak a greeting, but my voice came out in a horrible creaking, bleating fashion. Women shrieked and gathered their children under their aprons. Horses and cows bolted. Soldiers came at me with pistols and knives. I escaped back into thick forest foliage only because my strides are long, and even then, several bullets flew so close by that I screamed as if I were hit.

"Thus I resumed my wandering existence, marked by fury and hot tears. I betook myself to a hiding place deep in the woods, pulled branches and leaves around me, and for many a week wept like a child and felt like a child and was a child with no comfort nor any kind smile nor warm hand, and so I hid and howled as shy wolves and lost children do, and was all alone in the world. To comfort myself, I tried to bring to mind the stories and poems I had recited just weeks earlier, yet could recall only scarce phrases, which I repeated for hours at a time that they might stick in my mind, to no avail.

"Bitterness swept over me. I took up my wanderings again and traversed back to the St. Lawrence River, all the way up to Quebec. There I remained for some time in a cave near the riverside, for sturgeon and herring were plentiful, and numerous ducks and geese provided easy nourishment. I observed those who came and went upon the river. I learned about men called 'river rats' who live on flat-bottom boats—rough, strong, heavy-drinking men. They bought and sold every big and little thing, and lived free from regulation and oversight, which greatly appealed to me. I resolved to join this life, which could, I saw, take place entirely at night.

"I hunted for some weeks, collected numerous pelts, and traded them one moonless night for an old boat. Engulfed in my black cloak with its hood pulled tightly, I shrouded myself from curious eyes. To my benefit, rough men such as those have witnessed and done many an unspeakable thing, and thus are by nature rather blasé and incurious men. The ones with whom I fell in viewed me as unusually large in stature and forbidding in mien, and so they kept their distance except for conducting business. So, I had neither friend nor companion, but was close enough to see and hear them smoking, drinking, laughing, and carousing with women who came down to the river's edge from tents along the sand grasses on the riverside. They had frequent, bloody fights over money, women, waterways, cargo, boats, or nothing but foul temper.

"During this time, the last snippets of the book passages and poems in my mind drained away. My body swelled and burned and ached, and I was cursed with every manner of biting and stinging insect. Confusion filled my mind. I devoted hours to following my threads of cognition, but new lines of thinking crossed with the old, pulling me in discordant directions, crowding the whole of my conscious-ness with a collision of numbers, qualities of wood, effects of weather on curing hides, musical notes upon a page, types of spices, names of cattle feed until I near went mad.

"This produced a life lived in incoherence and, though I longed to, I could never say clearly to myself 'I am a preacher,' or 'I am a smuggler of rum,' or 'I am a shopkeeper,' or any such 'I' that I might take my place in a society of men, should I find one that did not draw back in panic and loathing at my appearance, so I ask again, again, your question: Am I man or beast? Sorely do I lack the natural ways of men I have observed—an easy intimacy with other men, fruitful work, affection for women and children, and the peaceful slumber I witnessed when families retreated to their open tents at night.

"I especially watched two men called Big Harpe and Little Harpe. I knew not if they were men or monsters, for they were ugly, their faces pitted from smallpox or worser catastrophes of body and soul. One was an enormous hulking brute with black hair; the other a slightly smaller man with unkempt hair like fire. Indeed, their locks grew long down their backs and their filthy beards had scarce ever been cut, producing an overall frightening aspect and causing me to wonder why I have no beard upon my face and why my hair does not grow long.

"The Harpe men carried muskets and tomahawks, and wore the fringed buckskin clothing of native peoples, along with big black fur hats festooned with feathers. Strung-together teeth and scalps, and even skulls, hung from their shoulders, waists, and horses. They traveled in a pack of smaller, but no less fearsome, companions, as well as very young girls, many with child.

"By observation, I saw that Big and Little Harpe had but one desire in life: to cause terror, harm, and gruesome death by light of day to those who crossed their path. I saw them steal horses, girls, and weapons, and slit the throats of any who argued. I saw them dash the bodies of their own infants against trees to cease their crying. I saw them disembowel and dismember men for no discernible reason and laugh all the while. Why was I drawn to them, even as I was repulsed? 'Twas because I feared myself akin to them—men so savage and alarming that their mere presence caused all to flee. And, like me, they wore billowing black capes overtop and made the trees tremble when they walked.

"For many a month, I lived among the river rats, witnessing the brawls, murders, thievery, and cheating. A poisonous cloud seemed to envelop them and 'twas infectious. At times, I was seized with the desire to likewise destroy all about me, for if this was manhood, I wished it greatly and my state of constant, torturing pain and swirling mental chaos drove me into great fits of rage that propelled me into the forest to catch game with my bare hands, break their necks, and tear off their hides. My thoughts surged in fretful waves and I was overswept with emotional disturbances. I seethed with anger for the evil predilections of men, yet also did I weep at the sight of women tending a soup pot over a fire and children splashing at the water's edge.

"That river was wide, dark, and deep, full of eddies and whirlpools and rushing torrents, yet the river children feared it not. One evening, I saw a child tip over backward on his father's boat and fall into the river. Three men on board drinking rum and playing cards knew not about the dire circumstances of the child. I navigated my boat nearby and slipped into the water, searching the depths and currents, but no child did I see or touch.

"So quickly was that boy snatched by some river demon and so uninterrupted were the men's shouts and laughter that perhaps I imagined what befell that little fellow, though I did see a small hat floating alongside me in the dark. Greatly tired from my exertions and weak with sorrow for that boy, I remained in the water, allowing myself to float with the current. My cloak and the rawhide satchel strung across my chest were heavy, but not fatefully so. I did not fight the river nor seek to head toward the riverbank, for just then I would have welcomed sinking to the bottom, so sick was I from the cruelty I have observed in my short time on this earth. But the river did not want me and I drifted a long way from Big and Little Harpe, the river rats, and the women and children in their riverside encampments.

"I was not cold, for my body seems insensible to temperature, except for its own internal furnace. All night I drifted and felt as near to peaceful as ever I had, for the water sounds and night sounds of owls and faraway coyotes soothed me greatly and put my fevered mind to rest, that intermediate state of internal emptiness which I know to be not death, not life, but a blankness during which I remember nothing and think nothing, as if my brain sputters out.

"Thus I departed from riverbank life. I traveled long distances, always on the outskirts of habitation, always seeking to fathom the ghastly feeling I had of possessing no center, of being a hollow man, like a scarecrow in a field, blown about by unseen forces. When I tired of trapping rabbits and digging roots for my supper, I crept into towns and villages at night, stepping soundlessly into shops and smokehouses and taverns to steal food.

"My expeditions always veered toward battlefields, which were many, though I knew not why. Truly 'twas torture for me there, for my body passed through agonies of sensation at the mere nearness of a bloody battlefield, as if I too then had been shot, stabbed, sliced, and ripped asunder in some kind of living dream. These fevered sensations were accompanied by shrieks, screams, and cries, not from my mouth, but silent cries in my distorted mind. My thoughts turned against men fortunate enough to dwell in these lush territories who nevertheless set peace aside and, even as boys, yearned for war and the blood of their enemies.

"Even when battlefields were quiet, I saw the degradation of man in their treatment of prisoners, how they flogged naked fellows over nothing, how they stood eye to eye with helpless hidebound men too weak to walk, carelessly shot or bayonetted them, then left them in whatever dirt they fell to die lonely deaths. At times, I came upon such soldiers and found their tears and pain unbearable, so I placed my hands around their necks as I did creatures of the forest until they drew breath no more. In this, I felt no killer's savagery, I felt... I know not what I felt or the why of anything.

"I carried these men to remote locations, as I had the bear person on your tower stairs, and sprinkled them over with leaves or flowers or sand or snow or whatever nature's bounty then provided. You draw back in abhorrence and call me a murderer, though I know not if 'tis true. Why do I not know myself? Truly, 'tis torture to witness the last breath of some poor soul at my hands, yet is this also not blessed peace? I beg you tell me true what brand of man or beast I be!

"Perhaps you think I know you not, my maker, but your name has not escaped me. Among the items I retrieved from the tower the night of my departure was a letter your father wrote to you, sealed with wax and never opened. I could not fathom its contents for many months, as my mind was in great agony and torment, as I have narrated to you. But at some length, attracted by its pleasing blue paper, I opened it and puzzled out its contents when my mind was calm. So many times have I read it that I know every word well. I have it here in my bag and you can see your father's name and residence embossed on top in a handsome fashion. By its content, I discovered how loved you are by an estimable and thoughtful man. I shall read it to you, for 'tis greatly wrinkled and torn from handling and the ink much faded. My vision is poor, yet I can read."

To Océane Frankenstein dit Belfleur

Princeton, New Jersey
February 7th, 1777

Upon receiving this, you may think it strange for me to address you on paper when we are here, side by side, in this Flying Hospital. But in these years of war, we have both learned that life is ephemeral, often catastrophic, and so I wish to reveal myself to you in this written manner so you may always hold this letter close to you. I have suffered in this life, as do we all, and by this I became an anxious, preoccupied man, working at my surgery until I collapsed so as to stave off the storm of emotions that reside, though you may find this surprising, in a well-guarded corner of my heart. Never could I forgive myself if I should perish without describing to you some portion of that corner as it relates to you.

Tender expressions of love from men to children do not always come easily, for we are mocked for evidencing soft feelings. 'Twas true in the homeland of my ancestors. They were well versed in the cruelties of life and so crushed any tender sensibilities they may have possessed when young. In Acadia, too, men are stalwart, with lives that are all external, requiring great physical strength and endurance, so gentle musings are oft' lost or forgotten.

I know not what you recall of me in your youngest years. You did not fear me, I believe, but neither did you find me patient and attentive. Too much did I grieve for your mother—my Beatrix Belfleur—and saw so much of her in you that it pained me to gaze too long upon your lovely face or listen overmuch to your baby stories of frogs and stars and buttercups. When we moved to Boston, I knew not what to do without Mimi, so you and Cristophé ran wild and saw things children should never see. My fellow surgeon told me of a man you saw who died and lived again one stormy day. I cursed myself that your angelic sensibility was shocked by that dramatic sight, yet I neglected to explain it to you that it might be stripped of any magical import you may have attached to it.

But my heart grew calm and comforted during your years at the Ursuline Academy, for they gave you constancy I could not. How intense and curious you are! What a beautiful, flowering girl! And me, I acquainted you with war, exposed you to every battlefield horror, to hunger, cold, misery, and deprivations of every kind.

Your excellent ministrations to those exhausted and injured soldiers fill us all with gratitude, for many times I have noticed how eagerly they accept your stitching, bandaging, poultices, and even more painful procedures, for you are far gentler than I. You are always at my side and Nicolas just behind you. When I lose hope or fall into black moods, I am only disheartened a little while, for you and your companion always cheer me. Even so, I berate myself for robbing you of the innocence and optimism by which a proper girlhood should be measured.

My darling child, should we in this war be separated by death or should life again take us in different directions, remember always that you are and have always been my precious, perfect girl—your beautiful mother's daughter. My heart, though pitiful at expressing itself, is entirely devoted to you, my dear Océane, my beloved child.

Your loving father,
Doctor Edgar Frankenstein

Eventually the paper drifted down onto my creature's lap and he closed his eyes. I grasped it, pressed it to my lips, kissed it, slumped to the grass, and wept for hours. When at last I comported myself, my creature was still there, waiting to speak yet more.

CHAPTER XIV

"Guided by the return address on your father's letter, I traveled to his city, as I believed that such a kindly man, a doctor, would not shy from me; indeed, perhaps he would take me in as his son. Thus I made my way to Boston and entered by daylight. My mood had changed, for I was weary of hiding in forests, peeking wistfully at the doings of mankind. Never had I seen a city; its noise and activity imbued me with a certain reckless feeling.

"I was tightly swathed in my cloak but left my hood loose, thus my face was visible. 'Twas a windy day, so great folds of fabric billowed around me in a manner I cared not. I strode quickly and people scattered as I passed. I neither pushed nor manhandled them, though my mood was dark, as not one I passed looked at me with other than shock. Yet no one raised a pistol nor threw rocks nor made other efforts to stop or chase me. I even detected a little glimmer on one or two of the faces of children, which gave me an unfamiliar feeling of hope. Perhaps in cities, I thought, people are all as kind and good as your father and, though initially unsettled at my appearance, their fears might fade as they became familiar with my presence.

"I could not readily find your father's house and, loath to ask anyone, I wandered many hours in the hope of stumbling upon it. I passed a large, verdant park and there observed a circle of brightly colored wagons. By then, dawn was near and all was quiet. Cautiously, I approached until I heard snores and sleepy coughs and sighs that indicated people not yet awake inside their wagons and carts. One wagon had no canopy and in it a woman slept upon a bed of straw. She had no arms or legs, yet was clearly a grown woman otherwise, breathing sweetly.

"Just inside the circle of wagons was another circle, this of animal cages, occupied by wild creatures such as one sees in books—two tigers, a panther, three lions, and an assortment of scruffy and dejected monkeys. I spied a slight movement behind a tarpaulin, and lifting it saw a young elephant chained to a post, shuffling his feet as far as the chain would permit. I had no fear and drew close. What a charming fellow he was! A badge hanging around his neck said 'Hobby,' and he was dear to me ever after. He nudged and searched me for pockets, that I might have some treat hidden there and for all the world I wish I had. He gave up on that, flapped his ears, huffed in my face with his long trunk, and overall seemed most interested in befriending me. I talked softly to him at much length of things no beast could fathom, things I did not understand myself. His scent and warmth brought forth a sweet aching sorrow in me. I wish he could have stayed near me always.

"Continuing my quiet perusal, I came next upon two half-naked men in a cage. They slept heavily and stank of rum. This inebriation allowed me to go as close to them as the bars allowed, for something held my gaze such that I could scarcely breathe. They were small, but not children. Their faces, arms, and torsos were covered with designs such as I had on my face. In their designs, I discerned flowers, animals, names, and sentences in a language I knew not. So eager was I to encounter men like me that I was but a nose length away when one of them shifted in his sleep, at which I jumped back and saw that, like Hobby, they were chained to the floor.

"I then heard a hissing nearby. A great beast stepped out of the shadowy corner of his cage, which gave me a fright, so unexpected was his sudden movement. His expression was woeful and he seemed desirous of seeing me. I approached until I was quite near and to my amazement heard him speak.

"'Unlock my cage, will you, mate?' he whispered. I crept close and saw that he was not a beast but a tall, stout man with a tremendous natural pelt of black hair all over his body. 'Have you got a light, mate?' he asked, and brought forth a tattered cigar, handling it as if 'twas his most treasured possession. 'I ain't had a smoke since winter,' he whispered. The brightening sky illuminated his pale face, which contained no malice. I was most surprised but knelt and used my flint to light a small pile of pine needles and thus lit his cigar and handed it back to him.

"I say to you, maker, that this, I believe, was my first comradely act. He puffed upon that cigar with an expression of joy and pleasure so wholesome that I felt wonderful happiness for him. He looked at me all the while and, though noting my size, strange visage, and half-burnt wounds, he was not fearful.

"'Take care,' he said, 'for they will lock you up too if they once catch sight of you. Go! Go quick, mate!' I backed away with all haste and tripped over the root of a tree, falling with a thud. The hairy man tried to hush me but began to laugh and could not stifle the sound. His laughter bestirred the big animals, who began to pace and roar. The monkeys put up a tremendous racket and a strange collection of people stumbled out of wagons in their nightclothes, carrying wooden bats and other ominous items.

"I safely made my way back into the heart of the city and, mulling over my adventures thus far, it occurred to me that the reason people had not reacted to me more violently that day—even unto killing me, loathsome as I am—could be attributed to their belief that I belonged to that circus and had temporarily slipped loose from my cage. This added to the other degradations of man I witnessed on my travels. My spirits fell low and I dreamed of fleeing to faraway lands where no men lived and beasts at least refrained from mocking one another.

"Yet I stayed. When at last I found your father's house, I watched it for weeks, from various vantage points, that I might gaze in different windows. The plentiful trees thereabouts provided many a hiding place. People came and went—a soldier with silver hair, though possessing a youthful visage, and a serious girl who every day wore a different color ribbon in her hair. I saw that she carried books in her basket in the morning and food upon her return.

"And I saw your father, Doctor Edgar Frankenstein, with his medical bag. I saw you there, too, especially at night when the lanterns were lit. I watched the four of you as in a theatrical play, going about the motions of supping, lighting a fire, reading aloud, creating handiworks, talking much, and in general depicting the perfect presentation of a happy family. I became preoccupied with the affection between you and the silver-haired soldier and stewed in an ugly state of envy and jealousy. I had not seen your face like that—pale and thin, yet expressing much ease, warmth, familial solicitude, and much beauty of countenance. Many blushes rose up in your cheeks when the soldier drew close to you, such that I abandoned my hope of approaching your family in any gentle manner and fixed instead on a desire to harm that soldier and, for that matter, all of you in your happy little scenario.

"In my study of people, I came to understand that human emotions often arrive one at a time. People have time to recover from each and thus have some clarity as to their state of being. Yet my emotions are like pieces of stacked-up shale that shift and totter. Pieces fall out of place by whim, break apart on top of other pieces, slip and slide. Thus at many moments, I experience a falling, clattering, mixed-up rubble of sentiments.

"Even when I was pleasantly lulled by your graceful, loving family and could scarce turn my eyes away, I hated you, my maker, for creating such as me who contains these slipping multitudes; thus I veered between lonely anguish and burning rage, for men made no place for your creature except, perhaps, to chain me to a post to endure the fun-making of onlookers. Those neat little squares of glass that comprise your windowpanes were a slippery wall I could not scale. Was my fate to evermore call myself no man's son nor brother nor friend?

"Then came a day when you and your friend, the girl with the hair ribbons, departed in a coach. I followed you. Did you feel me, creator, my breath not far behind? Did I disturb your dreams as you disturb mine? In the town you traveled to, I lived on a small abandoned boat much as I had on the St. Lawrence River, though absent river rats, drunken brawls, and murders by daylight. The river was plentiful with fish and I positioned myself in a small, secluded cove of no particular interest.

"The summer passed easily, for 'twas a most pacific place. Citizens behaved well and went about their business without overmuch joy or sorrow. I did not consider this the ideal human society, for the lack of laughter and delight imparted a somewhat stiff, polite, washed-out gloominess to all. I watched you and your friend with your pretty paints and picnics and sweet friendship. Your harmony and pleasure fed my jealousy, an evil and deplorable condition I could not control and, as the warm days passed and your cheeks took on the rosiness of health, the more incensed I grew, for you had clearly forgotten me, the most fateful creation of your life.

"Then came a fantastical day of darkness at noon, as you well remember. The townspeople all of a sudden were propelled to the extremes of life—screaming, running, drinking, beseeching God on their knees in the middle of the street, pushing and punching those who bumped into them, throwing sticks and rocks. This chaos disturbed me much, so I took up a lantern from a front stoop and headed for higher ground and saw you also, by yourself, climbing upwards. The dark bothered me not, indeed 'twas consonant with my foul sensibility. A peculiar rain commenced and I watched you hide beneath a precarious rock ledge to escape it. I wished to speak to you but feared that my loathsome, ragged voice might cause you to fall in alarm.

"Before I could gather my thoughts or sort through my confusion of impulses, you stood too near me and spoke with loud, shocking fury. Your cold tone brought tears to my eyes and I wanted to shrink like a bad boy, but hardly had this cringing feeling stolen over me than your voice grew quiet, but 'twas not a kindly quiet, more like a soft poison, so there my rage flamed up and I threw my lantern at you. You may curse me for that, but so boiling was my blood at your confounding questions that I could well have strangled you, so you should perhaps thank me for that mere gash on your leg.

"Now you are the one with hate in your eyes, for you know my tale is approaching the death of your friend and you believe that I caused it. 'Tis half true, if such abominations can be half true, but not in the way you imagine, so sheath the knife your fingers are creeping to retrieve and hear me.

"On the way back to the village, I came upon her in a dire state. She had stumbled on a dark path and mortally injured something inside her, for she was in terrible pain. Her hands clutched the area of her heart and the protecting ribs that were, perhaps, protecting her no more but had shattered and pierced some vital organs. That was my unschooled assessment, for I pushed her dress aside a bit that I might help her and saw her torso quite misshapen with a deep hollow where no hollow should be. I tried to lift her that I might transport her to town, for whatever loathing I felt overall for the four of you behind the windowpanes, I had no quarrel with her in particular, nay I liked her composure and the gentle interest with which she listened to others and offered kind words in return.

"She was near death, I tell you true. She bit my hand, kicked, and scratched me, for her pain had reduced her to a primitive state. 'Twas a hideous sight to behold in a young lady and distressed me more than the same in any man. Her agony echoed itself in me and I could not endure it. As I had with expiring soldiers on other paths in other forests, I wrapped my hands around her throat and remained thus until her body relaxed and her soul crept out and flew to the sky, away from the woes of earthly life. But I felt appalling guilt and shame absent with those others; I believe 'twas because she was a girl. I did my best to straighten her body, clothes, and hair, even attempting to retie her hair ribbon—green that day—but my fingers were clumsy and blistered, as they have been since the day of my creation. I left her there. You may blanch at this barbaric behavior, to which I say yes, because am I not unhuman?

"You who conceived a man in what I believe a most unnatural way, though I know not how, to you I say Listen! I am growing into a true self like the monsters of ancient legends, for they are made of parts, are they not? Man and lion, bird and goat, serpent and woman, bear and man. Am I made of parts, too? For I feel undone. Can you not be truthful? Did I ever live inside you, a tiny seed? Did I grow there many a month as human babies do? I feel that never have I been other than a giant, a mad creation. Are you dumbstruck? You loosed me in a world of war and cruelty. Did you give no thought to that, no thought as to how such as I would fare on this earth? Perhaps you thought I would be docile, like a barnyard dog.

"Again, again I ask, 'Have I a soul?' If I do, this world has burnt it black. And so I say Listen! Listen! as I stand naked before you. Am I not your calamitous progeny, rising up in bewilderment and despair, rising up in hatred for you, my maker? Evermore, I shall torment you and yours until your dying day and even then beyond. You gave me life, but in so doing, you cursed me to the eternal grief of all who search in vain for a place to belong upon this earth."

At this point, my creature seemed aflame with rage, so great he could speak no more, yet as I watched his fury drained away. His colors lost their angry brilliance and softened into pastels such as I had never seen. He came beside me. I drew back as far as possible to avoid him, but he fell upon his knees and, to my wonderment, curled up on his side and lay his head in my lap.

CHAPTER XV

Captain Galán, you who have become my abbé, have you done such a thing as that... rested your head upon a woman's lap? Ah, you don't wish to reply, for 'tis a man at his humblest, that gesture of surrender. A woman cannot help but be flooded in response with sympathy and caring—a sweet outpouring of tender feelings and a desire to pet and stroke the face and hair of one who reclines thus. And so my deepest womanhood stirred; I too was swamped with these desires, yet likewise with their opposite, for was he not a monstrous being who destroyed my friends and only a moment before cursed me, shaking and thundering with rage, pain, and hate toward me for giving him life?

My creature slept not, but had drifted into a middle zone of consciousness, his eyes blinking but not seeing the land-scape before us. I pulled my cloak around him and did not touch his face or hair, for his physiognomy was truly appalling up close—his scalp half-burned and bare, one ear sliding all the further down, and the many colors of his face swollen from new repairs and old wounds. I studied at some length the embroidered design on his face. Truly it stood on a razor's edge of beautiful and terrifying.

However much conflicted I felt about this creature, I could not stop myself from placing my hand upon his chest. This visceral nearness to the hearts of my Moses and Eugénie struck me as a thunderclap. Did this not sweep away all cares? Was this not the essence of my whole endeavor? How strong, how constant those heartbeats were. My soul filled with love as I looked down at him in his twilight haze. Was he not just a nameless shell for the true occupants of his flesh, the souls and spirits of my beloveds?

He stirred and sat near me then, but not too near. Those few moments of intimacy left in me a lingering fragility of emotion, which soon ebbed in the face of a creature with much to say, but no straightforward way to say it. His eyes burned with fierce intensity. He tried to overcome the loud, repellent, rasping stutter of his voice by speaking quietly and over-enunciating, which produced a direful, unearthly tone. That scraping, suffocated sound was more alarming than all his shouting and gesticulating.

"Think you not, my maker, that I have told my tale for good and all. Nay, perhaps you thought me gone; perhaps you know not that I became your shadow. I watched you suffer those months after your friend with the many hair ribbons departed this earth. Did you never feel me there? How ill you grew and wept so, and all the while I knew you cursed and condemned me with all your being. Murderer you called me in your feverish dreams, did you not, haunted by the ghosts of friends you believe I killed? Did their spirits not visit you day and night, crying and moaning until you near raved? Your sorrow did not rouse my sympathies; nay, my furies burst red-hot, for all this grief, yours and mine, is your doing, wretched girl.

"How slight you are and delicate. I could crack you in two with a breath. And why should I not? And why not too those you love so dearly–your father perhaps? Or that silver-haired soldier, so proud and solemn? No? This you could not bear? Well then, my maker, you must comply with my solution to counter the alchemy that created me, the dark arts that conceived a beast like me. I have come to believe that the only remedy for my woes, my loneliness, despair, and rage is for you to remain always by my side and treat me with the kindness all others in your life have so enjoyed. This will suffuse my soul with peace–if even I have a soul–and I shall no more trouble mankind. This is how I came to this realization, so listen well, for 'tis your future of which I speak.

"During my time with the river rats, I observed many wives upon the grassy banks, tending to their stewpots, washing clothes in the river, cleaning fish, and repairing the tents that served as shelter. These women struck me as weary on the whole, beaten by their husbands, bruised about their arms and legs, for those were vicious wild men with whom I could not find my place, monster though I am.

"I watched one particular woman much. She was young, as young as you perhaps, and fair like you, with an untroubled countenance and benevolent demeanor. How she came to live among that rough bunch, I know not. Her name was Deline, so I heard them call to her. She had a babe who crawled about the grass to toy with little stones and twigs with great interest, for he was at that age when every item big and small is of delight and absorption.

"Often he suckled at his mother's breast. Sometimes as he did so, he reached up to play with a locket around her neck. She found this amusing and held the chain back a bit so 'twould not break. Sometimes she opened it and showed him an object inside, which caused her to smile and hug him tightly. Every day, she brought water up from the river in a big kettle, heated it over a fire, and bathed him there, which brought forth laughing, splashing, and all-round merriment. She then rocked him to sleep.

"In these moments, a shadow came over her face and she wept a tear or two, for all who live have their troubles, but these clouds lasted only a moment, after which her face returned to its natural soft repose. The vile river rats did not agitate nor infuriate her as they did the other women; perhaps she was the daughter of a king, a river king whom I had seen not.

"To me, 'twas an exemplar of perfect earthly love. In my short, wretched life I have longed for such familial peace. Naturally, this caused me to ponder hopelessly upon these questions: Did I ever suckle at my mother's breast? Who is she, my mother? Does she have a locket containing a likeness of my father? Who, then, is my father? You who are mute on these matters have left me to conclude that my mother must be a hag, a skin-walker, a succubus; my father, a hellhound, a Minotaur, a gryphon, for only such demons could spawn the likes of me. Did you suckle at your mother's breast? Did a babe ever suckle at yours? Oh, why so stricken? Why weep now? Dry your tears, for your life will now begin anew and 'tis I who, this time, am the giver.

"You must promise to stay with me evermore with goodness of heart and tell me the truth of my origins. In exchange, I promise not to hurt you nor any person you hold dear. But mark me, you who unthinking gave life to one so foul, do as I ask or I will spill the blood of all with no regret."

He waited for some reply. My spirit drained away; I felt woozy and faint. Though I was in my body, I was not; though I was in my right mind, I was not. 'Twas as if I stood outside myself, watching a strange and distant play unfold. As such, my actions for some time had a sleepwalking quality.

"Say yes," he said, and so I nodded yes and he said, "Say it aloud," thus I croaked out the word *yes*, but my breath was foul with that unwilling word. I stared up at him as he loomed over me and despite his fearful wounds and pestilence and broken bones, that one word seemed to elevate his mood, for he shined again with magnificent beauty, his colors bright. In fact, his face glowed with joy, an expression I had never seen on his countenance.

"Again," he said, and this time his voice came out as a bark. I whispered yes. He bent to me and bid me repeat that hateful word thrice more, not out of cruelty but because he delighted in the reply. I saved myself from utter collapse by holding onto my ardent hope that the hearts beating in this creature I had loosed upon the world belonged to my beloveds and perhaps, if I did what he wished, their souls and spirits would reveal themselves to me. What is hope but blind desire? And my desire was truly blind.

As I listened, I found myself in a most uncomfortable physical state, desirous of a bath and clean dress. Seeing now this curious softness in my creature, I begged for an opportunity to cleanse myself in a nearby stream. He gave this request a long, silent consideration. 'Twas clearly a puzzle. My disheveled appearance apparently supported my appeal, for he assented.

I let Jack loose from his harness, tying him instead to a tree, for which he gave my hand a grudging nibble. I retrieved soap, a towel, and clean clothes from the cart and bid my creature sit near Jack with his back to the river and never turn around to look at me. This gave him a good deal of doubt and he near forbid me go, but I promised I would not flee and he believed me.

Like the mighty river it fed, the stream was swollen from the heavy rains, but I found a deep, still pool and gladly waded into the cold water, its mud now settling back to the bottom. I dove down many times, surfacing for air only when my lungs near burst, then submerging again. How beautiful 'twas, for looking up I saw sunlight filtered through the water, illuminating the depths with beams of green light, by which I saw fish and frogs going about their business and water bugs skating on the surface.

Why, you may ask, did I not flee? I could have made my way downstream to the river, then hailed some kindly soul to pull me from the water. Even the crudest of men, upon encountering a naked girl washing up on a riverbank, will hasten to offer his coat and assistance. My creature's threats of violence stopped me, as did those beloved items from my father, safe then in my belongings on the cart. Those two enormous books, anatomical fugitive sheets, and little ivory figure, along with my apothecary cabinet and recipes, held me fast.

My battlefield experience and Mr. Burton's *Anatomy of Melancholy* taught me much about afflictions of the mind. Some soldiers were stricken with nostalgia, that fever of the mind that tears a man apart with nightmares, despair, homesickness, sleeplessness, and worry. My father suffered many a year from that misery, as did I myself. In some, however, such illness deepens into madness, for which there is little treatment. Many men suffering from such calamities of the mind have endured being locked in dungeons, bled, shackled, plunged into baths, left in solitary confinement, or fated to wander the countryside as poor tortured souls—disordered, emaciated, agitated, fainthearted, howling, raging, given to sudden blindness or protracted stupors, hearing tormenting voices or sounds such as *vent du boulet*—the distinct sound of cannonballs rushing past, described so aptly in past wars as the confluence of a spinning top, boiling water, and whistling birds, a discord that in itself is enough to cause bedlam in any man's mind.

As I washed my hair and body, a revelation occurred to me. Hearing voices, falling into peculiar sleeps, savage moods—was this not that madness beyond nostalgia? Was my creature a mere wandering echo of the dead soldiers that comprise him? Had I, in quest of the spirits and souls of my beloveds, inflicted upon him every woe, hope, fury, and fear of men at war, boys at war really, half-tied to their mothers, half-tied to General Washington?

If so, does this not prove to all mankind that memories and sensibilities live in lowly flesh? If 'tis true, does this not mean that my creature contains within the vibrant lives and excruciating deaths of ten? If 'tis true, does this not also mean that Moses and Eugénie do indeed live inside my creature? Sire, I myself went mad then with horror and joy. Scarce could I bring myself to contemplate the nightmare of my creature's life, for 'twas as if the very breath and blood and voice and dreams of my beloveds stood before me whole, and thus I hastily made my way back to him.

That clean dress felt wondrous, as did my wet hair streaming freely past my waist. My creature, apparently inspired by my transformation, plunged into the stream, stumbling and splashing about like an elephant, letting out great groans of aches and pains. He stood before me then, trying to smooth his burned, unruly hair, and looked at me with an eager expression, a kind of trembling lunacy. My father taught me that when men are touched by madness, the best battleground treatment is to feign entering their world, that is, do not fight the derangement of mind and sensibilities, for 'tis a fool's errand. Nay, one should agree with such ravings and fears, become an ally and friend, and by this soothe their troubled soul.

Colossal, burned, scarred, seeping, hideous, sewn of flesh and thread, my creature rummaged through his satchel, pulled something from it, and hid his hands behind his back. He bid me stand higher than him on an incline that we might be eye to eye, and offered me one closed hand then the other, back and forth as in the child's game where one must guess which hand contains an object. At last, he relented and handed me his prize—Lara's green hair ribbon she wore on her last day. At this, I fell to wailing, which shocked him considerably.

With a frown, he bid me tie my hair with it and so I did. He took my hands, upsetting in itself, for the seams and stitches holding his hands in place at the wrist were stark signposts to the reality of his corporeal existence, should I slip too far into his magical dreamland. He had some idea of sacrament, reciting incoherent bits of psalms, causing me to understand that he was conducting a wedding cere-mony and by these scattered words, he sealed us evermore. I near passed out.

My creature thereafter led me to a large cave where he set up what you might call housekeeping in a pathetic, clumsy manner. Oh, I am loath to disclose this part of my tale! Forgive me, Captain, if I lapse now into maidenly rectitude regarding the next few months. You shall hear more of this before my time upon this earth is over. I was a prisoner, yes, for my creature oft' repeated his threats against my family and myself. Yet 'tis also true that his astonishing behavior could not help but engage me. Terror and fascination are kissing cousins, are they not?

CHAPTER XVI

Ultimately, however, words intended to be kind drove my captor from that prison and I too left. 'Twas a full moon the night of my freedom, softened by wispy clouds that drifted across its face and over-washed the stars too, creating a dreamy haze. I gazed up at Orion, Cassiopeia, and Andromeda—or thought I did, for stars can take on any design one imagines. In their nighttime adornment, the heavens happily ignore men's struggles below, for all who live on earth are but a brief spark that fades like fireflies.

As I mused on this, I heard a rude little snort and there stood my horse Jack who, though I had not seen him, had apparently kept to the cave environs all the while I lived there, if I may call that living. I caught his bridle and flung my arms around his neck, crying out his name, telling him what a good, good boy he was. He sneezed and bucked a good deal but suffered my embraces such that I began to get the impression that Jack was like a cranky uncle who, once petted properly and embraced, turns mushy and decides he likes you.

As the cart was nowhere to be seen, I mounted Jack directly, firmly strapping my trunk behind me, thankful my apothecary cabinet was compact enough to fit within. All the while I kept up a patter of compliments, so Jack stood quietly until at last we set off across the night grass, the soft moonlight guiding our path. My hair and cape flew out behind me and Jack picked up his pace such that I felt wild and free, as if no one could ever catch up with me. Jack proved a surefooted fellow. On we rode until dawn, sometimes at a gallop, sometimes at a sleepy walk.

We stopped to drink at creeks and while Jack grazed, I ate from nature's bounty of fruit, wild carrots, and quail eggs. I surrendered to the elemental; how primitive I felt, for the landscape was empty of people and settlements. I could have lived thus a thousand years ago on that same land, a girl and a horse wandering under kindly skies. For some brief time, I forgot all I lost, all I endured, and pretended I had no name nor needed any name. Instead, I harkened to the trees talking to themselves, voices of my childhood, and all the other sweet sounds of the natural world. This harmonious state lasted many days.

We traveled southeast, for I had in mind to visit that great city of New York, about which Father and Cristophé day-dreamed when we were young, for I wished to see it before returning to the bosom of my family in Boston.

Common sense stepped in and waggled a reproving finger as we drew near the city, for I had nary a penny. I sought out apothecary shops and soon came upon one called "Mr. Cobb's Physick & Apothecary Shop." Upon listening to the details of my background–those I chose to share–Mr. Cobb offered me a job despite my bedraggled appearance. He had his boy take Jack to graze upon the grass behind his house that his children might feed him sugar and brush him and enjoy his company. That good man even gave me an advance on wages to buy a presentable frock. He bid me stay on a cot at the back of the store.

Thus for some time I slept upon a lumpy, ill-covered cot which, though uncomfortable, bothered me not, for my room was filled with the deep, mysterious apothecary scents I knew from Acadia—gardenias, jasmine, tuberose, and the deep musk of forest roots. 'Twas chaotic with jars of potions placed slipshod on every surface, though each in itself was enchanting, gleaming gold or green or yellow in the light of a hurricane lamp at night.

Though I knew not one person in that great city, I relaxed amongst materials I knew well—guaiacum, sassafras, copaiba, cinchona bark, liniments, weights and scales, mortar and pestle, sulfur, wines, and oils. All in all, 'twas a companionable situation and I repaid Mr. Cobb many times over by organizing his shop from front to back, such that customers murmured in amazement at the now meticulous system of neatly labeled jars, tins, charms, and packets, that they might find all they desired with ease.

I strung a length of twine across the two long sides of the shop, causing Mr. Cobb to frown until I tied upon them dried bouquets of the sweet-scented flowers we used to make hair rinses and hand creams—lilac, roses, spicy dianthus, and such—for these items began to sell plentifully. I decorated each bunch with a ribbon and bit of lace, which set to trembling each time someone opened the door. Apothecary shops are quiet places, for people enter with their secret troubles, fears, and pains, and thus there is a hush. To find therein a place of beauty and order is already half a cure.

Though I had the skills and knowledge, I left the preparation of darker potions to Mr. Cobb, which he seemed to wish to prepare himself anyway. I had an aversion then to animal parts, fats, skins, mushrooms, odiferous bark, nor did I wish any contact with the rum, whiskey, and laudanum in so many preparations.

Have you noticed that when all has gone awry, awry becomes the natural order of things? If by some ill fate agony and terror have become everyday afflictions, we grow numb and stoic for, as a vessel does when overfilled with water, there is no space left for more. Our woes hasten into a little box in our minds and there they remain until unloosed by destiny or happenstance. Neither joys nor sorrows shadow us, nay we are dutiful, drowsy, half-listening, half-dreaming, half-seeing, half-thinking. A wayward carriage could knock us down in the street and we would merely brush off our clothes and continue on our way.

Likewise, when in that indifferent state of mind, a man could hand us a sack of gold and we would accept it as we would a sack of flour. Half the world or more, I think, lives in this sleepy, nowhere condition. Thus I was then—a neat, quiet girl. Pleasantly I looked customers in the eye as I handed them their items, yet I wonder now if anyone noticed that my eyes were blank.

Slowly, though, the city itself awakened me. Have you been to New York City, Captain Galán? 'Tis a wild, alive, dirty, fascinating, misbehaving place. Crooked streets meet at strange angles, leaving you immediately lost. Brawling men spill out of taverns and thieves lurk in the shadows. Part of my job consisted of hitching Jack up to a cart and delivering goods to houses and institutions. Families crowded into rough huts made of ships' canvas. Garbage piles impeded every intersection so that delivering potions and charms necessitated clever navigation.

New York Hospital was on my route and, after several months working for Mr. Cobb, I began to deliver materials used by medical students. This often included large jars of liquor balsamicum—a foul-smelling potion made of clotted pig's blood, Berlin blue, and mercury oxide—used to preserve anatomical specimens. I transported these with great care so their jars would not pop open, releasing abominable odors.

Upon entering the anatomy laboratory for the first time, I observed a scene—though much more expansive, of course—very like that in the church nave where I concocted my creature—limbs casually tossed about, torsos split open, their contents spilling over onto the floor, tops of heads sawed off with brains stacked in little slices like cheese, hand saws, metal braces, and preserved specimens from osteotomies, craniotomies, thoracotomies, pelvic hemisections, all with the telltale saw marks indicating angle and vigor of cuts.

These specimens comprised an extensive anatomical museum with hundreds of jars, mostly yellow in hue. The items therein had been dried in oils or resins, shot through with turpentine and mercury, or floated in liquids. I cannot aptly express to you how this affected me. Appalled though I was to find myself once again among this anarchy, those environs felt familiar. 'Twas a thrill to see others toiling in the same secret pursuit that so occupied me, but the students there did not toil alone as I had, for professors strolled about overseeing each cadaver, commenting upon and correcting procedures. Oh, that I had overseers, not to correct me, but to stop me. As I looked about, I wondered at the dark possibility that, in some obscure corner of the hospital, students were likewise attempting to create life out of death.

On my third delivery there, things were all amiss. Carts with their often-unsavory contents converged in front in a sweaty tangle of horses and drivers. Men upstairs in the anatomy room shouted and threw things out the windows to a garbage fire below. Mr. Arnet, the superintendent who oversaw the flow of carts—a crusty man with some manner of fungus sprouting over his face, arms, and calves—roared and waved his cigar around, trying to unclog the snarl of cart drivers attempting to proceed underground to discharge their unholy burdens.

I held Jack on the outskirts to avoid the fray, trying to gain an understanding of this furor. As I had seen in my previous visits, several assistants attended to Mr. Arnet's commands, often on hands and knees scrubbing the beds of empty carts with foul lye, then splashing buckets of water to wash the filth away. That day's assistant was a girl named Dido who dressed like a boy, for no lady's dress could survive that job. After some time, despite the general uproar, Mr. Arnet took a lazy break to sit upon a low wall by the hospital entryway, where he smoked and bossed others around at his leisure.

As I was about to depart, I saw Dido washing a particularly odious cart and crying. At first, I surmised that the stinging smell of lye had caused those tears, yet upon further scrutiny, I saw that she wept in earnest of some great sorrow. I gestured that she come around to the side of the building, out of Mr. Arnet's view, and upon my invitation, she accepted with a careful glance behind her. Through tears, she told me this story:

"Miss, perhaps you have noticed the uniformly dark hue of most of the bodies desecrated in this hospital by medical students. If you have wondered at this, wonder no more, for they are my people, slaves whose spirits have fled this loathsome life. 'Tis part of my job to remove the winding sheets in which they are buried and wash the bodies for anatomy studies. Miss, death stalks our people with especial glee, so we are accustomed to washing the corpses of our family members and friends for burial, that they might be lowered into the ground fresh and clean with their faces pointing east to assure their ascension to heaven.

"Those washings are done with love, and though we are

sorrowful, we fear it not, nor find it revolting. But here I do not love the stinking bodies of those who come through that door, nor cherish the necessity of these ablutions, which distress me much. Still, I perform this task with respect, for I know it to be the last careful touch their bodies will ever have. Occasionally, someone I know is brought here—a neighbor or a fellow churchgoer.

"This morning, I unwrapped a body and found it to be that of my Auntie Abigail who passed over just three days prior. That she was dead did not shock me, for I had attended her funeral last night, as did all who loved her, though the skies released heavy sheets of rain throughout. Slaves are forbidden to congregate, so we must tiptoe into graveyards like night shadows. So too must these resurrectionist grave robbers sneak in with their wooden shovels and ill intentions to snatch those barely cold.

"Auntie Abigail was a woman who prized her hair, which she braided and twisted into complex, beautiful coils in the manner of our ancestors in the old lands. This vanity, as masters consider it, is forbidden, so she hid it under a tightly wrapped scarf, as all slave women do. We buried her without her head wrap, that God might marvel at her natural, beguiling hair.

"When I unwrapped her not three hours ago, there she lay with her lovely hair greatly disturbed by clods of dirt and rough handling by the body snatchers, who are the brazen, shameless medical students you see here in this devil's school. I fainted at beholding her thus, but no one concerned themselves with this. After some time, I came to my senses and was ordered to scrub the cart that occupies me now. I know not where my auntie's body is, for she has been gone since I arose, probably to be manhandled and hacked asunder without even the semblance of a wash or prayer."

At this, she fell to sobbing yet harder. I fetched her a cup of water and bid her rest awhile in my cart, which she had never scrubbed, for I bore no unholy objects in my deliveries and thus the cart was clean save random escapees from my apothecary work—a branch of blue bachelor's buttons, a few mushrooms rolling about, a clutch of weeping willow buds. Thus she sat awhile and closed her eyes. I clucked my tongue at Jack and bid him home.

We clattered over the rough roads and when we reached the far edges of town, my passenger continued her story. I could not hear her well because of the clatter of Jack's hooves and the creaks and groans of the cart, so I stopped on a grassy lot and turned to listen to her. Jack nickered and complained much, for he was not a patient horse and was likely daydreaming of sugar cane and apples sure to come.

Dido continued thus: "I am not alone in my distress over this grave-robbing practice. Brawls have broken out and the city is most unsettled. Some weeks ago, free blacks and slaves submitted a petition pleading with the Common Council to call upon professors at the New York Hospital and Columbia University to cease allowing students their 'wanton sallies of excess'—that is how the writers described it—in digging up the deceased friends and relatives of my people. 'Twas ignored, as was a subsequent open letter in the newspaper. Soon enough, however, the body of a white man was stolen from the cemetery at Trinity Churchyard. Riots broke out.

"Then, some several days ago, a few boys played in a grassy area outside the hospital. Inside a medical student dissected an arm. Noting the boys at play, he waved the arm outside the window and yelled, 'This is your mother's arm! I just dug it up!' One boy's mother had, in fact, recently died, so the child ran down Broadway screaming to tell the story to his father, a mason, and that boy has not yet regained his senses. The man exhumed his wife's coffin and, after finding it empty, marched on the hospital these past few days with a group of angry workers carrying their tools. A cry of barbarity spread, a mob gathered, and the hospital was ransacked. In the anatomy room were found three fresh bodies—one boiling in a kettle and two others cut up with certain parts of their sex hanging from ropes in a brutal and lewd fashion.

"These circumstances, together with the everyday wanton and inhuman environs of that laboratory—which I myself have witnessed every day—enraged the mob beyond all bounds, thus they invaded the entire teaching wing of the hospital. They hauled bones and half-dissected bodies from all the anatomy rooms into a heap on the street and set them ablaze in a giant, stinking, foul bonfire. Although most of the doctors and medical students had already fled, those who remained to guard the valuable collection of anatomical specimens were also dragged out into the streets. How do I know this? Because I was there, hiding in a corner, witnessing the mayhem. Later, a rumor spread that some damage done could not have been done by men, for several doors were ripped off their hinges and a huge autopsy table was cleaved in two, but not with a saw. Some attributed it to the hand of God showing his displeasure at the goings-on at such a place. The professors, though, said 'twas a monster, a beast, or Satan himself, for they saw huge, looming black shadows fall upon the walls during the uproar. That was yesterday.

"This morning, hundreds more angry men overran the city looking for doctors, medical students, and bodies. A mob surged into Columbia University, pushed past the gates, and tore apart the museum, chapel, library, anatomical theater, and even students' bedrooms in search of bodies and bones. By then, the crowd had swelled to thousands of men armed with rocks and clubs. The militia arrived, opened fire with their muskets, and charged until blood ran in the streets.

"What you see now then is the hospital staff attempting to put everything back together and move bodies in and out as if it never happened. 'Twas into this climate that my Auntie Abigail arrived at this godforsaken place. Now, Miss, I must return to work, for should I be reported missing, a leaflet will be issued putting a bounty on my head."

I turned the cart around and retraced our route, though Jack was sulky and most contrary. My stomach dropped, my nerves lit on fire, and I could scarce contain a scream, for I knew well enough that my creature was that rampaging shadow and none other. I bid my passenger farewell and felt a great sadness for Auntie Abigail, her magnificent hair, and the girl who in her own way endured the inexorable quest for medical knowledge, which has neither heart nor regret for those it destroys along the road to enlightenment.

She departed the cart just before we reached the thick of town. I watched her walk away in her boy's clothes, eventually merging with the other citizens. Never did I see her again nor much of that chaotic city, for soon afterward I left Mr. Cobb's Apothecary and headed for Boston, that I might rest awhile with my dear family and tell what I could of the tumultuous New York City. 'Twas clear that my creature now knew of his true origin, as I shall soon relate to you. I trembled from a great sinking regret. Never should I have revealed it to him. Doom flattened me; I could scarce breathe.

CHAPTER XVII

To assuage my guilt at leaving Mr. Cobb's Apothecary so suddenly, I left Jack behind as a gift to his children. I shipped my belongings to my father's house and, carrying just a small bundle on my back—much like during my battlefield years—headed north. Many a soul offered me rides in conveyances big and small. I spoke little, so gloomy were my thoughts. Still, these journeys did not occur in silence, for certain kinds of silence are an invitation. Thus mine must have been, for I listened to many a tale from highborn and low, all on the single theme of those they had lost to war.

Poor fellows shot themselves or their fellows by accident, lost their feet in winter, froze to death for no blanket, were trampled by a horse, blinded by cannon powder, or drowned by falling in a river. Thanatos has many a way of snatching the lives of men, and each way engraves itself upon the souls of those left behind. Their grief, like mine, rides eternally upon their shoulders. How oft' the world seems no more

than a river of tears. I felt myself slide dangerously close to
that river's edge, thus I commanded myself to daydream
of the joys I would find at my father's house on Commonwealth Avenue. Never would I leave, for I wished to cease
my wanderings, henceforth cling to his side, and keep my
secrets locked forever within my tormented heart.

The sight of Boston lifted my spirits greatly. How comforting 'twas to pass the familiar sweet shops and other places
I knew so well and take pleasure once again from walking
under the lush green maple and chestnut trees gracing the
city and the summer flower boxes in windows throughout.
When I reached the house, to my shock, a dried-up black
wreath hung upon the red door and all the shutters were
closed, something that generally occurred only during
hurricanes and blizzards. Soggy, sunburnt newspapers were
scattered along the walkway.

I found the key in its usual place in the side garden. The
entryway was dim, the house forsaken, the air clotted, dry,
and desolate. I grasped the situation at once, yet grasped
it not at all, wandered past signs of life—a basket of apples,
now wizened, an open book, spilled ink across a page,
coats in closets, a half-smoked pipe next to a chair, a ball,
candlesticks burned to their nubs, an apron hanging on a
doorknob—Mimi's. My heart leapt at this last, for it meant
that she and Freddy had come from Acadia to stay awhile.
Upstairs, the bedrooms too were devoid of life; even the
mattresses were missing.

I turned my back on the clear evidence of calamity and
comforted myself with the notion that they must have gone
on a long sea voyage. Perhaps my father wished to show his
homeland to his wife and boy. Perhaps he had overcome
his repugnance for sea voyages and at that very moment
was standing upon the deck of a fine ship, restoring himself with bracing sea air. Perhaps he had arranged for a

thorough house-cleaning and new beds for his return.

I stood in the hallway a long time, spinning perhapses, then remembered that newspapers always carry notices about the comings and goings of prominent citizens. So, I brought them in, sorted them by date, and went about arranging them on the floor so that all their front pages lay side by side. There were twelve, the most recent dated two weeks earlier.

War and political news occupied many pages. Sailing news contained nary a mention of my father. The final pages, though—always printed last with breaking news—reported in detail the gruesome murders of Dr. Edgar Frankenstein, Madame Mimikej Frankenstein, nee Poulette, Captain Cristophé Savoie, and Master Frederick Frankenstein (body not recovered) at the hands of an unknown assailant. I vomited then, my whole body felt afire and I could scarce walk, so violently did I tremble.

Crawling into Cristophé's room, I saw his uniforms, weapons, and many badges of bravery in battle. Spread upon his bed frame was a soft blanket Mimi and I knit for him long ago. I took up one of his pistols and sat on the floor next to his bed, wishing to end my dire existence. All whom I loved had departed this life—savagely so—thus nothing more held me to this earth.

Shivering, I pulled the blanket around me and my heart split like broken glass, for it smelled of Cristophé. How thoughtless I had been to him, he who offered a different, harmonious life, which I threw away. I readied the pistol for shooting, for this I had been well taught. Yet 'twas heavy and I had no strength to lift it to heart or temple. Later, I thought, later, and lay down on the floor and slept a day and night of nightmares, except once I dreamed of Eugénie—my little seahorse girl—drifting in the sweet undulations and serenity of the sea. Surely she kept me alive that night, for 'twas no will of my own.

Once awake, I wandered downstairs as a sleepwalker moves, with Cristophé's blanket still around me, for no fire had warmed that hearth in many a day. I saw then what I had not before–a letter on a small table in the library. The handwriting was unfamiliar but it had my name on it. When I opened the envelope, bits of blue and gold thread fell from its folds, surely the signature of my creature. Until that day I knew not that he could write. As you can see, he wrote it upon my father's letterhead with that good man's pen and ink, sitting in the chair where Father had written many a loving letter to me all my life.

To CURSED MAKER YOU

Your Father's House

Once upon a time, I was dead; nay, ten times I was dead and in the ground. This I now know, for at last you confessed the truth of your demented undertaking many a week ago after you scarce spoke a word to me or gave me any sign of gentle regard, though I had pledged myself to you and poured myself into every effort to please you. Was not that cave high in the wilderness beyond the river, where no men walked except native peoples, was that not beautiful in its airy space and soft floor? And how agreeable was that nearby creek, which in our abode could be heard burbling in a pleasant manner? Did you not delight in the profusion of ivy that grew amongst the rocks, bringing the greenness of outside inside?

There I worked most earnestly to provide you with a fire always burning and a full stewpot. 'Twas more home to me than anywhere. 'Twas summer and warm, full of the songs of bats who shared our cave and the rustle of night creatures.

Many a day I spent building you a bower that you might rest in a hidden, sweet-scented alcove. Even in thunderstorms, I walked far in search of fragrant flowers of all manner, that you might use them as your pillow and weave them into your hair, as do girls in fairy tales. Every aching, burning step I took to charm you with the bounty of field and forest, I took gladly. I would have traversed one hundred miles to bring you a single strawberry. Know you the torture of these gentle acts? Violence, rage, and anguish—these fight for brightest within me. Know you I have lived tormented every day, for every hour of my life I felt that whatever earth I was made of 'twas foul, fetid, rotten; always I have lived in a raw, restless, dazed misery.

In my travels, I saw the river rats strike their women hard, then lay with them in intimate congress, laughing and breathing and slapping them playfully now, giving every indication of joy. Thus I yearned to find this joy and felt it my right, for when one person belongs to another, is that not the end to solitude and loneliness?

I write now of secret things, which men do not perhaps confess to women, but I am scarce human, so I will speak as one who knows not the courtly rules of human intercourse. Every night in that cursed cave I stripped you naked and myself, too, as husbands and wives do. Your body in the dim firelight was as a goddess, a statue—bewitching, terrifying. I dared not touch, for goddesses are not to be touched! 'Twas you who gave me not just the kiss of life, but also the kiss of love such as lovers do. Why kiss me then with warmth and promises of joy, yet turn mute and cold when we lay as man and wife with no eyes upon us but God's?

Sometimes you sobbed until you were feverish, causing me to draw far back into the cave for I knew not what to do. I feared crushing you and thus approached you tentatively and withdrew during the crying and fighting times. When this elicited not a glimmer of appreciation, rage burst up in me and I became rough and shook you and begged in a manner unbecoming man or monster. Never was I granted that bliss that is the birthright of all men.

Men, you say? Nay, I am a beast, am I not? Yet even beasts in the field experience conjugal joy, for they bear fruit in the form of lambs and colts and calves and all the creatures that populate this earth. But I, I have no seed, for no gush of life flows from me. Oh, maker, could you have contemplated a worse fate for me, your wretched offspring? Desire is the devil's own playmate, for though it arises, it does not always know how to ebb.

My rage poisoned all the air. Eventually, you wakened from your fear and one day, as I sat glooming in a corner far from you, boiling in my own misery, I noted a new look in your eyes—a softness I had not seen before. Have you any notion of the patience required to wait for your answer to my eternal question? Seeing that softness in your face, I thus asked, "Who am I?" I sat close and you gave me a look that could melt icebergs, so warm was it. I gathered my courage to hear whatever dire reply you might deliver, for though I knew not the exact substance, 'twas no doubt 'twould be awful; that I felt through and through, and all the wounds of my body burned and pulled and seeped and ached and cried out in dread anticipation.

Yet you spoke to me as to a child. What evil kind of person, when asked the deepest, heartfelt question one can ask—"Who am I?"—decides to tell a fairy story? Perhaps another day, any other day, I might have welcomed spinning tales and even told you bits of ancient legends my fractured memory recalls, but that day, the day you answered me so wrongly, 'twas as if the words swirled inside my mind in a language I understood not, yet did understand. So sick was I with the puzzle of it, the gentle-sounding mystery, that I could scarce fathom one sentence from the next. 'Twas as if your soft, slippery words slithered inside, curled up inside, to poison me forever after, for is it not a universal fact that the truth is a snake, the ruination of all that comes after?

Half your words escaped me, so oddly drowsy was your voice. At your bidding, I discarded my cloak and revealed my entire body to you by light of day—with its patchwork of colors such as exists in no other man—and felt then an excruciating shyness, for you looked at me as a net does a butterfly, a frog a mosquito.

"Close your eyes," you said, "and remember your creation." Your tongue tripped over itself to tell me something secret and hide it at the same time. Your words seared my soul—if I possess a soul—and never shall I forget that torment I already half-remembered. As you spoke, an anamnesis of the holy environs of a church rushed into my mind, bells, fire, again I remembered, putrid ashes, pieces of bodies strewn about, pieces of all colors—the colors of my arms and legs and all the rest of me. Struck with the truth, I suddenly knew all, remembered all, and fled the cave, howling at the knowledge of my unholy conception.

Fate directed me again to your father's red door. Surely when you entered this pretty house you felt the cold weight of absence. It now gives me joy to imagine you passing through each room, searching vainly for those who belonged to you. They will molder in their graves now as I once moldered in many graves upon a battlefield. My maker, I murdered them. Even your silver-haired soldier, who doubtless vanquished many a man, weakened once I put my hand upon him. I saw my gruesome visage reflected in the eyes of each as they drew their last breath and now you know that the image of my hideous, half-colored eyes, my pustules and freakish face will follow them to their resting places under the dirt and give them no peace.

Having dispatched your soldier, I strangled your beloved father and the woman beside him whose dark hair spilled upon the floor. I did not desecrate their bodies; in this, I am godlier than you, who defiled men as a butcher does a cow.

As I turned to depart their bedrooms, now their coffins, I heard a noise in yet another room—a raccoon perhaps, or city dog who had crept in from the cold night. But no, I saw a bare foot protruding from under a bed and pulled it toward me, thus revealing a boy so terror-stricken that he pissed himself and great gobs of secretions gushed from his eyes and nose. I bear no ill will against a child and even felt some pity for a little boy who thought he could vanquish me with a wooden sword. Still, I carried him into the other rooms and made him look at my handiwork that he might perish in heightened agony, then struck him a mighty blow and left him to die.

Forevermore, I curse you and swear by the earth, sea, and sky that I will torment you as you have tormented me. May you have neither friend nor family. May you neither sleep nor be free of nightmares. May your days be marked by despair and loneliness. In this, we will be companions, for I did seal our bond forever. All that I suffer, you shall suffer until the end of days, and even then may you never find peace under this green earth, for I will haunt your wicked heart now and evermore. May there be no flowers at your grave, nor any soul to mourn you, nor any clue that a wretch like you ever lived.

SIGNED HERE IN BLOOD, BLOOD OF ALL THE MEN YOU BEFOULED

SIGNED HERE IN TEARS, THE TEARS OF ONE WHO HAS NO SOUL

SIGNED HERE IN ANGUISH AND DESOLATION,

MY DESTINY AND YOURS

X

CHAPTER XVIII

'Twas that day I cut off my hair. I cut it close with Mimi's sewing scissors, then shaved my head with Father's razor, a slipshod job with numerous nicks causing rivulets of blood to trickle down my scalp and soak my collar. I stared long into the looking glass at my reflection that I might understand who I was, for by now my mind was no clearer on this point than was that of my creature. Into that glass I stared, nay fell into it I say, for I was lost. The sun disappeared, so I lit candles all around and a fire in the hearth. Again, I gazed into the mirror and said my name into the glass—Océane Frankenstein dit Belfleur—that I might find myself within.

Captain, had you ever seen a bald woman before I came upon your ship? 'Tis an unsettling sight. There is nowhere to hide. Grief and madness are not strangers and these were etched upon my face, along with a wash of paleness and deep violet hollows circling my eyes, all indicating illness and faintness, an absence of life's force. Thus I could call it the face of suffering, such as the faces of saints and the Virgin Mary in ancient paintings. Was I not wandering in the wilderness like Demeter, braving hell in search of her daughter? Was I not Niobe, eternally lamenting the loss of her beloveds such that she turned into a weeping stone? Blaspheme me if you will for likening myself in that moment to saints, virgins, and goddesses, but since time began women have borne the catastrophes of men and thus may be forgiven for feeling, in extreme moments of anguish, that we suffer as did biblical and mythical women who, in their female agony, served as our progenitors.

Logs settled in the hearth and in that looking glass I saw as in a dream the spirits of my beloveds drifting across the glass, then dissolving off the edges, leaving me alone again. All the night, I fed the fire and stared into the looking glass until in my exhaustion I had visions and hallucinations. When my eyelids drooped in sleep, my mind was bedeviled by the figure of my creature—his cloak a swirling tornado—screaming, cursing, blue of face, skin oozing different-colored purulence. At last, I cried out every tear and fell into a stupor upon the hearth.

My creature supposed that his mighty blow had neatly dispatched Freddy, but I felt him still alive and resolved to find him, for that dear child was a resourceful boy, as are all who spend their youngest years in the wilds of Acadia, thus I felt sure he was about and fending for himself. I wrapped my head tightly with several scarves and haunted the port for days, as Freddy had listened with fascination to the tales Cristophé and I told of our early adventures in that environ, which matched his own fascination with the sea and creatures of the wild. Boys scampered across the docks like pups, but none were Freddy.

I stood upon that spot where long ago I saw a man die and live again. Had I never witnessed that, would I be who I am?

Any given person can go mad by puzzling over all the ifs of life. Five minutes on this vast green earth, where time goes back to the time before time and will go forward to the time past time, five minutes or one minute in that endless sweep of clocks ticking can tilt the world askew, as I have done, all because of a man fishing during a thunderstorm. Where is he now, I wonder? Does he roam the earth dazed, covered with tattoos of ferns and roses as my creature does? I left those thoughts and that place and lingered then about the marketplace, for Freddy loved the candies sold there—iced almonds, candied cherries, barley sugar, and pastilles—but there too I failed to find him.

Some days later, my heart leapt, for I saw that dear boy through the window of a maritime supply shop, sweeping the floor in a manner that indicated he worked there. He saw me, raced out the door, and flung himself into my arms. We wept and talked over each other in an incoherent manner. Freddy spoke with the shop owner in an animated fashion, handed over his apron, and was mine, for that kind man bid him go.

We retired to a tavern crowded with cigar-smoking, loud-talking men and before long had before us heaping bowls of seafood soup, rosy with saffron, a whole loaf of bread, and a bottle of port. I poured Freddy a goodly portion and urged him to drink, for the words he had to share could not be said without reinforcement. I could have fed a pint of whiskey to a newborn in that tavern and no one would care, such were the upheavals of war in the great city of Boston. Once warmed and sated, I urged Freddy to tell me of his life.

"Ossy," he said—for this he called me since he was a babe—"Mama and I moved here after Papa left the war. I think 'twas because he was sick. He sat in his big chair so much and Mama fussed about him with teas and remedies. Cristophé was home, too. One night, we were all abed. I was reading *Robin Hood and His Merry Men*, although I had been told to put out my candle and go to sleep. I heard Papa snoring beyond the wall... you know how he does... how he does..." At this, his brave steadfastness broke. He leaned against me and, with a fistful of bread in one hand, shook with sobs, not quite child wails, but muffled sobs as men do, sorrow choking inward, tears swallowed. "...how he did..."

"Brave boy," I said, and we sat awhile, picking at the remnants of our soup, and forthwith he was able to continue.

"Nights always have scary things: groans, window glass rattles, curtain shadows on the walls, and animals yowling outside. I was afraid of those when I was a baby, but not now. At first, I thought nothing about a creaking on the stairs. Maybe 'twas Cristophé going down to the kitchen as he often does... did... for a glass of water. I put out my candle, hid my book under my pillow, and pretended to sleep, for he sometimes stopped on his return trip to step into my room and ruffle my hair or kiss me. I heard a door close and all was quiet and I was sleepy.

"'Twas then as if the house blew up, maybe hit by cannonballs... scary noises, terrible fighting, screaming, things falling and breaking, maybe the roof falling in. Great thumps, things smashing, men shouting, coughing, choking, hitting, cuss words, Mama screaming, and roaring, howling so loud I covered my ears. Lions, I thought then, lions are attacking us. I reached for my sword and put on my knight's helmet, but when I started to open the door, all went quiet. A long quiet. Maybe 'twas a nightmare inside a nightmare. Cristophé told me about that once. 'Tis when a person thinks he is awake and sees himself dreaming about some terrifying scary thing, but the awake part is just another nightmare. He told me that if I should ever find myself thus to pinch myself hard on the inside of my arm. In the dark and quiet

I did this, and it hurt. Twice I did it, twice it hurt, and so I knew 'twas no clever double nightmare.

"I was awake and tried to run, but my feet would not move. I heard jagged breathing and thought that the lions must be catching their breath. Papa and Mama and Cristophé were silent; I heard not a sound or movement, which surprised me greatly, for surely in the midst of danger they would have rushed to my side before all else. The panting lions stood outside my door, so I hid under my bed. My heart pounded so, for lions have very good noses!

"I said the Lord's Prayer, not out loud, but in my head. The door latch waggled. Someone entered and again I heard gasping and choking. Then it stopped a moment and something grabbed my foot and yanked me out until I stood before not a lion, but a horrible monster worse than from any storybook, a beastly demon in the shape of a mountain with the face of a man all burned and torn. I have read the words 'murder in his eyes' in many an adventure book and this I saw in that monster's face.

"He reached a hand toward me, a giant's hand. I swung my sword at him but my arm was shaking and the sword fell. That monster ripped off my nightclothes, so I was naked and crying and so scared I wet myself." Here he broke into sobs of humiliation. I whispered many comforting phrases and he continued. "He lifted me up by one arm until I thought 'twould break—see the bruises?—and dragged me into the other bedrooms."

Here his voice trailed into a whisper. His diction devolved into that of a younger child. Only as his sister could I understand him as he whispered his ghastly secrets—how the creature made him look at each by candlelight, the broken, strangled bodies of Father, Mimi, and Cristophé. "He hit me then or threw me. I remember looking into Mama's eyes as she lay falling off the bed, but then 'twas all black until I woke, pulled on my clothes, and ran and ran as fast as I could."

Oh, Captain, so struck was I with guilt after Freddy finished his story that I scarce could breathe. 'Twas I who murdered all those unlucky enough to know me. I gave that creature his hands—how carefully I chose them, one slightly larger than the other, one dark, one light. 'Twas I who gave them strength and infused them with life's blood. The dense cigar smoke in that tavern was choking and I could scarce keep my seat, for I wished to call to Satan to burn me as I had burned my unwitting creature.

But Freddy began to tremble and his eyes glassed over, so I held him close and at last he dozed. I brooded over my desperate circumstances and my mind drifted back to the conclusion of my habitation—if it may be called that—with my creature, for I promised to tell you of it and 'twill explain why, with the best intentions, I told my creature the story that set him upon a fate so terrible 'twas beyond imagining.

During his bridegroom period—if it may be called that—my creature carried so many roses, lilacs, and night-blooming jasmine into the cave that it had the appearance and heavy scent of a funeral parlor. The cave was more of a cavern and had a peculiar attribute. Fed by dribbling rivulets of water, vast quantities of some kind of living plant covered the walls, making them twinkle like stars. Between this and the flowers 'twas an overheated atmosphere with little to rest the eye.

So dedicated was he that he spent many an hour examining each stem that I might not accidentally prick myself with a thorn. So intent was he at laying gifts at my feet that one warm day he brought in a sackful of ladybugs; how many days of stalking through meadows had it taken to capture so many? He let them all loose at once and I will say 'twas an enchanted flying cloud of little red whirring creatures rising up like fairy dust. Some landed in my hair and on my hands, and I felt like a princess then, so light and lovely and innocent were they.

However, their presence awoke the bats from their daytime slumber and soon the cave was filled with hundreds of grotesque, swooping, chirping, clicking, and buzzing creatures diving in from the far reaches of a tunnel at the back of the cave where they lived. I fled then, but not too far, for my creature had me on an ankle chain. I have hesitated to mention this, for 'twas so reprehensible, so mortifying and debasing. I was able to stand a little way outside the mouth of the cave, away from the *mêlée*, from where I witnessed my creature flare up into a storm of ferocity. His ire directed at those infernal bats, he caught them barehanded and squeezed the life out of them; he even bit their heads off in his rage.

So confused and aroused were those hateful creatures that they formed a tornado of flying vermin gorging on helpless ladybugs, with my creature a flailing, shrieking giant within. Eventually, he too fled and leapt into the stream where he sat down so the water reached his shoulders and, his rage subsiding, cried bitter wordless tears for the destruction of his bower.

This ended his period of husbandly playacting—if it can be called that. We lived outside then, for he chained me to a tree and huddled some distance away, morose, glowering, dangerous. When he did approach me, 'twas roughly, and many a bruise and swollen eye and other unspeakable injuries occurred. Fearing for my life, I broke my silence and resolved to tell him of his origin. My weeks in chains provided me with much opportunity to contemplate how to do this. 'Twould be fatal, I thought, to explain it in terms of natural philosophy, surgery, and apothecary methods, and likewise perilous to name my beloveds, for would he not just fly into a jealous rage?

So, as one approaches a child whose sensibilities are too fragile to bear the cold realities of life, I told him a story in the hope that if I spoke it in a tender, hypnotic manner, he would receive the tale as a long-ago legend, perhaps to be puzzled over much later, long after I was gone, for having fulfilled my promise, my family would be safe evermore. Myths and legends are passed across time because they touch our deepest inchoate longings, and so I launched upon my fable, like Scheherazade, to save my life.

"Creature," I said, "come sit by me and think back. Try to remember your birth, for I will tell you now about your origin. But first you must unchain me, for I cannot think properly when I am thus bound." After much consideration, he complied and I continued. "Once upon a time, two souls wandered the earth—a man and his little girl. Too soon separated from their corporeal form, they searched far and wide for bodies without souls that they might enter those bodies and live out their long lives on this green earth. For many a year, they wandered, lonely souls crying out. The cold winds that people hear on winter days—those are their voices wailing and begging. Raindrops falling slowly down windowpanes, those are their tears.

"After many years, they came upon a wolf who promised them a body. 'Will you make it large enough for two souls?' they asked.

"'I will,' he said, 'but you must swear to go to the Northern Pole and live your life in the land of ice and snow at the end of the world and never reveal your secret to anyone.' They agreed and the wolf took them to a battlefield where brave men fell to their horrible deaths, never to draw breath again. The wolf gathered up these men and from their flesh and bones sewed a new body with beautiful thread, a body that looked like no other—the majestic, colossal body of a giant forged from earth and fire. And so the two lonely souls flew into that body and he lived evermore in the land of snow and ice, no longer lonely, for he is the only creature on earth with two souls."

I observed my creature carefully as I spoke and indeed my voice had a soporific effect on him until I finished and silence fell. Bewilderment then passed across his face, followed by a slow-dawning horror. He studied his limbs and torso as if seeing them anew, his colors grew livid, and his body and voice grew so enormous they seemed to block out the sun. "Corpses!" he uttered, "Corpses!" and his voice was a monstrous, agonized howl.

CHAPTER XIX

Hand in hand, Freddy and I walked back to the house that had been a touchstone in both our lives. I took off my cap and scarves to bare my scalp to him, but this caused no dismay; in fact, he wished the same and thus I shaved his head, too.

At first, we were as two recovering from a debilitating illness for which the remedy was food, sleep, and warmth. In this, we pulled all the contents of the larder and root cellar into the kitchen and arranged everything on the kitchen table to assess our provisions. We desired to create a fortress, for we had no wish to venture out into the city. We kept all window and door latches locked always. By day, we kept the shutters open that the sun might doubly warm us as we drowsed like elderly people in the soft chairs by the fireside, but at night we closed them, too. We dared not go upstairs, so we slept by the hearth wrapped in coats and extra clothes.

Domestic life took on a kind of holy, constant succor. We cooked together, seeking to reproduce the simple meals we loved best from Acadia. Some days, an onion was salvation, a jar of peaches elixir for the soul. We read aloud to each other as people in convalescent hospitals do, focusing on unfamiliar subjects in Father's library so as not to make our wounds flare up the worse. We read of ancient art, rivers in the world, and of the lives of great thinkers and writers. Sometimes, I told him stories of Penny and Jack, for he loved such stories and vowed that evermore Penny would be his favorite cow.

We spoke little about the evil that had befallen us, but by night our dreams spoke for us, if I may call them dreams, for they were truly sleeping terrors that caused us to sit upright and scream of falling off cliffs, of being chased by snarling, drooling forest creatures, of something tearing off our hands and feet as we tried to flee, of choking, drowning, burning, pistol shots, graves—of every wicked, agonized suffering man can endure. Yet by morning light, we did not speak of these, only mopped the sweat from each other's brow and prepared tea with ginger and sassafras root—our medicinal everyday breakfast.

Freddy had strange bouts of delirium, running through the house with his sword, barking orders, chasing shadows, lining up all his toys in perfectly straight lines, only to knock them about with a hard rubber ball, cursing and blaspheming everything big and small. I disturbed him not during these boyish occupations, for I understood from whence they came. He told me again how, on that terrible night, he was forced to look upon the splayed and strangled bodies of our beloveds, forced to put his little face right next to theirs and take in all the details of bulging eyes and cooling skin. How he endured that without losing his senses forever I do not know. I thought long how to spare him from a life steeped in melancholy and gloom, which I was sure a life with me would entail.

Over a period of weeks, I thus arranged the following: We would sail together from Boston to Halifax that he might experience life aboard a working ship, something he wished for often. A Frankenstein cousin, Nicolas's older brother, would meet us and take Freddy into the bosom of that Philadelphia part of the family, for they are a resilient, exuberant crew who I knew would give him the love and strength a child requires.

Upon receiving an inquiry from me, they readily agreed to raise Freddy as their boy. I showed Freddy their letter, but he did not wish to go. He begged that he and I might live in Father's house and continue our quiet refuge until he was a man. Finding me unmoving on this point, he came to realize that our beloved house was haunted by ghostly horrors. He asked then for me to live with him in Philadel-phia, but again I said no.

What cruelty I brought upon that boy, for upon the heels of losing near everyone in his life, I was now leaving him, too. I told him that doctors often prescribe long sea voyages for those with troubled hearts and spirits, and that I must undertake such a voyage north while he attended school and restored himself in the warm bosom of our relatives. I did not speak of my quest to rid this world of that mur-derous creature, nor of my connection to it. Perhaps fate would return me to Freddy's side when the deed was done.

Fervently did I wish to leave him with some bright hope, so, though I did not promise it, I said that I would attempt to undertake a very special project for him, something far dearer to him than my daily appearance amongst the numerous Frankensteins would come to mean. This piqued his curiosity and distracted him a bit from his sorrows, thus I expounded upon a make-believe idea that became real.

Like many a boy, Freddy was fascinated by the sea, adventuring, and exploring. Many a time he amused us with imaginings of known and unknown creatures living in undiscovered places. He could scarce walk before he wandered down the hill in Acadia to be near the harbor when whalers brought in great beasts of the sea. He listened until he keeled over as adults spun nighttime tales of bucks ten hands high deep in the forest, of birds whose wings filled the sky and darkened the sun, of whales that drank the sea, and of bears that lived on the moon.

I told him I would voyage to the far reaches of the Polar Regions, seek out creatures big and small, and write descriptions of each. These I would bind together in a book entitled *Great Creatures of Faraway Lands and Seas*, and deliver it to him so he would henceforth be the only person on earth to possess that book. So excited did I grow while musing about this book that by the end of the conversation, I half believed it myself. Why could I not fulfill this promise while pressing forth with my deadly assignment?

Even if Freddy were grown and thus fit for dangerous journeys, I would go alone, for by then I considered myself unworthy of the warmth and companionship of another. He who I brought to life must be mine alone to annihilate. Likely, I would lose my life, too, never to live more on this earth, and thus our story would be told.

Before we departed, I placed a travel bulletin in the *Boston Gazette* so that, should members of Mimi's family or old-world Frankensteins or Freddy's Boston friends or teachers go looking for him, they would know where to find him, which as you can see from this newspaper clipping that reads as follows:

> Master Frederick Frankenstein, son of the highly esteemed and recently departed Dr. Edgar and Madame Mimikej Frankenstein, has embarked upon a sailing adventure trip to Halifax, Nova Scotia. There he will be met by his cousin Mr. Abraham Frankenstein from the great city of Philadelphia, who will escort Master Frederick to Pennsylvania, where he will henceforth make his home among his relatives. Hearty wishes to this brave young fellow; may he have a safe journey and dwell always in the right hand of God.

The autumn colors were aflame as we left Boston. We were as moles blinking in sudden light, so long had we been indoors during our convalescence. Freddy was not the same light-hearted boy—how could he be? His expression had taken on a somewhat ascetic mien, so like Father's quiet, intense, beautiful, suffering visage. But he was still a boy, so the sea air lifted his spirits, as did seeing all the wonders of a great ship with its sails full of encouraging winds, all the clanking and hallooing of men, the groaning of ropes, and the sad singing at night when the sailors were in their cups and inclined to sing of homelands in faraway places. The bracing air brought blood to our cheeks and tears to our eyes, but not of misery.

Shamelessly, I used my feminine wiles upon the captain so that Freddy and I might study his maps and thus gain some familiarity with the Northern Pole—what little anyone knew of it—for that was, I believed, the destination of my creature, and there I must follow. I spent much time on deck staring out toward the horizon, hoping the cold air would freshen my mind, but fear kept ahold of me, for 'twas Beatrix Belfleur—my mother's ghost—whispering to me.

I'm sure I heard her, for we sailed right over the area in the great Atlantic Ocean where the death ships had anchored, right where began the sad story of my family's New World dance with death. Her wandering soul cried out to me and only Freddy's presence kept me from slipping over the side to search for her in the cold depths that no living man has seen. Perhaps one day great explorers will find cities in the sky and under the sea. I looked at Freddy as he likewise gazed off into the infinite ocean. Perhaps his descendants will be among those brave men and thus mark the name Frankenstein as a finder of new worlds. I found a new world, did I not, in the land of the living dead? May my dear Freddy never tread my path.

Knowing that he would soon depart for a new life with people who know nothing of my misadventures, except that Nicolas suffered an accident far out in the countryside while faithfully protecting me, I determined to write the boy a letter, that it might be sealed and given to him in his full manhood. Long did I contemplate the content of such a letter. Should I tell my dear little brother the truth about how the monster came to be, for is he not the only person left to carry such a tale unto future generations?

The name "Frankenstein" has been long known for the nobility of good works by such as my father and his father, and back to our earliest ancestor, who first extended his hand to help his fellow man. Yet love and loss, grief and pain, propelled me—also a Frankenstein—to the pits of hell from whence came the aberration of my creature, and that too is our story. Had I confessed it earlier, my loved ones who fell one by one to earth like stars might yet live.

Is confession really good for the soul, as learned men proclaim? If I revealed the truth to Freddy, would my soul rise to heaven? If he knew all, would he then find peace by understanding at last what cataclysm struck our family?

Conversely, if I wrote him a rosy letter full of happy remembrances of our lives that he might not forget them in old age, would he remain forever tortured by questions that for him had no answers? In the end, I told the truth. Some of the truth. I wrote of Moses and our baby, and briefly did I describe the creation of the creature and the madness that drove me to that infernal endeavor.

Mostly, with many words and tears upon the page, I begged his forgiveness for introducing that creature into our family. Likewise, I pled with him to tell this tale to his children and their children, for it brings with it lessons for those who follow, lest they one day be tempted to use their skills for vile purposes. And, is it not better to know someone truly rather than believe you truly know them? I sealed this letter with much candle wax and wrote upon the outside: "For Frederick Frankenstein, When He Is Of Age." I tucked it in my sleeve that I might easily hand it over to Cousin Abraham when we docked.

We sailed into Halifax Harbor on an exceptionally beautiful day. Mother Nature showed off with agreeable blue swells and a cold but gentle wind that steered us easily toward shore. Freddy and I grew melancholy as we watched the harbor draw close, for we knew that parting was upon us. I stroked and kissed his beautiful face many times, so greatly did I despair that never again would I gaze upon it, and so 'twas, for as clearly as you look upon me in this dire condition, surely I shall never return.

Still I saw a light in his eyes, for children cannot help but eagerly greet new adventures. I had told him much of the rowdy, happy cousins with whom he would now reside, and had described the wilderness that stretched far west of the Louisiana Territories—its beauties and mysteries, and plentiful creatures and potential for exploration and discovery. By this, perhaps, I dissuaded him in some small measure from exploration by sea, that he might fulfill his adventurous desires yet keep his feet upon the ground.

By dint of nervous energy, I must have buttoned and unbuttoned his coat a dozen times, and likewise pushed and pulled his scarf about his ears, yet he let me fuss in this woman's way. So busy were my hands wrestling with his clothing that my letter slipped out of my sleeve and, itself a little vessel, flew round and round out over the sea and settled upon a wave. For a moment 'twas visible, then the sea swallowed it, the ink no doubt already washed away.

He asked me if it had belonged to me and when I replied 'twas nothing important, he looked at me and knew full well that 'twas not true, yet he permitted this secret to go to its watery grave. Thus fate kept my dear brother forever ignorant of the true birthplace of his sorrows. 'Twas best, I now see, for what he was forced to witness that one catastrophic night, was that not enough for any one boy or man to bear? Sometimes whys and wherefores are but pointless agonies.

Off my Freddy went with Abraham, whom I had not seen in many years and scarcely remembered. He was a smaller version of his brother—short and stout, but with a face so like my Nicolas that he set me at ease at once, for he embraced Freddy heartily and gave him a fine pocket watch which, according to the language of men, as you well know, means "you are now a man." Freddy was much younger than is customary for such an inheritance, but he understood the meaning and tucked the watch deep into his breeches pocket, fastening the chain to his belt. We embraced one last time and he had tears in his eyes, but they were a man's tears, shining with courage and hope.

CHAPTER XX

Thereafter I traveled by coach from Halifax, through Quebec, far up to Baffin Island, for on the ship's captain's map 'twas the dividing line between land and ice, and 'twas there I must acquire a sledge and dogs. In towns along the way, the autumn leaves had fallen early, presaging a stormy winter. People stacked the last few logs into their high woodpiles and bought carded wool, boots, lanterns, and big blocks of wax for candles. I required similar items and provisions for my arduous journey into the remote unknown.

This journey took some weeks and 'twas a silent one, for the driver was not a talkative fellow, nay I scarcely ever saw his face, for his entire body was swathed in layers of fur, as was mine. When we stopped in towns and villages to sleep, he smoked a pipe and thus I saw his hands and eyes and a gigantic beard, but little more. When I first unwrapped my numerous furs in a tavern that I might eat, he was surprised to discover that his passenger was a girl.

The landscape was severe, all white, with screaming winds and endless swirling snow, and when my traveling companion—if he can be called that—hunched upon the coachman's seat shrouded in caribou furs, he loomed as an immense shadow against the sky. In certain kinds of light, alarm surged through me and I feared 'twas not him, but my creature, whipping the horses to fly across the inhospitable land.

At times, I fell into terrible dreams from which I had difficulty awakening. Once, I dreamt of a journey within a journey: a dream of long-lost places Cristophé and I often spoke of as children. When the dream began, I fell through a narrow entrance to the bottom of the sea, to the mountainous island of Atlantis. Carved into a mountainside was a great palace and there I wandered. I could not reach my destination—whatever that might be—for guards blocked every passage, and violent earthquakes and floods shook the island and caused it to disintegrate until 'twas no more than flotsam floating on a tide.

I called out for someone—I know not who—and found myself then in Avalon, where all the earth's apples grow. Again, I called out. Again, I followed many paths, but all ended at the edge of a deep black hole. Into that hole I fell, falling up, not down, screaming and crying until I landed on Mount Olympus and there traversed through lush forests like those in Acadia, roaming among trees I knew and loved. How beautiful their scent and dancing leaves that spoke in whispers!

I then came to a great, severe mountaintop splitting the clouds apart, yet no gods dwelled there. I threw a rock and the vibrations echoed and echoed until years seemed to pass, then at last the ringing died away. I called out again but my voice was silent. The vast forests below turned to deserts and the earth was hollow. Again, again I called out, but no one heard and there I was doomed to cry out into the void evermore.

As we traveled on, my silent coachman nevertheless proved himself a good companion, for he helped me amass several boxes of provisions necessary for my onward journey and took especial care of my books, which as it turned out, were my life's most constant companions.

When we ran out of land, he handed me off to a boatman, who carried me across the choppy waters of a bay to Baffin Island, a most primitive land—forbidding, beset by voracious beasts, wailing tempests, and ice rising up in places to form towering cliffs hollowed out by the wind. Still, I felt a stirring of courage crossing that bay, so clean and untouched did the world feel then. So far was I from anyone I had ever known, anything I had ever seen, so stripped was I, slight as a babe, slight as a bird, and gladly did I hold onto this floating sensation until land was once again in sight. Scarcely had I set foot thereupon when the boatman swung my boxes ashore, turned his little ship, and sailed back across the bay without a word. Was life in this frigid land conducted in pantomime?

I made my way to Frobisher Bay, the only town of any size on Baffin Island, after which the whole great unknown stretches forth with only scattered settlements along the west coast. Somewhere there I was to step from land onto the land of the frozen sea by way of dog sledge and thus I made my way to the taverns, of which there were three.

I knew not the Inuit language, and to forestall this impediment I brought with me a children's book from Halifax, which depicted Husky dogs and sledges. This I showed the barkeepers and other men who frequent such places and, while they admired the drawings and found my non-verbal efforts to communicate amusing, they did not seem to understand what I wanted.

Thereupon, I brought forth the little silk moneybag from

my bodice and placed it on the counter. This caused a good deal of curiosity amongst the citizens. The barkeepers emptied the bag and placed the bills for all to see, a lordly sum that I had taken from my father's house before leaving, but this too drew forth no offer of assistance. I repeated this demonstration in the second and third taverns, with the same result.

Discouraged, I sat to warm myself before the fire of the third tavern and requested what I thought, by hand gestures, was a pot of tea. This came to me in a warm, heavy flagon containing a dark concoction of herbs and leaves with which I was not familiar—rich and heady with a deep musky taste provided by the addition of fermented reindeer milk—Labrador tea, 'twas called. 'Twas so potent I felt a buzz in my ears and a great, hot burn in my chest.

My life had taught me well to eat and drink what was offered or on hand, but here in the land of the frozen sea I had difficulty reconciling myself to the taste of seal and bear, despite my hunger; nor did I find a reindeer milk potion easy to swallow. I hope my aversion did not show in my expression, for I was most keen not to insult my hosts.

Before long, my discouragement was replaced by a flush that lightened my spirits considerably. A man approached as I sat in this warm bubble of herbs and alcohol. "You have money?" he asked in French.

"Oh," I said, "*oui*," delighted to hear my native tongue.

"Dogs?" he continued. He sat next to me and rubbed his hands vigorously before the fire. So dry and battered were they that this motion made a quite unpleasant sound, wood scraping wood. I admired this gesture anyway, for simple, elemental things are often the only true things in a world of war and chaos. I witnessed this on the battlefield many a time, for amidst the crack of pistols and boom of cannons and drums hide the secret elemental aspects of war—a dying soldier feeling the dewy grass beneath his cheek that he might touch one last grasp of God's good earth; or the baby of a camp follower tied to her back, its head warm against the skin and fragrance of her neck; or a skinny cow licking the bark of a tree to taste its sweet sap.

I showed this fellow my picture book, which elicited a rumbling laugh. He bid the barkeeper bring him whiskey and introduced himself as Mr. Harry Bourgouin, a surname I knew from Acadia. I likewise told him my name and inquired as to his homeland. St. John's Island, he told me, and tears flooded my eyes, so greatly did I feel an unexpected kinship to find him in these parts. He took off his hat and there I saw his Acadian black hair and gray eyes, and in his grizzled countenance was a shadow of the handsomeness of his youth, which all Acadian men possess. "How came you here?" I asked.

"Well," he said, and settled further into his chair with the pleasure of a man who loves to tell a story. "I killed a man with these bare hands, Mademoiselle; let me state that outright, for hearing it you may not wish to listen to me more."

A most peculiar feeling came over me then, for well do I know another who kills men with his bare hands. 'Twas such a chilling parallel that I near ran out of the place, but this man from my homeland appeared quite congenial and even gentlemanly. I do believe he saw my sudden panic, for he bid me rise and placed a fur pillow upon the hearth so as to cushion my seat and bid me sit again, so I could not help but nod for him to continue.

"I was known in my hometown as a man strong and courageous enough to fight a bear with my hands alone. I did this twice, both times leaping upon the beast from a tree, thus taking the creature by surprise. I used that instant of surprise to shove my hand down his throat and bite him on the jugular vein, which caused the beast to topple over with a great crash, as does a tree, whereupon I beat him to death with a rock. Both times I had a friend with me, one who often accompanied me on hunting and fishing forays. So quickly did this ambush occur that my fellow moved not until 'twas over. Thus he witnessed the whole thing and spread a story of strength and audacity possessed only by the likes of Atlas. I admit to many a subsequent tavern brawl, but no man thereafter has challenged me in a serious way. Thus I stepped into the world fearless.

"Mademoiselle Frankenstein, a man's downfall may come from another kind of fear." Here he refreshed his drink. "By the time I reached manhood, Acadia was too small for me, so I struck out and joined the Continental Army for several years. There I was fearless, too. Upon completing my service, I traveled to Charleston, South Carolina, and took up work as a dockman at the harbor. There I lived for many a year.

"'Tis a rough job, dockman, for fellows knock about with unsavory types—thieves, slavers, rum runners, and such. Many a woman drifted through my life. I saw everything that came in and went out of that harbor. One particular man sent me into foul moods, a slave auctioneer named Mr. Browning. I was a hard man by then, but still my Acadian blood ran sour at the rough manner in which he presented the strong points of each slave who came before him, that he might get a maximum sales price. He tore off their clothes, crowed over the number of lashes a muscular man had endured, or the good posture of a girl barely ten years of age.

"These displays—common enough in that nasty business— were exacerbated by this fellow, for he put his hands on them and agitated them to further debase them. Sometimes he would poke at a man's sexual parts with a prod, causing those tender parts to flop around in a mortifying fashion. He squeezed women about the waists, breasts, and nether regions, ostensibly to tout their good looks and breeding potential, such that buyers might look forward to the propagation of more slaves.

"His gestures were prurient, sneering, leering, and he was plainly aroused himself. Pardon my direct talk, but I wish to impress upon you the true nature of these goings-on. This man was well regarded amongst the prosperous men of the town who possessed big money bags and stately houses and much land to be planted and harvested. Whenever a slave ship neared, Mr. Browning posted advertising leaflets notable for their exaggerations and so-called humorous tone. These too irked me; indeed, the whole endeavor turned me poisonous. Summers burned unbearably hot and the docks stank of tar and hemp and open carts of night soil slopping and oozing everywhere as they headed to the hills to bury the fetid loads spilling from their wagons. Men grew surly and prone to fight at the slightest provocation."

At this, he rose, stretched, and blew hot foul wind from his top and bottom orifices. He waved his hand for food and forthwith the tavern keeper brought a pot of seal meat. Mr. Bourgouin ate heartily and I downed what I could as I pondered his bear-killing tale. Despite the extreme nature of his description, I believed him. Eventually, he wiped his mouth on his beard and continued.

"As I was saying, I watched these revolting theatrics play out for many a month and year. The numbers of incoming slave ships never slaked. One day, I saw a girl on the auction block suffering Mr. Browning's manhandling. She was, I would say, pretty, though not beautiful. I believe fate stepped in then, for once I beheld her, I swear to you that I heard birds sing and my innards floated out to sea on a happy wave. I sought to purchase her, though my stomach even now turns at the very word. Now, Mr. Browning had a particular loathing for me, for he had observed me many a time glowering at his activities. Seeing me step forward with haste, he called out for other bidders and put up his hand to stop me, into which I put a goodly handful of gold pieces and drew that girl out of his clutches.

"Thus began a magical time in my life or, I would amend, I thought it magical at the time. Once before, many years ago, I married a beautiful devil girl who turned me inside out and upside down, yet still I loved her long after she turned her back on me and vanished into some other life. So, I was filled with joy those many years later to discover that gentle slave girl and be able to treat her in a kind manner. Our time together was full of delights and I felt a deep surety that 'twould last my whole life through.

"I loved that girl, plain and simple. Her name was Emilina and we lived together as man and wife. Here is where fear crept in for the first time in my life. Happy though I was, I lived in fear every one of those days, for 'twas wartime and any untoward thing could happen any day. Most of all, though, I lived in fear because she was a mysterious girl who scared me witless. I never knew what she was thinking and this alone is sufficient to throw a man off his normal course.

"She was neither my slave nor servant, though she did all those same domestic chores, which in a later chastened mood I understood were, admittedly, a scarce difference from the work she had done before. In my sunny state, I believed that if a man loves a girl and lies with her every night in his own bed, she cannot then be his slave. For nearly a year, despite my fears, we lived in a blissful state of agreeability. Never had my little house been kept in a clean, orderly, shining manner. Emilina even scrubbed off some of the encrusted filth and stench from my dock clothes and boots. All I wished was to sit by the fire and hold her hand. In the confines of those walls, I became soft, domesticated.

"As happens in the normal course of life, she became with child, which was all the more blessed for me, for I resolved that that babe would not be born into slavery. I would officially free them both with a written document filed at the courthouse and thus they would be as all should be—masters of their own lives.

"As it turned out, however, Emilina felt none of the sweet regard that I felt. In her forays to the marketplace, she learned that her husband—yes, she was long married—and two children were field slaves at the large plantation owned by none other than Mr. Browning, who spared not the whip, not a single day, for he beat her children until they could scarcely stand. One day, her belly swollen with my baby, she disappeared. I later discovered that they fled together and thus a bounty was on their heads and much danger faced them. So, I lost my love, my child, and every last gold piece I had.

"Still, I worked on the docks and saw Mr. Browning every day, up to his usual no good. There beside him many a woman and girl stood, cringing with shame, and I could only withstand this for seven days after the departure of my Emilina. At twilight on the seventh day, as we moved barrels and crates into their rightful places, he wound up his day by peering at his account book with much glee. I charged him then as I had those bears and likewise rammed my fist down his screaming throat and bit his jugular. Men are easier to kill than bears, so very quickly he lay sprawled upon the dock in a puddle of blood with his eyes rolled at the sky.

"I ran then and by any handy conveyance traveled north as if pursued by a wolf pack. In truth, 'tis doubtful that anyone looked for me once I reached New York and beyond, especially as I now had this beard and let my hair grow long like a woodsman. And that, Mademoiselle Frankenstein, is how I came to live in Frobisher Bay on Baffin Island as a purveyor of dogs and sledges."

CHAPTER XXI

So cozy and diverting was the hearth in that tavern that I was of a mind to sleep the night right there. The barkeeper showed me to another room, however, and there I slept on a thick mat on the floor with the cook and scullery maid close beside me. I knew them not and the smell of their bodies, hair, and breath were strange to me, yet how comforted and safe I felt! So much time had passed, so many dire events, since I last lay abed with women or girls, such as Lara and I did in Newburyport, such as with the girls at the Ursuline Academy when we slipped into the beds of our dear friends to whisper secrets and stories and provide sweet slumber apart from the world of men.

I shed tears that night for Lara and for my lost youth which, upon reflection–something that these long journeys have provided me in abundance–I believe was lost on that death ship the moment my own beautiful Beatrix Belfleur was thrown overboard to choke and die alone with my name upon her lips.

Was not my innocence stillborn? Are events such as occurred on the death ship not seared into even the youngest child's bones and blood? Was that not the first day of my ruination? Did that not show me that there is no true mother's milk in this world, that losing the touch, breath, and beauty of those you love the best—is that not the ground upon which all agony walks? Is that not the ground upon which we fight and break every law of man and God to cling to some part—however ephemeral—of those ripped from us, not in the natural course of age or illness or accident, but from the depravity of man? Was that not where the first inkling of my creature came into being—a yearning for life undying—on that cursed ship out to sea? Those questions occupied my mind for a little while, but soon enough I was lulled to sleep by the soft landscapes of bosoms and hips and the gentle breath of women whose names I did not know.

As dawn neared, however—though one can scarcely call this eternal twilight dawn—a frightful dream crept in to occupy my sleeping mind, thusly: I walked along a Boston street in my father's neighborhood on a sunny day. All the trees rained down cherry blossoms, even non-cherry trees such as maple and chestnut. Pretty white fence posts demarcated each yard along the roadway. As I passed one particular front gate, the posts on each side grew immensely tall and turned into humans hovering in a funnel of fire and smoke and winds that blew the cherry blossoms into great tornadoes.

The being on the left was an enormous man, hideous, misshapen, dissolving and reforming with discordant eyes and limbs in wrong places and a half-face melting away like candle wax. An endless howl came forth from him, similar to the one my creature made when first he took breath. The right post transformed into a girl—likewise grotesque, contorted—with babies falling from her open belly in a river of blood flowing out to the horizon. In vain, she tried to catch those babies, but they slid away. She too screamed, but what emerged was a soft, haunting tone, like a faraway ship's bells. The two creatures became a tangle of writhing flesh until they decomposed into mud. Then 'twas again a sunny day raining cherry blossoms.

I scarce could breathe and awoke sweaty and shaking. My bedmates exchanged a few words in their language, gestured toward me, and rose to dress in numerous layers of clothes and caps. Soon I heard the sounds of stove and kettle and crepitating fire bringing the day to life, and returned to my place at the hearth. For some time, I sat before that fire sipping Labrador tea. 'Tis soothing to sit amongst people speaking a foreign tongue. I listened and at first sought out roots of words or cadences of sentences that might link with French or English.

Making no progress, I let the conversation flow around me like music and instead began to puzzle out the relationships between speakers, some family, some friends. I concentrated much effort upon this so that the night's terror dream might evaporate from its prominent position at the front of my mind and it pleased me to observe how friendly were these strangers, much hardened from the climate and much inclined to josh and touch each other in a friendly manner.

The men's palms were crossed with deep lines of healed scars from pulling their own monsters—such as polar bears and walruses—from the ice holes that mark the white landscape on this floating continent. The women bore scars as well, on their hands, forearms, and faces, as is true for all women who cook over an open fire—teardrops of burns where years of scalding fat and red-hot embers have marked their skin.

The sledge dog fellow rapped upon the glass of the tavern window and gestured for me to join him. My bedmates helped me don the complex arrangement of skins and furs until I could scarce move my limbs. Mr. Bourgouin grinned upon beholding me, for I had yet to learn the suppleness of my attire and stood as a scarecrow does. He led me to a large cart into which he had already loaded my chest of provisions. 'Twas drawn by one muscular white horse whose belly and back were wrapped in a white fur blanket. In this, the animal blended into the landscape in an eerie manner until he seemed like a ghost or dream horse.

Mr. Bourgouin—"call me Harry"—hiked me unceremoniously into the seat beside him and we rode along thusly for half a day. He too was not talkative in the early morning; this I discovered soon enough, so I occupied myself by gazing out across the landscape. All around, snow had hardened into small peaks, like meringue on a cake. With gulps and coughs, I tried to modulate my breathing to the environment. 'Tis difficult to describe the air at the end of the world, is it not, Captain? Except to say 'tis blue and can shiv your lungs on certain days and make you drunk with beauty on others.

At length, we came upon a compound of three round snow huts, Harry's home and business. 'Twas in disarray, with sledges parked higgledy-piggledy and debris strewn about—pots, bottles, bones, dog excrement, leather straps and buckles, and, I presumed, other accouterments of dog-sledge travel. Harry saw me examine this disarray and muttered something about the embarrassing habits of solitary men. Rough fellow, his expression was suddenly so sweet and boyish that I smiled and then laughter burst from me like some foreign thing in great clouds of warm air that immediately froze and vanished. I became quite hysterical, such that I fell over and could not get up because of my attire and the laughter turned to tears that froze upon my cheeks and I snuffled into the snow, feeling like the most pitiful wretch on earth.

"What ails ye, girl?" asked Harry. He pulled me up and half dragged me into his hut, piled dried dung and rendered blubber into a fire pit, and before long smoke chugged up and out through a pipe protruding through the roof and I was able to remove my outermost furs. Eventually, I got ahold of myself with many shaky sighs. Harry warmed some seal stew, which struck me as tasteless, salty, and odiferous. The little room warmed and I removed more furs until, in its unfamiliarity, I could move about with ease, though I would not remove my cap.

"What then are ye up to?" Harry asked. "Why does one such as you wish to meet sure death alone in the frigid north?" I had practiced a reply, for I was still disinclined to tell of my creature, though of everyone I met Harry might have accepted it easily, for surely he who rams his fist down the throats of man and beast and draws quick-rushing blood from their vulnerable necks, surely such a man is half monster himself.

Still, I could not bring myself to speak of it, so I told him about deaths in the family and about a despondent little boy in Philadelphia and my vow to travel to a land of wonders and mysteries and create a book for him. I explained the content of this project and even rummaged through my traveling chest to show him a sheaf of blank parchment papers rolled up with protective newspaper sheets; likewise, I opened a small wooden box to reveal several pens, pencils, and three bottles of ink, all of which I had procured in Halifax. He listened and tipped one of the inkpots to and fro in front of the lantern, creating little crescents of blue light upon the snow walls. "As long as people pay good and proper, I ask no questions," he said. Still, he looked at me a long time, waiting for me to elaborate, but I did not.

We wrapped ourselves in furs again and I followed him to the largest of the huts. As we approached, a thunderous barking ensued and I was jolted by a fear that packs of dogs would leap upon me as I entered. But there were no more than twenty dogs, which Harry quieted with a shrill whistle. They settled down and I saw that they were not running free, for partitions separated them into small groups according to some peace-keeping scheme. He wandered among them and each became a tail-wagging, hand-licking lover of Mr. Harry Bourgouin.

He sold me seven dogs—two Samoyed, two Kamchatka, and three Siberians—hustled them outside, and—with just the smallest hand gesture—bid them line up in a row, still as statues except for their lolling tongues.

"Name them if ye wish," he said. "Here we do not, for most will freeze to death or be eaten by the other dogs or even by you before your journey ends. Therefore, to us they are mere means of transport,"—here he smiled—"except for the occasional favorite that propels our affection. But ye, being a girl, might feel different about naming living things." He put the dogs through paces, turns, and positions in order to demonstrate hand motions and orders I must learn. "Tomorrow ye will meet them one by one," he said, "but for now let us rest inside, for a storm is coming from the east." He sniffed the air. "Yah," he said. The dogs returned to their shelter and so did we.

'Tis disorienting when, day or night, the sky is always the same color which, the further north I traveled, was increasing shades of blue. All was the same soft blue-gray in Frobisher Bay—sky, air, ground, snow, dogs, people. 'Tis a strange, eerie world, oddly soothing in its soft monochromia, despite the arctic cold. By contrast, the interior of Harry's snow hut was like stained glass, as firelight and lamplight ricocheted off each glass or metallic object and reflected color on the snow walls.

Since the day of my birth, I have felt like a vagabond. Though facts may argue, 'tis the truth to me. I do make the distinction, as I'm sure must sailors at sea, between solitude and loneliness. Solitude can be every man's friend, for by that inner quietude we may find ourselves as none other knows us. But loneliness… sometimes the exhaustion of loneliness is unbearable. Every last tear inside me is insufficient to express the depth and breadth of the loneliness I have felt and struggle with to this very moment, despite your kind attentions and care, for loneliness is not always relative to being alone or in the company of others.

You have my gratitude, Captain, but I cannot seem to let your warmth into my soul, for I myself have destroyed that delicate entity by my own actions. My creature has asked me many a time if he has a soul, but never has he asked if I have one. Should he ask me now, I know not what reply to give.

At such times, when I am overcome with loneliness and emptiness, I lose the fear of my creature. I care not what he does or feels. I cannot conjure or remember or hope for anything good, for life seems built for extraordinary suffering. No one knows me except one faraway little boy and one so monstrous he has no name. In this mood, every breath is a crushing labor; every thought weighs a thousand pounds.

I felt myself sink into one of those spells in Harry's hut. He had gone out, perhaps to feed the dogs, whose muffled barks I heard from time to time. The fire needed tending, yet I tended it not. And so the room cooled, darkened, and took on an indistinct tone, as through a veil. At length, Harry came back, glared at me, and cursed over the fire gone down. Once it roared again, he shrugged off his furs and lit an oil lamp, which he brought close to me. He handed me a paper and a pen–his own–and said, "Name your dogs."

My eyes filled with grateful tears, which he ignored, and I set about this pleasant task and never again did I feel so low during my days at Harry's compound.

For some days, a fierce wind blew endless ice needles across the landscape, yet still we trudged every day to the dog hut, though we could scarce see two feet forward. Upon entering, Harry performed a ritual, which was to coax each dog near, crouch down to ruffle their coats, greet them, and exchange the occasional kiss or two. Our second day there, Harry corralled my seven dogs into one partitioned area and bid me sit upon an upended bucket just alongside.

One by one, the dogs sat politely before me and let me look at and pet them. I had little experience with dogs; in Acadia, they worked as farm dogs, and in the cities of New Orleans and Boston they were skulking, hollow strays to be avoided for fear of bites, fevers, or infectious sores. How beautiful and strong Harry's dogs were, how richly colored and intelligent, their eyes soulful and patient.

Each sniffed my hands and gave my fingers a little lick. I wrote down identifying descriptions and gave each a name, and so my faithful new friends became Echo, a beautiful, clever dog with blue, liquid eyes; Unmak, a lop-eared black and tan plodder who never looked back; Gus, a long-legged, speedy youngster; Empress, a roan-colored, slim dog with tremendous endurance; Neptune, a great black wolf with sharp-pointed teeth and perpendicular ears; Indigo, a quick, eager dog, so affectionate in his overtures of joy that he often sent me sprawling; and Eski, a gentle-natured dog more like a retriever, who always ran next to the sledge with her nose to the ground.

One by one, we hitched each to a small sledge and circled the compound that I might get the feel of a dog sledge and familiarize myself with straps, hitches, and the proper calls and commands. My natural voice was too weak to fight with the wind, so Harry taught me to shout from my belly, as if to a faraway crowd, but even that, he determined, was too insignificant to penetrate the weather I would encounter, so he gave me a carved whalebone whistle on a cord to hang around my neck.

Each progressive day, I came to know the particularities of my dogs a little more. We progressed to larger sledges pulled by two, then four dogs. So eager were they, so unmindful of the stinging ice, that they would have traveled many miles with no care in the world had Harry not held them back. Black crevasses appeared around the compound as the snow and ice began to melt. Bits of black, lifeless earth were visible deep inside each crevasse, but 'twas scarce an inspiring presentiment of spring.

Harry was as tough as cowhide, a crude, loud killer of bears and men, living in utter freezing disarray, yet he also heard birds sing for all the wrong people and kissed dogs with much affection. I discovered another of his remarkable attributes one day when a cruel wind bit to the bone and the snow was dirty gray and all was miserable and unpleasant. As we put the dogs through their paces, Harry opened his mouth and a sound issued forth that nearly felled me, for he sang a ballad in French such as one hears tell of in romantic days when a man stood beneath a girl's window to pour his heart out and beg for her eternal love else he would languish and die. He sang loud enough to cause the dogs to lose their pace and howl as if the moon had just then called to them and they could not resist.

His voice was a deep, clarion call such as I had never before heard; I felt it strike as a physical, not aural sensation, causing a gorgeous pain such as sometimes happens when church choirs send forth unearthly music to the heavens. His face contorted with emotion, and so contagious was his feeling that I shed tears that turned to icy diamonds and tinkled to the ground. His voice, booming and flying out over the land of ice and snow with no boundaries, marked the end of my affiliation with civilized life. All restraints of the comfort and pleasant mediocrities of social life—so valued in the world of cities—were gone. So far was I from nearly all humanity, from all that had shaped me—for good and ill—that for some little while I felt beyond good and evil, bare I would call it, free of artifice, free of all my woes, strangely innocent there in Harry's Garden of Eden.

So, I did not return to the tavern at night to slumber with cooks and maids; nay, I remained in Harry's hut and before even one night had passed, while Harry labored over some small leatherwork, I stood close to the stove and shed all my clothes, even my cap, until there I was—bald-headed, naked, sidling so close to the fire that I felt my skin reddening from the warmth. Harry—one must give him credit here, Captain, think you not?—calmly set aside his work, came toward me, ran a tender hand over my shorn head—a gesture that said a thousand things to me—and drew me to his bed and there we stayed through days of storms.

If I may expound upon this delicate subject a moment: girls and women of my class in general have a decorous approach to intimate matters with their husbands. Many, I knew, had husbands who had never seen them naked. Christian shame has a mighty, dampening effect on a woman's participation in the conjugal aspects of life. Pleasure for one; babies for the other. 'Tis the way of my world. My too-brief marriage to Moses was born and died in that world, for he had a tender ardor and adoration of my heart and soul, and 'twas all the sweetness, comfort, and joy I desired as I recovered from the battlefield. He was my beloved; every touch of his hand bound me to him, every kiss was gentle and loving. Beautiful, perfect, and sublime. My Moses, ever and forever my beloved. You may ask how my creature fits into this disquisition, but of that aspect I can say nothing, for 'twas unspeakable in its... unspeakable in its... its... ah, nay, I cannot even complete that sentence without falling into a fit of abashment and woe.

Some may call my many wanderings unusually, even unnaturally free, but such sojourns were plagued by the terrors of war and my creature. Now, at the end of the world, the end of my life, I yearned to kick aside shadows and fears to feel—for once—free. Harry opened his door and took my fury and tears with equanimity and a steadiness that kept me from dissolving or breaking or drowning in regret or shame or inhibition.

Men of the world who reach a certain age and have had many women in their beds are like doctors of sexual inter-course—eyes open, expert, confident, unflappable, with all the controlled time in the world. Death beckoned me from the icy doorway of Harry's hut and though I felt that fatal breath at my heels, I turned toward Harry and with fierce, rough desire 'twas as if my too-tight stays had at last been cut with a knife.

CHAPTER XXII

That spate of storms passed and all was muffled and cold, with a strange white darkness at night. We resumed dog training and when I glanced at Harry, his skin was blue from the color of the air. When I took off my glove, I could see by my hand that mine was, too. This appealed to me greatly, for as the time for me to depart for the unknown drew near, I wanted to be anyone but myself.

I spun long daydreams about how my creature had likely already died. Despite my occasional ministrations, were his wounds not suppurating? Was he not literally falling apart at the seams? How long could any living thing survive in that condition? Perhaps he had perished here in the land of ice, failing slowly, falling hard like a polar bear or walrus—alone, friendless, silent forevermore. Thus I began to dawdle in my preparations, upon which Harry did not remark.

One blue day or night, he said "Come, girl," and taking Unmak and Empress with us that they might get a bit of air, off we walked across the ice with no landmark or horizon in sight, nor any distinction between earth and sky. As Harry fiddled with his boots, I walked some distance ahead until he was obscured by fog. I stared into the nothingness to test how my onward travels would truly feel once all vestiges of human settlement were gone. 'Twas terrifying. Would I not soon be just an umbra, a trifle in this vast territory?

I hurried back to Harry and put my hand upon his chest that I might feel his warm solidity. I believe he saw the fear in my face. "Come let me show you something," he said, so onward we trudged across the slippery ground. Eventually, he stopped at a place that to my eye appeared the same as any other icy spot. "Look under your feet," he said. I did and saw ice. He stepped a few feet away from me. "Look under my feet." I did and likewise saw ice. "Deep under the ice you stand upon is land. Deep under the ice I stand upon is the unknown sea, upon which you will traverse."

Perhaps this was his way of trying to deter me from traveling onward alone. I opened my mouth to reply–I know not what–when we heard an appalling outcry nearby–louder than a person or a wolf, more blood-curdling than a bear. Harry drew a knife from his belt and crouched such that his body was compact, ready to attack, though a foe was yet invisible. Perhaps 'twas an incorporeal ghost. All was hushed.

Harry–bare-fisted killer of bears and men–had no inclination to wait. "Show yourself, whoever ya be, for if ya be human, I shall not kill ya. If ya be beast, I will gut and skin ya and sup upon your liver this very night." His voice boomed across the ice.

A monstrous blue creature–my cursed creation–distinguished itself from the general blueness and caused my knees to buckle from his loathsome appearance which, though I knew it well, shocked me anew each time I laid eyes upon him. Many a new, deep wound had slashed his face and body, and instead of forming healing scars, the raw edges of flesh were black and frozen. "My maker," he said, and his cracking voice shook with rage.

Harry sprang as a lion would, knife flashing. This took my creature by surprise and I saw a spurt of blood run down his neck. With dreadful cries, a fight ensued on the ice over the frozen sea, so fierce that the fissures grew wider and the terrible sound of cracking ice intensified far below. Both were in a fury and ignored my exhortations to cease. The knife went flying. Bones broke. At the last, my creature trampled hard upon the ice until it gave and an abyss opened, whereupon he dragged Harry to it and kicked him into the pitiless sea.

Shrieking, I ran toward him until the ice felt unsteady, then lay down on my belly and slid the rest of the way, right up to the edge. Harry's heavy furs and boots now became his burial shroud, dragging him down. I tried to grab his collar and pull but made no headway. He held onto the rim of ice with one hand, as if to claw his way up. I called his name but he seemed unable to hear and I saw the life drain from his eyes. I begged him to come back and, leaning toward the black water as far as I dared—why, why did I not slide in after him and end my tormented life?—I kissed his cold, cold lips. That kiss near tore my heart out, for 'twas for Harry, yes, but too for all my beloveds who died unkissed by me.

My creature had crouched quietly nearby to watch Harry's final struggle, but that kiss aroused his temper and he burst forth with a stream of curses and threats and a gasping, ragged dissertation about kisses—dead kisses, lovers' kisses, kiss of life, kiss of death. Harry sank then into the unknowable arctic sea, leaving me disoriented as to the location of his compound in the blue gloom. I grasped the whistle from under my furs and managed only a weak trill, for my throat was choked with ice and tears. Nevertheless, those faithful dogs appeared, barking furiously at my creature, hurtling themselves at him.

Roaring, he swatted them away. They squatted to jump again, but I blew the whistle more clearly and they came to my side snarling, all teeth and foaming mouths. I turned my back on the chasm that swallowed Harry—the bravest man in the Northern Pole—and headed in what I thought was the direction of the compound. The dogs nudged me southwest and thus we proceeded, though I was numb and blind with grief and frozen through and through.

My creature could have leapt upon me and this I half expected, but he refrained, I think, to torment me yet longer. While he did not follow, his voice did. "Think not we are done with each other, maker," he cried. "You made me, devil, cursed wretch. Chase me then to the farthest end of the world and try to end my life, for if we meet there I will lie down upon the ice and let you take my last breath as you gave me my first." The dogs bumped against my legs and on I went. Yet my creature's voice followed me, now just my name... "Océane... Océane..." over and over until 'twas just a hollow wave of sound, an apparition whispering from hell.

For my onward travels, I kept some of Harry's belongings—his compass, extra fur hats and mitts, and a polar bear rug—and sorted through items that might be useful to others: his bedding, a bit of cookware, extra oil lamps, his leather-working materials, and more. There on his workbench lay the small, secret pieces he had toiled over during my time with him—seven leather tags hanging from collars, each with the name of one of my dogs chiseled onto it. How touching were those labors that took place unbeknownst to me while I wrote my promised animal descriptions for Freddy, and even there he helped me by providing scientific details that only a hunter would know.

"Harry," I said aloud in the empty compound, "you for

whom lovebirds sing, may you find a place in the spirit world where you can kill beasts with your bare hands and love all the wrong girls, for though they were wrong, you loved them all the more."

It took me many hours to load his things onto one of his large sledges. I divided the dogs into three groups—mine, whom I tied up to keep them apart from the goings-on, six others I wished to harness to the big sledge, and the rest. This I did with great difficulty, for most of them were not my dogs and knew me only by sight from my visits to the dog hut. I was terrified to approach all but my own, for they were in a foul mood from Harry's conspicuous absence. I threw bits of frozen seal meat to the six and by this method enticed one at a time into harness while the others howled in protest.

Once this was complete, I let the remaining dogs loose—not my seven—and blew my whistle "mush" as Harry had taught me. The six hitched dogs leapt forward without a driver and off they went with the rest running free behind. 'Twas my hope they went to Frobisher Bay, a route they knew well, but I shall never know. I fed my own dogs and tied their leather nametags around their necks. They wagged their tails with great excitement, for they felt a journey imminent.

I spent one last night—if night 'twas—in Harry's hut and the dogs stayed with me, too, harnessed. I did not wish to struggle with that task on the day of departure, for 'twas a laborious and cumbersome endeavor. Too, I found the prospect of lying alone on that ice floor unbearable. Better to have the night noises of dogs, whatever they may be, for I knew not even that. They circled around, chose favorite spots, and relaxed greatly, for Harry's scent was evident. Thus I had seven sentinels about me. 'Tis strange to sleep in a person's home without them. Their rooms are steeped in their habits and ways. Harry's disorder was distasteful to me, but now the remainder lay strewn about, sad little remnants of a big life, and 'twas heartbreaking.

Bedding gone, I curled up next to the stove with my coat bunched up under me. I could not but fidget, so fearful was I of falling into the black pit of a nightmare. Periodically, I rose to gaze out at the landscape–a sapphire world near untrod by man. Cold and forbidding though 'twas, I was eager now to go, for I desired only to forthwith end my creature's life in the frozen sea. Fate could do with me as it wished. By ice and fire, our agony would somehow end.

I studied Harry's portolano charts, the only onward guides I had. How beautiful, how fanciful they were! There, for the first time, I saw the origin of my name–Oceanus, a figure of antiquity, the personification of the sea in the form of an enormous river encircling the world, font of all the earth's fresh water, such as rivers, wells, springs, and rain-clouds.

The northern territory into which I ventured alone was not an empty continent, for by the meticulous colored drawings on those maps its seas contained splendid ships with their sails overfull, shape-shifting finfolk, fire-breathing leviathans, krakens, octopus-dragons, and supernatural water horses. On the icy land lived giant wolves, hairless dogs that caused people to fall down in fits, avenging bears, and flying sea serpents. Perhaps a drawing of my nameless creature should likewise decorate that map, for he is no less a fantastical monster than any of them. I tucked the charts into my leather satchel and dozed fitfully in that cold air redolent of dogs.

Morning arrived, as evidenced by a lighter shade of blue-white brightening the ice. The dogs and I set out in a north-westerly direction, toward the endmost end of the earth. For some time, we traveled smoothly, for I was well provisioned and warmly clad, and though snowstorms blew across the ice, the worst of winter was over and they were not severe enough to break apart the sledge nor discourage me from my mission.

Each night, the dogs sprinted off to hunt for baby seals or walruses, returning when I blew the whistle with blood on their muzzles and full bellies. They slept in a warm huddle next to the sledge where I lay inside a sheltering bearskin enclosure Harry had built upon its rear section.

Some nights when the wind was low, I opened that canopy and watched the mysterious sweep of heaven in its nocturnal activity, as did my ancestors and all man's ancestors back to the time before time. Mythology, astrology, celestial navigation... how slight are these in penetrating that black emptiness and its riot of lights skittering about, flaring, flying, being born, dying. Are they the same stars I wished upon in my childhood purity in Acadia? Does one particular star have my name on it, as some folk say—born when I was born, fated to die when I die?

Bereft of human companionship, I sought out certain stars, such as Polaris, the North Star, leading me to my destination, and the Great Bear, created, as Lara once told me, when Hercules threw a troublesome bear into the sky by grabbing its tail, swinging it above his head, and flinging it up to join the stars.

Captain, you of all people know this far better than I, but I have found it most surprising to discover that this ice continent is not a silent place broken only by the howls of wind and wolf. No, this infinite expanse is a living thing. The ice itself groans and cracks with booms like distant cannons in its restless construction of floes, icebergs, ice drifts, and deathly crevasses. 'Tis most alarming and I could scarce rest by night or day for the constant turmoil beneath the frozen sea. How odd is this unknown territory!—deafening gales, snow tornadoes, and the strange white darkness and blue light to which I will never become adjusted. At times, I knew not whether I pursued my creature or if he pursued me, thus in this endless open space I sometimes felt a paradoxical suffocating confusion.

Still, 'tis beautiful. Whatever evil men are up to, however severe the land and season, nature's beauty cannot be denied. Even at this dire moment of my life, my mission undone, my breath ebbing away, I can say I have been alone upon a frozen sea and watched my breath turn into sparkling ice splinters that fell to the ground. If my life has taught me anything, 'tis that beauty abounds everywhere. I saw this on the battlefield, in the very creation of my creature, and even when storms here blow awful hurricanes of snow, for they are awful in the other sense of the word—awe-full.

I envy the man who in his one lifetime will see the deserts, forests, mountains, plains, glaciers, and valleys of this earth. Will I, as I take my last breath, see something beautiful from your little bunk? Perhaps the gods of the night sky will give me one last glimpse of their glorious dark eternity.

My mind wandered much during my travels in this vast space of nothingness. Holding fast to my compass, I steered my faithful dogs hour after hour. When the wind was low, I heard them panting and the clink of metal on their harnesses and the scraping of the runners—'twas hypnotic.

Where there are no landmarks, the mind's eye creates its own. One day, I swear I saw a summer river and gentle hill, and the farmhouse where I had lived with Moses and Nicolas. Truly I saw the barn, Penny with her little bell tinkling, Nicolas chopping firewood, and Moses—my beloved—sitting on the porch with his nose in a book.

Did I mention that he kept an old silver coin in his pocket? 'Twas an odd item for a Quaker, for they place little value on acquisitiveness. One twilight after supper, we lingered at the kitchen table. Nicolas, belly full, already lay upon his mat snoring softly, for he loved sleep as much as a baby.

'Twas spring, the air so clean and sweet. Moses emptied his pockets, as was his habit, so that his essential items might be there for morning.

I loved this... the little parade of men's belongings—a pocket-knife in its leather case, striking steel and flints, a handkerchief, a folded notebook in the back pocket, a pencil, and that coin. 'Twas called an Elephant Token, made of darkly tarnished silver. A tusked elephant filled one side and the other side contained the motto: *God Preserve Carolina 1694*. I had seen it go in and out of Moses's pocket many a time. Though he handled it absently, 'twas my sense that 'twas more of an anxious burden than a fond remembrance or lucky piece. A spring rain began to fall that particular evening and with the doors and windows open we watched it fall silently into the new grass. This and the softening light created a gentle, contemplative mood. I asked Moses about the coin and he confided this story:

"We are so alike, dear girl—deserters, runaways—shaped by war. 'Tis my personal failing that I could not cling fast to one of my people's basic tenets, which Quakers all memorize as children: *We utterly deny all outward wars and strife and fighting with outward weapons.* As the war grew, so did the dire need for soldiers. Both Loyalists and Patriots assaulted my people, for both thought us agents of the other. I burned with fury at attacks against our great William Penn and the city he built, and I could not tamp down a growing flood of patriotism I felt for our new world, for freedom from oppression.

"Thus I left with only this poor knife, knowing I could never return to my people again. I joined the Army under General Nathanael Greene, who was likewise a Quaker and, like me, disowned for taking up arms. 'Twas not the time of snappy uniforms and well-trained and supplied soldiers; 'twas early on and as thee know thyself, my brave love, 'twas freezing and soldiers had neither coats, nor mufflers, nor boots; indeed, after some months through heavy terrain, some of us had no shoes at all, for our leather had worn clean through and we walked with rags bound to our feet.

"Had thee come upon us on a country road, thou would have thought us a band of ruffians, so ragtag were we. Yet we burned with the mad fire that surges through the hearts of soldiers. 'Tis shocking, Océane, that spilled blood and fear and brotherhood of war create their own heat and thus in packs like wolves we fight to kill or die. Nothing in my gentle Quaker life prepared me for this. I am not complaining, darling girl, only expressing my confusion that the aspirations and practices of my religion, shaped to produce kind hearts and gentle souls, is a grievous lie, or more kindly I might say a daydream. Would it not be better if from boyhood we were trained like the great Stoics or Vikings?—to feel no fear, to have no wants except to kill, for war seems to be the most damned and eternal thing on earth.

"Dearest, I learned to use a pistol, for all we had were pistols, knives, clubs, axes, and hammers; 'tis how ill-equipped we were without the defense of rifles, bayonets, and cannons. At that time and place, we were some long distance from the benefit of Flying Hospitals or saviors such as thy father and thee. Had I only known thee then, only had one moment to fall into thy arms and feel thy kiss upon my cheek!

"Still, we did the abhorrent things that soldiers do. Thou hast witnessed enough such that I need not elaborate. Many a day I had blood on my clothes, in my hair and beard. Many a day, when night at last forced fighting back on its heels, I fell on my knees and washed my face with snow and wondered if 'twould ever end.

"What caused me to break? Well, one hundred men can die at the hands of a regiment and 'tis just a blur of blood and sweat and screams. But take one life when those around you slumber and all is still; 'tis another tale to tell. One night, as our fires burned low, I took my turn as lookout. Under the conditions in which we found ourselves then, 'twas largely a matter of trying not to freeze to death. Being on watch when nights are warm and food is plenteous, even then 'tis the dark night of the soul, when all a man has been and done and thought and felt rise in one's throat like ragged shards of glass.

"During the early weeks of soldiering, men comfort themselves with fond thoughts of home, reading letters until the pages tatter and blow away, telling stories of home, of amusing friends, and of girls left behind. But these then slip into private dreams, then brooding, then vanish altogether, overtaken by the realities of war, cruelty, and deprivation. Then, on night lookout, there is no comfort from secret thoughts. Bitterness, fury, pain, anguish, blood, death, and loneliness—these are a soldier's daily lot and hurt all the more at night lookout.

"So, as I say, one of those nights as I paced in circles, slapping my arms and jumping up and down to keep warm, cursing fate, staring out over a blank landscape of snow as my regiment slept in the forest behind me, I heard the crunch of snow. Soldiers do not typically venture away from camp at night, but I raised my knife, for perhaps 'twas an edible night wanderer such as a farm animal or fox. Or perhaps 'twas an Indian, in which case my life would end before I heard or saw anything more.

"A figure then appeared startlingly close. In the moonlight, I saw a small man with a damaged drum slung over his shoulder and the gleam of many buttons marking a British war coat and hat.

"'Sir,' he whispered, 'sir...' 'Twas a drummer boy, holding a drumstick out at me as if 'twere a bayonet. I leapt forward and drove my knife into his chest. He fell at my feet and there

I saw his face—he was perhaps nine years of age, though he wore the uniform of a large man. Thus he fell, that boy. I fell, too, from shock, and knelt beside him.

"Still he breathed, and looked at me with trust and innocence. 'I am Ephraim,' he said, and his spirit left his body. Hot tears sprang to my eyes, yet by rote I conducted the usual search for shoes, flints, and other items that might be of use to us. All I found were his other drumstick and, in his waistcoat pocket, this coin thou see me carry every day. I left that night, at dawn, after another soldier relieved me at watch. At every moment, I expected someone to holler 'Ho, soldier, where go you?' but no one did. I was invisible, with the name Ephraim on my lips."

CHAPTER XXIII

The Arctic world then began to smell of salt, for as the ice continued to split apart, the melting sea below tinged the air and every breath was sharp with it. I learned many things that you no doubt discovered long before me. A place can be empty yet noisy, blue yet colorless, endless yet visible only an inch at a time. 'Tis easy here to forget your mission and even, at times, the whole miserable story of your life.

I slept poorly, plagued by terrors of my creature creeping up beside my sledge, beset by fears of freezing to death alone in this purgatory of my own making. By day, though, the scent of salt cleared my mind and there rose up all manner of reflections about things I scarcely knew or had long forgotten, messages from long ago, from ancient ones, from ancestors I knew not. When I was a child, my father told me of those who came before us—the people, places, and events that shaped our very cells and deepest hollows of our hearts. Once upon a time in faraway lands, he told me, our family was represented by the "Ancient Arms of Frankenstein," a coat of arms marked by a golden heart shield, oblique red battle axe, a crowned knight's helmet, and a great castle in the Rhineland region. He often told me of those who proudly wore that shield. One year, he said, a great war spread fire and death across the land, causing the youngest of the family—twins no more than five years of age named Adelina and Gunne—to flee the castle for the safety of the mountains.

They wandered far and wide and found themselves at the edge of the mysterious Pădurea Hoia forest in Cluj-Napoca, Transylvania. Villagers offered them shelter and begged them go no further, as a shepherd and his two hundred sheep entered that forest only three moons before and never returned. But they ignored this good advice and entered anyway.

At once, they were overswept with intense anxiety. Tormented, haunted green eyes watched them from unnaturally crooked trees cloaked in black fog. Disembodied female voices giggled. The wind spoke and the children were beset with all manner of rashes, nausea, vomiting, migraines, and lightheadedness. Burns and scratches plagued their skin. Strange orbs of light spun through the forest and vanished.

They reached a circular clearing where no vegetation grew and stepping there suddenly knew things they had never known about their ancestors from the time before time, when the earth was warm from the ever-present breath of gods who themselves remembered when stars and planets swirled in infinite darkness and restless, unnamed forces collided and joined, split and formed, were born and died.

A dozen years passed. One day, those children emerged

from the forest and never had they aged a year nor a day. They met a man upon the path and spoke as children waking from a dream. They told him all they knew and had seen, then promptly forgot it all. They were returned to the castle, to the arms of their kin, and, though hundreds of years more passed, never did they age a single day nor lose the sweet innocence of childhood.

Recalling that barely remembered tale caused me to understand myself as a direct descendant of those children, linked by blood and fate. They too were blown about by the winds of war. They too wandered into a dark, foreboding place. They too were then beset by terrifying things not of this world. But a blessed God who no longer believes in me rescued them with sweet silence and eternal youth. Would that this outcome was my own! After perhaps two weeks of solitary travel, I came upon a village. Nay, I cannot call it a village, for it contained only two large families. They lived upon the ice in spacious square icehouses built on runners, surrounded by a herd of reindeer, their subsistence and livelihood. They greeted my dogs with eager smiles and affection, and escorted me indoors.

I gave them one of Harry's knives, which had a beautiful floral carving on its handle. They admired it much and shared their meal of shaved blubber, which I ate with difficulty. Two days I remained there that my dogs might rest and I restore myself from my frigid travels. I gave them other items from my provision box as well, each something they had never seen before—a length of frilly pink ribbon, an illustrated book about whales, and city-made fur mittens—and this they repaid with the kindest hospitality. I observed their daily lives with great interest, for Harry had told me of these descendants of the mighty Thule, who he admired for their fierce strength and fearlessness.

Four children lived at that compound, named Yuka, Jissika, Kumaglak, and Akaka. So round and cheeky were they that the most cold-hearted of men would have stopped to pat their heads and smile. They enlisted me in their chores, which I was glad to do, such as milking reindeer, scraping hides, and carrying pails of chipped ice indoors to melt for household water.

My second day there coincided with a greatly anticipated event—the bathing of the children. The adults joined in the task of gathering and heating ice until hot water sufficiently filled a wooden tub. The children crowded in together, along with a couple of pups, and their mothers scrubbed them with hard black soap amidst great splashing and giggling. Covered with suds, the children scampered outside where adults rubbed them all over with handfuls of soft snow until the soap was gone. Once dressed in their furs again, they fell into a rosy heap by the fire and slept. The elders then relaxed against each other with no inhibition, spoke quietly amongst themselves, and shared with me a stinking mug of fermented reindeer milk.

Even in this friendly warmth, I could not sleep, for I was tormented by the ghost of my own sweet girl, who would never lie rosy-cheeked before a fire. One night, I lit a candle—my own so as not to deplete their supply—and composed a letter to my creature. Why? All travelers write to their families and friends, do they not? Yet what living being did I know, save Freddy? So, with pen and paper I addressed the only being who knew anything of my life... such was my aching loneliness.

To MY CREATURE

North of Frobisher Bay
Baffin Island, deepest winter 1781

I will not here recount the horrors you inflicted upon me and mine. Instead, I wish to tell you of the goodness I sought in your construction. You know now of the mechanics of your origin in that faraway belfry, but that is not your full true origin. You were truly fashioned out of sorrow, lamentation, tears, longing, and love, and of this I tell you now. Before I dreamed of your existence, I had a beloved husband and unborn child. I did not reveal this to you until now for fear you would react violently and rampage further. They died... oh, 'tis excruciating to even write those words. I so longed for them to live on that I placed their hearts inside a constructed man that they might live anew and be my beloveds in a different form. 'Twas my crime, my black arts, my unnatural grief, and my blasphemous actions that brought this calamity upon us all.

Creature, to impress upon you the purity of your creation, I want to tell you of just a single afternoon. 'Twas midsummer and never was there a sweeter day. My husband and I lay on our backs in a meadow some distance from our farmhouse. My belly was rounding then with our baby. The sun warmed us so kindly that we removed all our clothes, held hands, and rested in the long, soft grass with all manner of life around us—flowers at their most flamboyant bloom; insects, birds, mice, rabbits, and deer frolicking about; extravagant, lazy clouds; willow trees whispering along a nearby creek.

My love, how beautiful he was and strong, his arms and face golden brown. That was my Garden of Eden, my Paradise. I knew it then and know it now. As we departed the meadow, Moses went a step or two ahead and extended one hand behind him without looking back, for me to clasp his hand. That casual, unconscious gesture you may never know yourself, but I will tell you, 'tis an act of pure ease and togetherness that only truly pledged people experience. I urge this memory upon you that you might comprehend that the love and beauty I describe here were, truly, the seeds and cells from which you sprang.

Your Maker

Postscript
Monster, murderer, 'tis not forgiveness that makes me write thus gently. Never to my last breath will I forgive you. Yet do I not always call you "my creature"? Does that not make you mine? Whatever you are to me, you are of me and of my beloveds. He who is of a woman's breath cannot ever be separate from her.

O

I folded the letter into a small square. Never would I give it to him. Would it not just cause him to fly into another murderous fit? My candle burned low. Before it extinguished, I dripped a bit of wax on the letter, pressed into it the top of a wooden thimble in a sewing basket near me, leaving a little round mark, and tucked it in the leather bag around my waist. On the low table, I saw three other thimbles carved from bone, whalebone perhaps, or the tusk of a narwhal. How carefully they were fashioned, with polished surfaces, cool to the touch. I slept then, comforted by their very ordinariness.

The following morning, the air was calm and no snow fell. A great bustling ensued, for my nomadic hosts were on the move to a better hunting ground. They harnessed a score or more reindeer, strapped their reins to one side of the larger hut, and, with much yelling and arm-waving, urged the animals forward, which was quite a task as they were not domesticated. Still, at last they pulled in unison and off across the ice went the merry caravan.

The second hut was secured behind the first and behind that my sledge, for through examination of the stars and my map they determined that they could transport me one day west before I must continue northward alone. The children rode in my sledge with me, sprawled like royal children, for their sledges were smaller and lacked the fur roof mine possessed.

My harnessed dogs ran behind my sledge, for if let loose they would have felled a reindeer for their dinner. Though they were cranky with this arrangement, my hosts had fed them well and early that morning gave them big rounds of pemmican to chew on. Behind them trotted the remaining reindeer, kept in line by two herding dogs, prized possessions of that family. Behind them, their sledge dogs ran in a pack, and at the very rear an old man rode in a small sledge pulled by one dog, that he might alert the others ahead should something go amiss.

'Twas a circus! I caught the contagion of happiness and goodwill, perhaps too much, perhaps hysterically, for I believed these were the last humans, the last sweet-faced children I would ever behold. I likely petted them overmuch. Maybe generations from now this family would tell tales of a strange, sickly, bald being who prevailed upon their hospitality that she might steal their children, so ardently did she clasp, embrace, and kiss them.

That singular interlude ended, as all good things must. The arctic night fell hard and frigid when they cut loose my sledge and dogs. The children ran back to their mothers clutching gifts, for I gave them the picture book of dogs and a braided candle, that they might study those pictures in the long nights of the Northern Pole and dream of mighty hunters and their faithful companions.

CHAPTER XXIV

Spring is one of Mother Nature's great fakers. A flower can bloom or a bird sing, or here at the end of the world fissures of water can appear, then a last blast of winter slams back with bouts of dense, wet, heavy snow that obliterates the landscape and causes sledge runners to clog. So, a series of blizzards then overswept the landscape and, unable to use Polaris as my guide, I relied upon my compass.

Often, we were forced to stop our onward trek due to exhaustion of the dogs, for 'tis most difficult to run in that kind of snow. We were at times snowbound for days, and I learned how to use my sledge as a barrier by situating it broadside to the wind and raising the roof so that the snow forthwith gathered in a towering drift along the backside and overtop, thereby creating a temporary cave on the leeward side where I could burn dried animal dung and pass the time until the wind changed, the snow stopped, and we were able to continue. Our provisions were low and bellies empty. We ate a good deal of snow to slake our thirst.

Once, while I languished in that little snow den, I thought about a story Harry told me of the ancient Vikings, their belief about the beginning of the world. He related this as we lay abed watching the fire throw lights upon the walls, our bellies full of a delicacy thereabouts—the vomited contents of a reindeer's stomach, composed of select mosses and grasses in a semi-digested, sharp, and aromatic stew. Fortunately, he did not explicate upon this dish until 'twas well eaten. Thus went the tale of the Viking cosmos:

"Before there was soil, or sky, or any green thing, a chaos of perfect silence and darkness lay between the homeland of elemental fire and the homeland of elemental ice. Blowing flames from the fire and frost from the ice crept toward each other until they met and the drops formed themselves into Ymir, the first of godlike but destructive giants. He was a hermaphrodite and could reproduce asexually; as he slept, more giants leapt from his legs and the sweat of his armpits.

"Thereafter appeared a cow feeding upon ice-licks, from which emerged half-god, half-giant men and women. Three of these brothers slew Ymir and set about constructing the world from his corpse. They fashioned the oceans from his blood, soil from his skin and muscles, vegetation from his hair, clouds from his brains, and the sky from his skull. From this, the first man and woman sprang from tree trunks and built a fence around their dwelling place to keep out the giants."

Is the human psyche, then, not eternally captivated by dreams of men born of pieces, men sprung from earth? My creature was likewise born of pieces and sprang from the earth. Will men ever learn that things that live in dreams, things that hide deep in mystery and imaginings, ought never be brought to life?

A day came when, scavenging my provision box for any bit

of dried meat or pemmican, I found therein an enormous black egg that had not been there before, in some sort of casing. A dragon's egg? A sea serpent? 'Twas the strangest I ever saw; I could scarce hold it in my arms, so heavy was it, bulbous in shape, like a supernatural beetle. Though frozen solid, the exterior was brittle and I was able to shatter it by hurling it against a block of ice. Inside was a frozen aquatic creature, somewhat like a giant tadpole with the broad flat head and barbed fin of a shark.

Also tucked into the provision box were a group of smaller eggs, round on one end, somewhat pointed on the other, cone-shaped, blue with black speckles—bird eggs, I would say... a very large bird. I gave one to each dog and kept one for myself. I smashed the shark—surely a whale shark for its size—into smaller pieces and shaved them then yet smaller, tossing them to the dogs, who fought each other as enemies for the slightest sliver or even the dust of a sliver. I then huddled in my snow cave with my stinking, choking, smoking oil lamp at my side and ate my own portion with difficulty, for I had to use the utmost power of my teeth to crack the pieces or suck on them like candy—a horrifying, lamentable meal.

Those eggs came from no one but my creature, that I knew. Often did I feel his shadow looming over me. Did he creep near my sledge while I slept and place those eggs, silent as an apparition? Was he then friend to me, he who was my foe?

Every night now, from twilight to the deepest dark of midnight, the sky split open and out rushed billowing, rippling bands of color—green and yellow below; purple, red, and pink above—shimmering curtains, steady glows, pulsating globs, ribbons of light streaking across the sky.

Whatever the outcome of my mission, however soon my own demise might be, had I never endured this long journey to the end of the world, never would I have witnessed this luminous beauty, this restless, ethereal, gorgeous, faraway heavenly landscape beyond the reach of man. But for one little boy who I would likely never see again, nary a soul did I have to call my own, nor any human companionship or solace. Nevertheless, I drowned in rapture during those hours when I watched the heavens, for were not the ancient gods sighing, their breath painting the sky?

Whatever mystical thoughts the nights brought with them, speeding by day over a frigid, undiscovered ice continent imparts an odd, pervasive giddiness, perhaps from the rarefied air that no other man has breathed. Inhaled too deeply 'twill sear the lungs; taken in little puffs, though, it lightens the head, so light that all is floating—sky and ice, memories, dreams, imaginings—divinely effervescent.

Sometimes, I smelled food, strongly, as if a laden table were only a foot away. This occupied me with much nostalgia for certain delicacies. Mimi's specialties in particular wafted over me with especial vividness, food of my second mother and her people, the same simple food back to the time before time.

During one of these dreamy episodes, I saw myself at the Ursuline Academy. Which of my demure playmates could have foreseen my fate? My early years there, I put my wild ways in my pocket to love the sweet solicitude of my friends and teachers. Had I by some accident died in the bosom of that innocence, 'twould have been a life well lived. Would that Lara was beside me now! Dear soul, she would not damn me as I damn myself. Nay, she would still be my truest heart's companion, resting close to me in my little snow cave, telling tales of stone-cutters, fairies, kings' daughters, ice-maidens, goose girls, water spirits, and laughing babies born under cabbage leaves.

During those weeks, I had a traveling companion of sorts, a polar bear I named Franklin—a huge, dirty, lumbering, sorrowful fellow, he trod alone, parallel to my little caravan. One leg was lame, so his walk could not be mistaken. At times, he roared so plaintively that the ice echoed his lamentations and my dogs set to howling like wolves.

Sometimes I hollered to him, which was difficult, as my lip had split, sending shooting pains across one cheek every time I moved my mouth. Nevertheless, I called to him, "Franklin, Franklin, how goes your life today?" Did he reply? Sometimes I thought so, believing that the wind or loud shifting of ice could be his voice. Then he disappeared. If Franklin could have told me his story, I believe 'twould have been thus:

"In the time before two-legged creatures, polar bears were kings of all you see. For eons, we ruled over the dominion of land, sea, and ice. So great were our voices that one roar sent the moon to the dark side of the earth that the sun might rise again. So great was our speed that the ice beneath our feet scattered to the sky as stars. So sharp were our teeth that we carved mountains out of stone. So brave were our hearts that all other creatures bowed down. Now you see me broken and bedraggled, but the time after time will come when two-legged creatures no longer walk the earth and once again we shall rule the land of ice and snow."

One day, in the worst of those spring storms, long after the eggs were gone, my dog Indigo gave birth to six puppies and promptly ate five of them. 'Tis a shocking, cruel world for helpless creatures, be they man or beast. My poor dogs had little to eat then, as did I, for 'tis difficult to catch a seal or any other creature when storms shriek so.

The dogs had grown bony and their eyes took on a surly desperation. They watched each other for the slightest sign of weakness, that they might attack and devour each other. Two broke their traces and vanished into the beyond. When Indigo's pups were born, the scent galvanized the remaining dogs as if a shock had hit them. As much as their traces would permit, they hung about her hindquarters, jaws dripping, eyes burning. But she herself snatched up those pups one by one, leaving me with but a brief glimpse of each poor, wet, naked bit of life who fate handed only one breath of frozen blue air before extinction.

'Twas a very peculiar period overall, Captain, for at this same time a snowy owl began to circle around, following us for days. I named her Lea. At night, she perched upon my sledge top, for when the wind died down, I heard mewling, tongue clicking, and the occasional noisy feather fluffing. I felt myself losing all sense of human existence, so surrounded was I by creatures.

You may ask what of the sixth pup? At the moment of its birth I felt sure that my creature was near. I fired the pistol in his direction, what I thought was his direction. The dogs, already riled over the scent of blood, reared up and lurched in divergent directions. In the mayhem, my sledge tipped and threw off numerous possessions. Down flew Lea. She dove out of the sky and with feathers flying and a barking *krek-krek* grabbed the sixth newborn pup and flew into the clouds, never to be seen again.

That pistol shot was all for naught, for truly I only shot at a ghost. After the general confusion of pups and owl and infuriated dogs died down, I sat a long while listening, thinking I might hear screams of pain or a great crash as my creature's body fell through the ice from a bullet wound, but no such sound occurred. The dogs curled up at last and slept, leaving me alone with the cold wind and groans of troubled ice beneath.

I too slept then, though not properly ensconced in my usual night protections. I did not care to call the dogs to circle me, nor shield myself under the fur roof nor even light the little oil lamp. Sincerely did I wish this journey over. That day, with the echo of a pistol retort, the whole of my existence fell upon me. I could scarce breathe with the weight of it. Hating is exhausting. How I wished to say farewell to it all.

But fate is cruel and does not let you give up on yourself until it gives up on you. Day came round again and there I was. 'Twas evident the ice was divorcing itself. Once hitched, the dogs roused themselves and took off at a great clip, perhaps catching sight of a distant seal. So eager were they that, in one fateful moment, Neptune, the lead dog, missed her footing and down we slid into a crevasse, dogs falling, claws scratching desperately to gain a footing.

Howls and barks echoed off the vertiginous walls, ricocheting down to a great distance below, where embankments of ice had parted, creating pale blue slicks of glass that seemed to extend to the middle of the earth. The sledge had slid sideways, its runners caught against hard ice ridges that prevented it from tumbling likewise into the crevasse. Many of my belongings disappeared into the abyss, including my precious books and apothecary cabinet.

My body was tangled up with dog traces and I could not move. My cheek pressed against the snow and all the while I heard the savage cracking of ice and the desperate cries of dogs, and within my sight the blue glass walls of the crevasse. I believe I began to freeze to death, for I have heard tell 'tis a sleepy feeling, full of slow, random thoughts. I thought of Lara, how she knew all the ancient gods and made me memorize them: Chaos (the nothingness from which all things spring), Deimos (dread and terror), Erebus (primordial god of darkness), Tartaros (god of the deep abyss), etc., and how each suddenly seemed to keep me company there. Lara, dearest friend, she knew the secrets of the old ways and 'twas clear to me that the old ways had shaped my life and sealed my fate.

The dog whimpers grew dim. I blew and blew into my whistle but soon my breath was spent and I fainted then and remained thus for I know not how long. Long enough for the ice pan upon which I floated to dislodge itself and slide away from the crevasse with the dogs heavy and inert on their leashes trailing behind; long enough, I suppose, to bang against the side of the *Valor*. I remember only the shouts of men and my heavy cloak of ice, and being unwillingly lifted back into a life full of black despair.

Captain, I must rest now and forevermore, for I feel too weak to utter scarce more. If you ask me what most embodies my life—my breath, my song, my echo, my poem, my epitaph, my perfume, my prayer—I would say: *The longing for something that can only be longed for.*

April 26th, 1781

God willing, dearest Sister, you have now read this dreadful tale. My visitor seems to have no words left for now, or maybe forevermore, though my heart sinks upon considering this prospect. She slept, though not a gentle sleep, for awful dreams and visions beset her. She sobbed and cried out names and places I now know. Her cheeks burned with fever, yet she was cold.

At times, she woke and gazed upon the cabin boy and dog with great affection. The boy had heard most of her long story, for he tended to her need for food and drink and cold compresses upon her forehead. She had forsaken her cap; perhaps vanity had deserted her or at last she felt at ease to do so in our company. In any case, her auburn hair stuck out in all directions and, because of the extreme fragility of her frame and state of mind, she looked like a lost wood nymph or pixie.

I had neglected my ship and men, as I could barely take my eyes off her while she spoke of her life, such was her supernatural appearance and expressive manner of speech. Every hour of listening I broke a little more and, despite the horrifying outcome of her actions, I did not damn her. One rarely, in the course of human intercourse, hears the totality of another's life, even back to the sweep of a person's ancestors. Regardless of the events narrated, a recitation of this sort is hypnotic, for every person's life is a tragic story in whole, is it not? Were the words she spoke recorded in a book rather than my poor scribbles here, I would hold it close, read it at every opportunity, and again fall in love with the teller of the tale.

I found as many occasions as possible to speak her name, for though she addressed me always as Captain Galán, she long since bid me call her Océane, and this I did. 'Tis impossible to speak that name in anger, for by its vowels and whispery sound 'tis by nature itself a kiss. Many a time I reflected upon her mother—the beautiful Beatrix Belfleur—bleeding, ill, starving on the filthy floor below decks with her newborn babe, nevertheless bestowing on her the most beautiful name under God's great sky.

During the recitation of her story, when Océane became too overcome with sorrow, anger, or regret to speak, she broke off to work in silence upon a sheaf of notes and a letter for Freddy. This was a laborious task, weak as she was, and I sometimes found her asleep, her fingers stained with ink, smudges marring her pale cheeks. At length, she gave me Freddy's letter, bid me read it aloud to her that she might gauge its tone and content, and begged me to see it delivered.

To Master FREDERICK FRANKENSTEIN
in the care of Mr. ABRAHAM FRANKENSTEIN

Philadelphia, in the Colony of Pennsylvania
The Good Ship *Valor*
Edge of the World, April 26th, 1781

I write to you from the captain's quarters of a brigantine named *Valor*, which is bound to discover an Arctic passage between the Atlantic and Pacific oceans. Men have died in quest of this mission in the past, but Captain Galán is brave and stalwart and determined to succeed. His sleeping cabin, which he has kindly given to me, is small, yet comfortable enough and similar to our cabin in the ship upon which we sailed to Halifax.

There is a porthole through which I gaze at this splendid frozen sea, its icy cloak, the black fissures winding off to the horizon as the ice melts, cracks, and throws off towering blocks of ice. The long winter has passed its apex and the sky is lighter a fraction each day as a sliver of sun peers briefly over the landscape. I am kept company by a cabin boy named Percy who reminds me so of you, and a dog named Eski, who has a friendly, gentle nature.

I have seen so many creatures, dear Freddy! Polar bears are by nature formidable, yet somehow sad and pensive as they navigate the ice, mostly alone. Once I saw an eagle swoop down, grab a bear cub, fly up, then drop the cub upon the ice far below, which alas ended the life of that poor little bear. The eagle circled back down, lifted him again, and flew off into a bank of clouds. This plagued my sensibilities for many a day, for babies of all kinds ought to have a chance to live and grow for at least a little while.

Narwhal, the unicorns of the sea, are most peculiar-looking, for their spiral tusks break the surface like swords rising up in the hands of Neptune and his companions. Often have I heard the howling of wolves, but have not laid eyes on them, for here they are white as the ice—ghost predators. Seals are plentiful, slipping in and out of the frozen sea. I swear that mythical beasts live here, too, for many wind-formed ice constructions take the shape of colossal bears with wings, walruses the size of elephants, birds with the head of a man, sea serpents, centaurs, and more, as if those mighty creatures froze in place and, over the eons, turned to ice.

When traversing this cold, blue, mysterious land, one sees all manner of fanciful things. I have described them as thoroughly as I can, given the inimical writing conditions, and I enclose those pages here. You will see—the parchment itself tells the story of a great adventure! The smudged ink and water spots are caused by ice melting off my cap or cloak as, after a long day of travel, I sat near a fire each night with my pen and paper.

One of my greatest joys while crossing this undiscovered territory is imagining you in a new school, with new friends, new books, and boisterous cousins to bring you much noise and life. Freddy, as you grow into manhood, I pray that your grief turns into sweet memories and your anguish and horror fade away until they are faint shadows that may cast a little sadness over you from time to time, but not poison your life. It takes tremendous courage and fortitude to remember our beloveds without being flattened by the manner of their death. I have more faith in you than I do myself in this.

I love you, dear little Brother, now and forever and even after that. Whether I am corporeal on this earth or not, my spirit will always be with you, for love cannot be vanquished.

Your dear loving sister,
OCÉANE FRANKENSTEIN DIT BELFLEUR

Sea captain though I am, I came near bawling when I reached the end of that letter. My visitor and her people suddenly seemed worth all else on earth. I dozed in my captain's chair with the dog at my feet as my mind concocted a world with Océane as my wife, Freddy as my son, Mimi as my mother, then fathers and brothers and aunts, then all Acadians going back to before the beginning—as Océane might say—propelling me forward with sons and daughters unto the far edge of eternity.

May 2nd, 1781

Today, my men revolted, gave Master Percy a black eye, and stormed my cabin, for they have suspected my death or great illness, and surely dereliction of duty. Océane lay upon my bunk swathed in her cloak. The dog leaped upon the men in a fury of barking and snarling. 'Twas some time before all was sorted out, after which nearly a score of my strongest men—weak from our long ice incarceration—crowded together, glaring at me, ready to launch into a litany of complaints.

I stepped toward them, exposing the bunk and the pale figure upon it. My men grew quiet, for all grow quiet when the specter of death hovers nearby. The eye believes what the mind has been told, thus they saw her still as that boy they pulled from the sea—Master John Willoughby. They backed out then, fearing both death and the contagion of lice.

To my sorrow, I have these past two days spent little time with Océane, for I found terrible disarray throughout the ship. Mr. Dawson has been ill and without direction, my men lacked the will to organize and clean, which are essential tasks to the maintenance of a ship at sea, even one currently ice-locked. They grumbled at my exhortations that they scrub from bow to stern on deck and below, but not long after regained their spirits at this physical activity and an orderly task at hand.

While I was thus occupied, Océane stayed with her faithful watchers, Master Percy and Eski. The boy has been furiously working on some secret drawing project that is affording him much pleasure.

May 5th, 1781

One of my men went mad today. Though his limbs were weak and he was half-starved, he lowered himself over the side of the ship onto the ice, then called to his comrades above to accompany him to a place called the White Horse Tavern for a hand of cards, a round of billiards, and a hearty meal. He flung off his coat and raced across the ice like a boy—running a few steps, then sliding, running then sliding.

'Twas not even a solid expanse of ice, for we could see black uneasy margins all around where a large floe had worked itself free of the overall ice cap. As he skated, he called out details of the tavern menu, for which he seemed to have great affection—lamb pies, fatback cornbread, stewed pork, ale. This last especially delighted him, for he described in detail the types of ale, their origin, color, and degree of bitterness.

Two sailors went after him with ropes to bind and hoist him back aboard ship. This amused him no end; he ducked and feinted and mocked them with expletives I shall not repeat here. The floating ice upon which they struggled drifted away from the ship. As they captured him at last, a loop of rope caught itself on the jagged edge of the iceberg and they could not free themselves. A wind came up and the air filled with blowing snow until we could see them only as ghostly white figures that then vanished, never to be seen again.

This event greatly disturbed the remaining sailors. During these long, ice-locked months, we have ventured onto the ice to cut holes and fish for any living thing we might eat. For such excursions, the rats aboard became our living bait, for tied alive to fishing line they tempted seals, walruses, and other beasts of the deep. These expeditions, however, were planned and executed with care, involving ropes, whistles, torches, compasses, and dark feed bags flapping from the high masts that the hunters might locate the ship against the white sea ice.

Men strung themselves out like clothes pegs on a line, that no one might be deprived of immediate visual contact with the next man. But today those men attempted a rescue without any of that. Though I would privately call their actions foolhardy, the remaining sailors saw it as a heroic mission, a godly errand. Therefore, the outcome was the bitterest pill, the end of their fortitude, the last of what little hope remained.

I bid the men knock to pieces every chair on board, carry the wooden pieces to the galley, and wait for me there. Pale, weak, sickly, poxish, coughing, shivering men with their teeth falling out and skin sloughing off–'tis a sorry sight, Sister, one a ship's captain prays never to see. But there they were, suffering like the damned while I remained ensconced in my cabin listening to fantastic stories told by a dying girl with my heart in her pocket.

Overcome with guilt, I ordered the men to stuff the cook-stoves with wood to their maximum capacity and the cooks to use every crumb in the larder if need be to fill every belly. Soon those woeful adventurers sank to the floor for the lack of chairs and in the gathering heat held out their bowls–orphans of the eternal night. No one spoke of the actual content of their thick and stringy meal, for all knew 'twas the meat of rats and the cats kept on board in a vain attempt to keep the rodent population in check. Despite an infernal infestation of weevils in all the flour on board, they dipped hard biscuits into this concoction to soften them enough to eat.

In a flash of inspiration, with her permission, I loosed Océane's dog Eski into this gathering. Tame by nature and by the gentle ministrations of her mistress and the cabin boy, she did not now bare her teeth nor jump upon the men. Instead, she roamed amongst them like a princess among slaves, allowing them to pet and talk to her, to marvel at the beauty of her coat and her soulful eyes. They fed her bits of meat, which she took from them with delicacy, so as not to bite their fingers. Thus for one hour were my men saved from despair and my guilt assuaged in some small measure.

May 7th, 1781

Lest you think me now an exemplary man for this kindness to my sailors, let that thought fly from your mind, for upon the heels of this magnanimous gesture I fled back to my cabin, to the silken thread that binds me to my visitor as in a fairy story—a magic thread that cannot be broken, for its mistress sings a dark and dangerous song as did the sirens to Odysseus.

May 12th, 1781

What was the deep groaning of ice is now a cacophony of frightening bellows from below, fracturing and splintering the ice floes as they collide into each other and move apart and knock each other in random directions. The spiderweb of black margins between floes that we have seen for some weeks has become visible expanses of churning water. Because of this, the ship now jolts and rolls such that frigid water often sweeps up and across the deck, drenching all who venture there.

When dozing, my visitor now misses the occasional breath, sending me into fits of anguish and, I confess, tearfulness. Perhaps I am next to lose my mind, or have already lost it. I now spend most of my time hunched upon a footstool at the side of the bunk, listening to every sigh and muttered syllable, awaiting ever-briefer periods of lucidity.

As the ship tosses about, she still gazes much out the porthole until it fogs over with her breath; she then wipes it clean to gaze out yet more. At times, she thinks her creature has appeared beside the ship and tears and regret then shake her. At times, horror overwhelms all else and she asks for her pistol that she might keep it by her side. I comply, though it has been ruined by saltwater and will likely never fire again.

Master Percy has completed his project, allowing me to help at the end. During one of Océane's wakeful periods, he handed it to her with much shyness and ceremony. 'Twas wrapped in a rumpled length of linen and tied with strips of scavenged leather. So exciting was the giving of this gift that the three of us—dog, boy, and man—crowded close until Océane scarcely had room to move. 'Twas a loose-leaf book with its pages clumsily bundled together on the left edge with fishing line.

Seeing my handwriting upon the title page, she let out a happy gasp, which filled my eyes with tears, as I had never seen this free expression of delight from her before. The boy and I elbowed one another, each with foolish, satisfied smiles, and honestly, we felt like the most splendid men on earth as she read the title aloud: *Great Creatures of Faraway Lands and Seas*—exactly the title of Freddy's promised book, her accidental book.

The lines after the title read "*Written by Mademoiselle Océane Frankenstein dit Belfleur and Illustrated by Master Percy Lyne on the Great Ship* VALOR *on its Voyage to the Unknown Northern Pole*." She leafed through the parchment pages with tears streaming down her cheeks, happy tears, for Master Percy and I had combined her pages of notes describing the creatures she saw on her travels with his charcoal and colored pencil drawings of those creatures and all the ones she spoke of in the recitation of her life story.

I captioned each drawing with inscriptions for each creature—"Penny the calf," "Hobby the elephant," "Jack the horse," and so on—for though my cabin boy was skilled in the sketching arts, he had little knowledge of script and spelling. Océane read the captions aloud, for she was suffused then with rosy-cheeked vigor and the desire to recollect the creatures she scarcely knew numbered enough to fill a book in its entirety.

Upon reaching the penultimate page, Océane closed the book and drew Master Percy close, for he had drawn her creature there. 'Twas a terrifying beast with fangs and claws and a giant's head with zigzagged face and an ear in one hand. The edges of that page were filled in with rough charcoal strokes, as if the creature were trapped by night or fog.

Seeing Océane threaten to sink back into sorrow and terror, Master Percy bid her turn one more page. There she saw the boy's version of Eugénie—baby of her sweetest dreams—a little seahorse with a girl astride, lightly drawn with colored pencils worn down at that point to their nubs, the figures pale, seeming to float across the page. The caption read "Eugénie, girl in the sea."

Océane slipped that page out of the binding, kissed it, pressed it to her bosom, and nevermore parted with it as long as ever she lived, which was only two days more, during which she was largely occupied with fevered murmurs, uneasy sleep, and much gazing at the drawing of her daughter. Once, she called to me as I dozed in my captain's chair. I leaned close and heard her whisper, "Beg him to forgive me." This threw me into great turmoil, for were that creature's actions not unforgivable? Was he not worthy of only rage and hate and fantasies of retribution? As if to quash my protests, she whispered again, "Beg him to forgive me."

To my everlasting regret, Océane drew her last breath alone, for I was working with my men on deck at that last desperate moment. Alone! After all the misery and horror and loneliness in her life, alone! I realized this upon returning to my quarters, for Isabel, she was blue, blue as the frozen air. The drawing lay against her heart. I touched her cold cheek and wept like a baby.

Eski, her final companion, whined and licked her cold hand, and when I entered the room howled with an agony that matched my own. Never have I felt such violence of emotion—I can scarce describe it. 'Tis a crime I committed by leaving her alone, a crime; 'tis what plagues me every hour now and even after I am in the ground or under the frozen ice, 'twill no doubt count as unforgivable, the worst of my sins.

Master Percy was absent, too, for I had ordered him back to regular duty so that whatever of innocent childhood was left in him might be spared the death of the mademoiselle who enchanted us both. I yearned to breathe into her mouth as she had her creature's, breathe my life into her, but even I—who learns the hard way—have learned from my visitor that the dead do not wish to be disturbed from their eternal sleep.

Still! All I left unsaid and undone! Had I kissed her hand or lips? Had I told her of my love fever? Is not love given freely, even if not returned, succor for the soul? Would it not have comforted her a little to know that a flesh-and-blood man loved her as her flame burned out?

I gnashed my teeth and flung things about my cabin until all was disorder. The dog snarled and snapped at me as if she knew me not. At length, I slumped to the floor; 'twas as if sorrow itself were corporeal and had knocked me down. The death of my fiancée so many years past... I once thought that was a pain with no salve. I mourned for her most grievously and even, as you know, redirected the course of my life thereafter, but I now see that those tears were a green young man's tears.

The despair I feel now upon the death of my visitor is seasoned by time and experience, and the realization that I am of an age closer to the end of life than the beginning. Only now does my body and soul understand what losing really is. Her tale was so fantastic—half the time I knew not if she spoke from delirium. But now I apprehend the agony from whence her creature sprang. My heart filled with tenderness and compassion that had no outlet but in tears and thus I brooded many an hour.

Midnight came round and another storm blew in with great violence. Reluctantly, I left my visitor upon my bunk and proceeded on deck. The ship rolled and knocked so violently that I feared my beloved ship might split asunder and drag one and all to the bottom of the sea. A few faithful men remained at their posts, cursing and puking and turning half to ice themselves. I bid them go below and made my way forward hand-over-hand, for the storm obscured the heavens such that I could not see even an arm's length ahead, and clung to the leeward side.

There I called out like a madman to gods I scarce believe in, not for the lives of my men, not for the survival of my ship, not for my mission to an undiscovered Northwest Passage. No, I begged that I might live long enough to turn my ship around, retrace my route, then travel overland to Philadelphia that I might deliver Freddy's book to him by hand and see, perhaps, a glimpse of Océane's face in his.

The night was full of monsters. There on deck I was beset by all manner of phantoms and lamentations—the cries and visitations of sea demons I heard tell of in childhood—grindylows, kraken, leviathan, panlong dragons, rusalka ghosts—I swear they were about that night. Sailors are brave men, though, so I called myself a fool and tried to dismiss these fears and fancies, yet still I jumped at every shadow and sound.

I stopped in the galley and downed a goodly quantity of whiskey, then moved onward with an oil lamp in hand, down the corridors leading to my quarters. There I saw my men choking on the ever-present smoke of candles, tobacco, mold, tar vapors, and bilge waste, some smoking, some practicing knots—hitches, bends, and splices—some tattooing their fellow men with crosses, mermaids, or names—a painstaking pastime on the calmest of seas, a fool's errand under such turmoil as that night.

The door of my cabin was ajar, thrown open perhaps by the violent pitching of the ship. My lamplight threw shadows in all directions and strange billows of cloth or sails blew out into the hall, pushed from behind by a funnel of wind. A window must have shattered therein, forcing snow and seawater across my quarters, out the door. I stumbled over my belongings now strewn about the floor and fastened the metal casing over the porthole, thus sealing it.

'Twas as if all the air had left the room, creating an uncanny, hollow sensation. I stuffed wood into the stove until it blazed up that I might see more clearly. My Océane lay as before, curled up on her side like a little sleeping girl, Master Percy's drawing clutched close. You see now how I boldly call her "mine"? 'Tis easy to reject or claim the dead with one's full force of emotion when they are no longer sensate to dissuade, correct, or inhibit such proclamations.

My mind began to fashion its own self-forgiving story: Yes, I neglected to say, "My dear, I love you for all eternity with such violence and ardor that I can scarce look at you without wishing to crush you in my embracing arms and kiss you until my lips are numb." Even so, surely she knew of my adoration. Of course she knew! Why else would she confide in me—only me—all the secrets of her life? This contemplation assured me in some small measure.

Slowly, though, I became aware of breathing—ragged, shallow breaths. 'Twas the dog, I thought. I whistled for her but she did not come, nor seem to be in my quarters at all. Instead, stepping out of the dark alcove that held my books came forth the creature of my Océane's life and nightmares.

At first, he was just a swirl in a black cloak, but forthwith that slid to the floor and there stood a giant dressed in scarce tatters, showing me the many hallmarks described by his maker: the face tattoo, though now drained of color; the drooping ear; gaping seams; the patchwork of skin colors; seeping, bleeding abscesses, sores, and putrification; skin sloughing off; fingertips gone. How shocking was his size, extreme ugliness, and state of disrepair!

Yet I did not scream nor flee, for I knew him. I knew him! He was no stranger to me, this unwilling creation, for I knew to the most intimate detail of his confusion and loneliness, anguish and travails, pain and rage and murder. The stories I had heard swept over me as I stared, and for a moment, I thought I saw right through him to the rosy big and little hearts beating, giving him life. If you know someone's deepest torments, sorrows, bewilderments, and longings–what then? Is it not natural to feel pity?

The creature knelt that he might fit more easily in my cabin and began to speak to me with a voice so harsh and torn and stuttering that my sympathy was rapidly replaced by revulsion over his monstrous appearance.

"I know you to be captain of this benighted ship," he said, "for I have lived upon this ice and watched you and your men. I saw those three pitiful sailors tangled in their confusion of ropes. I could have saved them, but why? What men have ever saved me from my terrible destiny? You may go or stay. I have no interest in nor care for you, for I am now compelled only by a desire to speak to she who gave me life."

At this, he gestured toward my visitor, who lay exactly as she had when I last left the room. "She sleeps now and I shall allow her this slumber before I tell her that, while I hate this life she gave me, I do not hate her, nay I love her, for however cursed I may be, I belong to her. As a wretched cur slinks back to its cruel master, likewise do I now return to her in the hope of some gesture of acceptance."

"But sir," I said, "alas, she sleeps God's eternal repose, as you will see if you approach."

He leapt to his feet, knocked his head against the ceiling, and stepped to the bunk. Pulling Océane's blanket back, he saw her unnatural hue, how wasted away she was, her chopped hair. "Nay, 'tis not her!" he cried. "'Tis not my maker, for whatever cruel fate she inflicted on me, she is a beautiful girl, fair of face, with long auburn curls." Even as he said this, I could tell from his expression that he knew 'twas truly her.

His knees buckled and he seemed unwell. He touched her arm but recoiled at the coldness of her flesh and fell upon the floor, screaming piteously. Gingerly, I rose to add wood to the stove and by its light saw pools of blood on the floor where he leaked from his seams and sores. 'Twas a hideous sight and I could scarcely cast my eyes upon it. I sidled toward the door to call for help in removing this monster from my quarters, but he seized my ankle and bid me stay.

"Captain," he said, "what do you know of me? Why do you not shrink in terror at my presence? Are you a man who fears nothing?"

I did not reply, for right then I feared that if I spoke, my grief would bubble over, uncontainable. I did not wish to give him the slightest hint of my sensibility. Some mistake a quiet man for a strong, courageous man, and though not always true, it suited me well enough right then that he should think so.

"Hear me," he said, "I was nothing, I was no one, yet too I was many men, I was earth, I was dreamless sleep. I was untroubled, wordless, beyond the reach of man's cruelty and hate. What possessed this girl, my maker, to unearth stinking flesh and bones to create one made of many, to breathe her hot, sweet breath into a new being—too beastly to be a man, too manly to be a beast? Never did she bless me with a name. Never did she call me son nor brother nor sweetheart nor husband nor friend. Never did she happily converse with me as I saw her do with others. She repaired my wounds and listened to my story once, but my words then were a furious rebuke, all accusation and sorrow, leaving her no room for tender reply. By then, 'twas too late anyway, for her friend had fallen down the stairs and set my foul destiny upon its course. Or was it my creation itself that set my destiny?

"Sir, I am all confusion. You are a man of the world; 'twill not dismay you if I say that, scarcely had I first risen to my feet than my maker drew me to a straw bed and ran her hands all over my flesh in a most alarming, provocative manner, my flesh which was flaring and sparking and raging from its unholy birth. Some might say she then made a man of me, for I know that phrase from somewhere, but I contend that she made a monster of me, because ever after my blood was up, dooming me to loathing, desires, and furies from which I cannot rest. If a being yearns for tender regard but by every act of his own pushes that regard further away, that being should indeed remain nameless, always a beast, never a man."

He lifted Océane as a father would a child and lay upon my bunk with her in his arms. Her head lolled against his chest, her cheek directly over where beat the hearts of her beloveds. I cannot amply describe that sight—a creature and his mistress, both born in agony, both yearning, tormented, terrified, skin-to-skin. 'Twas pure love there, hardened by fire, petrified by ice. Love given too late, multiplied by two.

Icy rain beat against the windows, on and on went the grinding and banging of ice careening against the hull. My cabin tipped this way and that with the swells, and the oil lamplight threw its nervous shadows all the more wildly. In the presence of those shadows, the howl of the frozen sea, and the monster before me, I went mad with jealousy, as does a child thunderstruck to realize he is not the favorite, or a lover who through misplaced rectitude lost his chance upon this earth to claim his love.

My eyes went blind with tears and I heard myself cry out as if I too were a creature. Plain and simple, I wanted then to kill that misbegotten giant, to strangle him. But this red-hot fury was soon felled by shame. Was this not their story—the monster and the maiden? Was I not an accidental interloper? The monster touched Océane's face with his filthy, awkward hand and my jealousy turned to tears of longing that I instead might lie close to her extinguished body. He coughed and blood spattered the blankets. Weary, debilitated, he asked, "Did she speak of me?"

Oh, Sister, I battled all my demons then, for I desired to relate to him all the hatred, loathing, and fear she felt for him and that her sole wish was to dismember and scatter his cursed flesh across the earth that never again could they form themselves by some black magic into the shape of a man. But 'twas as if I heard her quiet final words. I could not give lie to them. I handed him Océane's small, folded-up letter. He broke the seal and read it with difficulty, as his vision was poor. "Oh, how cruel is fate," he said, but I could scarcely hear him.

Again, I felt pity well up and so I told him all: "Creature, she spoke these final words, 'Beg him to forgive me'... that is what your maker said... 'Beg him to forgive me.'"

He stared right into my soul, that illegitimate demon, and never shall I forget the burning anguish in his unnatural eyes. He then took up her cold hand, kissed its palm, and drew his own last shaking breath, the breath she breathed into him to give life, now exhaled as a sigh. There too I witnessed a tear travel slowly to the pillow, the tear shed upon his birth, shed yet again, forevermore part of the great unknown that awaits us all.

I sat in my captain's chair with the whiskey bottle in one hand and a cigar in the other, trying to gather the bits of myself together again. The dog crept in and lay beside the bunk. Over the course of hours, the storm abated and a sliver of sunlight appeared for its brief rendezvous with the horizon. I heard men shouting from the deck, keen to see that bit of light, now readying ropes and sails for the continuance of our journey. Master Percy wandered in, his face stained with tears, and curled up with the dog, emitting little hiccups of sorrow for his dear mademoiselle.

At length, I rose to write of my ongoing plans in my captain's log, which is absent of all I have written here for you.

My men will happily turn their backs on Polaris, eager to attend to their health and families. But I resolve to you that I will come again to this frozen landscape when my newer mission is complete. I will return Master Percy to his father and give Océane's book, letters, and dog to Freddy and tell him of his cherished sister, for no child should have to wait forever for someone who will never return. He will weep, I know, but her tale will be told, except for that which is best unspoken.

Sister, will you and your husband and children make the journey across the great Atlantic to New York or Boston, that I might embrace you before I set off for the Northern Pole once again? You will beg me not to go. But I am not the same man I was some months ago, bristling with foolish pride and ridiculous suppositions about fountains of youth. It has taken Mademoiselle Océane Frankenstein and the terrible, inexorable force of Mother Nature, mother of all who live and die, to break and humble me for whatever my future may hold.

That day passed in a haze of liquor and melancholy. The dog—faithful sentinel—remained always close. At length, Master Percy and I dried our tears and went about the business of a burial at sea. I called in several sailors who I believed would take to heart any oath to secrecy I bid them take and thus did swear them never to reveal what they had seen and done.

During our months of fighting the frozen sea, blizzards, and ice-locks, their fevered minds, like mine, had seen all manner of towering sea monsters real and imagined, so perhaps 'twas not such a shock to behold that dead creature in my quarters. And they still believed that Océane was the poor boy they had pulled from the ice, so never was her identity revealed otherwise. Furtively, I removed Harry's whistle from around her neck and slipped it in my pocket.

'Tis now all I possess of her existence on this earth.

I tucked that drawing within her bodice and we bound their bodies separately in their cloaks and sailcloth and lengths of ropes and chains, then transported them on deck when night came around again and all were sleeping. 'Twas still and clear, the stars extravagant. The ship continued to rock at the will of the sea, but less violently. Then appeared the *aurora borealis* I have spoken of before—green and yellow that night, bright, billowing, gorgeous, mysterious.

So devastated were my thoughts that I could not bring a single word of God's prayer to mind. Instead, I spoke my own thoughts. To the monster, I said, "Your cursed life has come to a welcome end. 'Twill be as if you never existed, for innominate creatures are never spoken of in history books nor in tales around a fire. The furies of perdition will tear you to pieces and cast you down that you might for all eternity call hell your home."

At this, the men threw him overboard, where he landed with a watery disturbance so great that the sea objected and sent an immense wave over the deck. Wet now and gray with cold, I bid the men leave my side and take Master Percy with them. I fell upon my knees as the green lights flared above and the sea spoke its enigmatic language. Then I lifted my visitor; even with chains winding around her body, she was small and light. I looked to the heavens. My blood was hot with grief and I could barely speak.

"Océane..." I breathed her name. "Océane... farewell from one who adores you evermore." And so, I gave my precious visitor to the ocean, the ocean from which came her name, her second ocean, for did she not first swim in the ocean of her mother?

I watched a long time as she rocked in the arms of the sea and floated away from the ship toward the sliver of horizon far away, which would soon brighten to a brief rosy yellow;

watched until I could see her only bit by bit as the broken ice floated past and around her, then saw her no more.

So great was my devotion that I felt myself float down with her, down through the cold black sea, down to a different sea, calm, far from the restless furor above, pale green, past a forest of long-whispering undersea trees reaching up to the sun, ever summer, warmer now, 'twas the sea of her dreams where, free of her chains and shroud, she drifts gently–beautiful, nude, hair flowing as it once had–drifting down past bright fish making way for her, drifting down past spinning starfish, drifting down to the deepest deep where her mother glides like a mermaid and her daughter rocks for all eternity on her little seahorse.

254

AFTERWORD

Mary Shelley's novel, *Frankenstein; or, The Modern Prometheus* (1818), is the most important novel of the 19th century. It is not the finest novel, nor the best written, nor the most elegant. But it is the most important. It articulates the cultural anxieties underlying the advent of the Industrial Revolution, the concerns about rapidly evolving technology, the dehumanization of an industrial society, and the limitations of humanity gaining a growing power over the natural world. Those are the fears that struck a societal subtext of too much social and technological change happening too quickly. Even to this day, Frankenstein's monster haunts us; our "monsters" are pollution causing devastating global change and the ability of complete self-destruction through nuclear weapons and war. After all, Frankenstein's creature does ultimately destroy everything surrounding its creator's life.

Robin Solit's brilliant novel, *Mademoiselle Frankenstein*, works within this Gothic dystopian tradition, something that I term the "Frankenstein Syndrome" (a concept where arrogant conceit and the application of destructive knowledge creates catastrophe), providing a dazzling retelling of the Frankenstein story.

Frankenstein's monster is one very popular horror icon. There have been countless films, TV shows, comic books, and theatrical adaptations relating to Shelley's famous creation. Frankenstein has become part of the vocabulary of our culture, one of the most prevalent images of science gone terribly wrong in the hands of an overweening pride. Shelley reminds us in her novel that humanity is not God and is incapable of possessing the power of life over death.

Solit's novel reexamines Shelley's work through a different lens than any of the Frankenstein appropriations, a unique perspective that does more than just add to the Frankenstein canon. She literally reinvents the Frankenstein Syndrome. Her approach is to use Shelley's original cautionary Gothic tale and shape it in captivating ways.

Solit begins her story's plot similarly to Shelley's, with a sequence of the epistolary communications of Captain Gabriel Galán as he attempts to chart a passage "across the St. Lawrence Gulf and up into the uncharted Northern Pole," analogous in nature to Shelley's Captain Robert Walton's venture in the opening correspondence of *Frankenstein*. The desire of both men's misguided attempts to accomplish the impossible reflects the wish of the creators, Mademoiselle Océane Frankenstein and Victor Frankenstein, to generate life from dead human flesh, thus becoming godlike. But such an attempt, the reader understands, is doomed to fail. Like Shelley's, Solit's novel is also a cautionary tale, but that is where the similarities end.

Solit places her story at an earlier time than does Shelley, and in the New World rather than the Old World. The person who creates the monster is a female, rather than a male. The creature is born out of herbalism and mysticism instead of scientific technology. In addition, the creation of the monster is decidedly feminine in scope (women were practitioners of herbal medicine at that time), and not technologically male-centric, as with Shelley's novel. Mother Earth is the womb of Océane's creation.

Furthermore, Solit uses the American Revolutionary War as her setting, the dead soldiers of that conflict providing Océane with the raw human flesh for her creation. The revolutionary act of the American colonies declaring their independence from Great Britain reflects the alienation of the newly formed monster's initial conception, an unnatural birth by a mother without a father. Thus, not only is Océane's monster an outsider from humanity because of the dead human flesh with which he has been constructed, but he is also a twisted child of his time, a child of war and destruction, a child without genuine human connections, a child of dying and death. Océane's creature is consequently representative of "the Other," of the outsider archetype, a being both astonishing and pitiful.

Solit's novel is unique—a warning about female pride and arrogance, artfully packaged in the young protagonist, Océane.

Solit's characters are haunting. Her use of narrative gripping. Her descriptive language both beautiful and horrific. Her argument for the power inherent in women compelling. Her story encompasses both the horror of the other (artificially-created life) and the beauty of imagination that attempts the impossible, even if that attempt is doomed to anguish and ultimate failure.

The monster's creation, or "birth," in *Mademoiselle Frankenstein* is, of course, unnatural, or more precisely supernatural (which illustrates another major difference with Shelley's *Frankenstein*). The creature's unnatural existence is given a physical representation as the narrative progresses, evident in his physical deterioration. The reader is reminded that, regardless of Océane's skills in bringing life to dead flesh, she nonetheless is not a perfect creator. The limitations of her ability to create perfection reflect the limitations of the human condition itself. Women can become pregnant and give birth, but no mortal female (or male) can resurrect the dead; it would violate the fixed natural order of the world. This ability exists only in the realm of the supernatural.

In the finest Gothic fiction of the 19th century, human transgression is punished by suffering and death. The big three—Shelley's groundbreaking *Frankenstein*, Robert Louis Stevenson's moralistic *Strange Case of Dr. Jekyll and Mr. Hyde* (1886), and Bram Stoker's fin de siècle *Dracula* (1897)—provide perfect examples in the literature of that era of the cost of such natural/supernatural transgressions. The violation of nature and the natural world comes with a terrible price for the person who ignores the ordinary temporal sequence of things: birth, growth, aging, and death.

The implication is that only God can play at being God. Human imposters or transgressors are severely punished. This holds true in *Mademoiselle Frankenstein*. Following the strange creation of Océane's patchwork monster, Océane herself undergoes an epic, fantastic journey, one that takes her to the point of physical and mental torment, one that literally takes her to the edge of the world, and to premature death. Her ambition at the beginning of the novel is magnificent. Her ability to control the product of that ambition is constrained. Her death is a consequence of that ambition.

Ultimately, Solit's *Mademoiselle Frankenstein* unveils a superb, catastrophic chronicle in the guise of the Gothic narrative genre. Océane's journey is tragic, and completely damning for its protagonist. The novel's plot defies the circular and happy ending of Joseph Campbell's monomyth, but it is nevertheless a Byronic hero's journey, an unerring voyage downwards from lofty heights or ambition to the deepest depths of despair. Solit's novel recounts the tale of an angel falling as a result of overreach and hubris. But because Océane's desire to create her creature is impelled by love and grief, there is a certain nobility in her fall, a grace revealed in trying to achieve that which is forbidden (or impossible). She is a creature of Eden reaching for forbidden fruit. Alas, she is forcefully expelled for her efforts, but what a magnificent attempt...

With *Mademoiselle Frankenstein*, Solit provides not only a brilliant retelling of the Frankenstein story, but also an interpretation of Gothic horror that is as romantic as it is suspenseful. She has given us a novel every bit as good as Shelley's original, better even because it drops Shelley's narrative flaws. Robin Solit has delivered something quite exceptional.

Professor Gary Hoppenstand
Department of English
Literary Studies, Film and Media Studies, Popular Culture
Michigan State University, USA

9 798991 635806